DIRTY LIAR
MARISSA FINCH

Copyright © 2019 by Marissa Finch

All rights reserved.

No part of this book may be reproduced in any form or by any electronic or mechanical means, including information storage and retrieval systems, without written permission from the author, except for the use of brief quotations in a book review.

ONE
PRESENT DAY

Someone is following me. I don't know how I know, but I do.

I turn around, expecting to see a spandex-clad jogger or a mountain biker or even an overly aggressive grey squirrel, but the trail is empty.

Completely, totally deserted.

Exactly the same as it's been every other time I've turned around this morning, every other time I've been positive that I could hear or feel or sense, somehow, the presence of someone behind me.

Empty. Deserted.

I strain my ears, trying to hear, but the only sound is the snorfeling noise King makes as his nose skims the ground, searching out God knows what. He barks once and cranes his head to look back at me. He's grinning that dumb doggy grin of his and it thaws something in me, the way it always does. Anyone who can look at a dog and not smile doesn't deserve to be called human, at least not in my eyes.

"Whatcha got, boy?" I ask, forgetting, for the moment, my nagging sense of unease.

His ears twitch at the sound of my voice and he lunges forward and then back at me. Still grinning. He wants to make sure I'm with him. My therapist would call that behavior 'checking in', and she says it can be healthy up until it's not, and then it's just co-dependent. I don't mind being co-dependent with my dog. He's better than most — if not all — people I know.

Right now he's 'checking in' because he wants to go for something that's off in the bushes, and he knows he's not allowed to leave the trail. He thinks if he can lure me into following him, he'll get to pursue whatever it is he's got his nose hooked on. I'm not falling for it. "Get back here," I tell him, and I point to the dirt path beneath my feet.

King gives one last look into the forest beyond and pads over to me. He shakes himself good, like he's trying to get his head back into the game, throw off whatever was so enticing to him. In the slant of sunlight, I see dust and fine golden hairs flying off him. *He needs a brushing,* I think. *As soon as we get home.*

"Let's go, you goofball," I say. We start to walk again. I only glance over my shoulder a couple of times, and each time, the trail remains empty.

It's Sunday morning. Early. Not quite seven o'clock yet, according to my FitBit. We've already logged over eight thousand steps. Well, I have. I'm not sure how many steps that is in dog steps.

We come out here almost every weekend, King and I. *Here* being Capitol State Forest. It's our favorite place to hike, even though it takes an hour and a half to drive here from Seattle. We prefer it over the city parks. It's wilder out here, untouched by the usual yuppies that crowd the city's green spaces with their screaming toddlers and their overpriced Swell bottles filled with cheap wine. Beacon Hill, where I live, is overrun with them. But Capitol Forest is a logging forest, which means it isn't nearly so precious. It's a rugged, working forest, but there are plenty of trails for mountain biking, ATVing, horseback riding, and hiking. Plenty of shooting ranges, too, and hunters in the fall.

We like to hike. It's not something I was always that into, but these days I find it's the only thing that clears my head. I also consider it my penance for keeping King in the house all day during the week, when I'm trapped at a job I used to love but now can't stand going to, a job where I spend three-quarters of my time daydreaming about flinging myself from the seventeenth floor window of our mirrored monstrosity of an office building, thinking about what it feels like to fall from such a colossal height. So, yeah. When I'm not at work, I walk. And on weekends, we come out to the forest, where we can really stretch our legs.

We do five miles most of the time, sometimes as many as ten. Today the weather is so perfect — sunny, but temperate, and with a gentle breeze that blows my hair and King's fur off our faces — we'll do at least eight, easy. It's only the end of August, but Mother Nature has gifted us with a perfect September day.

The trail isn't busy. It almost never is, and this early in the morning, it *definitely* isn't. Plus, we're far out now, at least two miles from where we parked the Explorer. In the first mile, we passed a couple of early morning runners and an elderly couple walking a miniature white poodle with muddy paws and a mean streak, who lunged at King, baring her teeth and growling like Cujo. King gave her, and then me, a long-suffering look and marched on. We haven't seen anyone else since.

King strays over to the edge of the trail, his nose low to the ground, sniffing at the grass and shrubs that grow up along the edge of the trail. Mostly salal and boxwood, the grey skeletons of the spring's lupins. His tail swishes with metronome precision. We keep walking. The pace is meditative. It's strange; you'd think being out here on my own would give me too much time to think — to ruminate, as my therapist would say, which means dwelling on things I can't change — but it isn't like that. Just the opposite, actually. Walking out here helps me forget. My thoughts roll away with the rhythm of my steps, beat, beat, beat, and somehow that softens them. Makes them feel more distant, less frantic. These walks are as good for me as they are for King. They make me a better person; I don't think it's a stretch to say that. Maybe it's the physical movement or the massive dose of Vitamin G — that's G for green, as in green space, an idea my therapist likes to tout — but either way, it goes a long way toward keeping me sane. And these days, I need all the help I can get.

Today, though, I can't get into the rhythm of it. Something nags at me, hovering at the edge of my consciousness. I turn and look behind me again, but the path remains empty. It hasn't rained in days so the trail is dusty, and I can see the prints from my sneakers and the more winding trail of King's paw prints. I keep walking.

Still, it nags.

I don't know if it's a sound or a smell or something more subtle. I turn once more, sweeping my eyes over. Not just the trail but the trees surrounding it. There's no one. We're all alone out here. I stick my hand in my pocket, taking out my cell phone and patting the can of pepper spray I keep holstered to my side in case of bears or bobcats. You never know what you're going to encounter in Capitol Forest; it's over a hundred thousand acres and huge swaths of it are still untouched and untamed.

King is oblivious to whatever is causing my unease. That means it's probably not an animal. One time, we came upon something that might have been a lynx and he completely lost his shit — barking, lunging, growling. But now he's ten feet ahead of me, nose working, tail wagging. Unconcerned and happy. So not an animal, then.

I look at the woods that line the trail and think, *there could be a person in there. There could be someone in there and I'd never know.* The trees are dense, the foliage thick. A thousand hiding places. You wouldn't even really have to hide — you could stand right in between the pines or behind the sagging branches of the hemlocks and not be at all visible from the trail.

I shiver and force myself to put one foot in front of the other. Keep moving.

I've never been scared out here before. Not even when the investigation was in full swing and I had every reason to be on high alert. The trails were my happy place. My *me time*. Solitude for the soul.

Now I have the uneasy feeling that the solitude is only an illusion.

I keep walking. It's the birds, I tell myself. All those damn birds.

The woods are teeming with them. They screech, warble, coo, caw, trill in the treetops. I imagine them watching me as I walk along the trail, their beady little eyes following me, exchanging messages and plans of attack. I don't like birds. Never have, never will. I read somewhere once that it's because the way they take off into flight is very startling; not liking birds is a sign that a person doesn't like to be surprised. I suppose that's true. I'm not a big fan of surprises, either. Even the good ones provoke anxiety.

The birds are the only thing I don't like about these woods. The solitude doesn't bother me; its half of why I come out here. And the black flies tend to leave me alone. I'm lucky that way, I guess. Once, my coworker Daphne ventured out here with her boyfriend — on my recommendation — and she came into work on Monday with huge welts all over her legs and arms and she glared at me and said "Never again." But for me, they're not so bad. King doesn't seem to mind them, either. Maybe the wag of his tail keeps them away, like it does for horses.

Something rubs against my legs and I scream, almost dropping my phone, but it's only King, doubled back to join me. I reach down to pat his coarse fur, but he trots away again, back to the edge of the trail. His tail swings back and forth.

"Get back here," I hiss. I find that I don't want to speak too loudly. I can't shake the sensation that we're not alone out here. And I don't want King getting too far away from me. Maybe we should turn back. We've logged enough miles already.

King doesn't hear me, or maybe he chooses to ignore me. He's deeper into the tangled bush, his dark nose rubbing against the dirt. Whatever scent he's been tracking is stronger out here.

"King!" I force myself to say it louder. "Come."

King is a good dog, and usually when I say 'come' he comes. He knows his name and he knows his basic commands. Something's got his attention, though, and it isn't me. He ignores me and keeps padding along. There's even a joyful spring in his step.

"You dumb beast," I mutter. I follow him a few steps off the path, past the thick perimeter of scraggly weeds and beyond the first line of trees. The only way to get his attention when he's in the zone like this is to grab him by the collar. Sometimes if I wave a hotdog around he'll catch the scent and that'll be enough to lure him back, but mostly I have to physically interrupt him to draw him back to me. And wouldn't you know it, I'm fresh out of hotdogs.

I look back at the trail, six feet from where I'm standing. The trail represents safety, knowability. But King is ten feet, now twelve feet in the other direction, getting deeper into the dark and looming forest. My concern for his safety overrides my own unease. I couldn't live with myself if anything ever happened to him. I start to follow.

He, of course, thinks it's a game. He starts to run faster. The dumb beast.

It's amazing how much you can come to love an animal in just a few short months. That's what I think as I chase him, clambering over moss-covered nurse logs and tripping over tree branches that King scales easily. King is both my baby and my savior. I couldn't have made it through the last six months without him. I'd gone to the animal shelter intending to get a cat — something living and breathing to distract me from the deathly stillness of my apartment —but as soon as I glimpsed King's soulful brown eyes, his bushy blond eyebrows, I was a goner. An absolute goner. His name had been Alvin, but I'd changed it to King, and neither of us have looked back since. I never saw myself as a dog person, never mind a lover of German Shepherds, but it turns out that we can surprise ourselves in all sorts of ways. Sometimes you don't know what you want until it's right in front of you.

Or until you're threatened with losing it.

"King, get back here. Please." My voice sounds desperate, and it's because I am. We're fifty feet off the trail now, maybe more. I will not be able to live with myself if something happens to him.

King thinks this is maybe the best game ever. He looks over his shoulder at me, grinning. Checking-in. *Isn't this fun? Catch me if you can!*

I groan in frustration. I run faster, lunging for him, but he dodges my grasp and pulls ahead. I should have kept his leash on. It was stupid to take it off out here, but it drives me crazy how he's constantly criss-crossing in front of me and I have to keep switching leash-hands. Plus, when I hold it in my left hand, my FitBit won't track my steps. So, all for the sake of a few thousand steps I'd unhooked his leash and strung it around my waist. I could kill myself for it.

King bounds over a fallen tree stump. He's far more graceful than I am. I catch my foot on the rough edge going over and almost fall. King glances back, and I swear to God he's laughing. I've lost track of where the trail is or how far we've come. We haven't gone straight into the woods, but on a diagonal. I think. We might have even doubled back at some point. The trees are even thicker out here, and King bobs and weaves around them with an animal grace. I lurch and stumble, out of breath. Panic fills me, a desperate kind of hopelessness. I'm not sure how much longer I can run for, and I'm afraid he's going to get away from me and I'm never going to see him again.

"King!" It comes out in a sob. Maybe he hears my agony, because he stops and watches me. "Yes," I plead. "Stay there."

I lunge toward him, but he bounds out of my grasp and I let out another groan. I've got a stitch in my side that's threatening to take me down, and I press my hand there to try to work out the cramp while I start to run again. If you could even call it running. It's more of a drunken stagger at this point, holding my sides and trying to avoid all the branches and roots and brambles that threaten to trip me up.

Finally, a clearing. Not a big one, not a field or anything, but a small patch where the trees don't grow as thick and the ground is covered in ferns instead of deathtraps. It should be a relief, with the sun beating down and that overwhelming sense of claustrophobia letting up, but my sense of unease only intensifies. My forearms prickle with goosebumps, despite the heat of the sun. I look behind me, somehow sure I'm going to see someone standing right there, but there are only trees, shadows.

King barks playfully and starts to circle the clearing, his nose investigating the tree line along the perimeter. He's still moving at a good clip, like a sidewinder, muscles rippling in his flank. I move straight through the clearing, thinking I can head him off.

It's a good plan, and I force myself to take huge running leaps through the cleared area so I can get ahead of him.

That's when my legs give out.

No, not my legs, I realize in the instant after it happens. The ground itself. There's a heart-stopping moment of weightlessness, of falling, and then I'm hitting ground. Hard. Every bone in my body jolts and I bite down on my tongue, so violently I think I've crunched right through it.

I don't scream. I'm too shocked to scream. My mouth wells with blood and my eyes blink against the darkness as I try to figure out what the hell just happened.

King barks. It sounds like it's coming from far away. He barks a second time, a short sharp shock of sound. Darkness envelops me and my eyes aren't adjusting. Did I hit my head? Maybe I have a concussion. A traumatic brain injury. King barks again and I realize the sound isn't coming from anywhere around me but from above me. *Above.*

I stare up. Brightness. Blue sky and the tips of trees and King's face grinning down at me.

I look around, at the earthen walls encircling me, the dirt floor beneath me. I'm in … a hole. A fucking hole. And not a shallow one, either. King's got to be at least twelve feet above me, maybe more.

"What the actual fuck?" I say, or try to say, before I realize how much my tongue has swollen. I spit onto the earth floor and see blood mixed in with my saliva.

King barks again, delighted with this new twist on the game. Adrenalin courses through me — leftover from my chase-induced panic and sparked again by this. Whatever *this* is. I look around again and try to take it all in, even though my poor brain feels doused with gasoline and ready to blow. Maybe I *did* hit my head.

It's all real, though. I'm actually in a hole. Eight feet by eight feet, maybe, in terms of the space I have to move. Not exactly square but not exactly round, either. Sort of haphazardly-shaped. But distinctly man-made. This isn't a natural crevice or sinkhole or whatever. Shovel marks — or tool marks of some kind — line the sides. The bottom, where I'm sitting, is craggy and uneven.

What the hell is it? Some kind of abandoned well? But wouldn't a well be better constructed? They usually drill them, don't they? So the sides would be uniform. I think. I've never exactly found myself at the bottom of an abandoned well before, so what the hell do I know? That famous news story from the eighties comes to mind, the baby caught in the well. Baby Jessica. She survived, right?

I spit again, see blood again. Less this time, so that's good. I stagger to my feet and test the various parts of my body. My wrists, my shoulders, my legs. My ribs hurt, but I think it's because I knocked the wind out of myself when I landed. It doesn't feel like anything's broken or fractured or whatever. The worst pain is in my tongue, and even that's starting to fade to a dull throb.

I look up at the top of the hole again, where King is leaning over and grinning at me. I fell twelve feet. This could have been so much worse. I could have broken multiple bones. I probably could have even died, if I'd hit my head or my neck the wrong way. What if I had fractured my spine and had to lay here paralyzed while I waited for someone to come and get me? Another wave of anxious adrenalin surges through me.

I'm fine, I tell myself. Just fine. Nothing broken. Some day this will be a funny story I'll tell at work. *That time I fell into a hole, haha, remember that?*

All I have to do is figure a way out.

I reach for my phone but find my pockets empty. I pat them down, frantic. The two side pockets of my windbreaker, the hidden pocket on the waistband of my runner's leggings, even though there's no chance I would have put the phone in there. I'm pretty sure it wouldn't even fit. I strip the jacket off and turn it inside out, as if somehow the phone might have gotten caught in the sleeve or the lining or some other mysterious hidey-hole. There's nothing. No phone.

For the first time, I feel a surge of real fear. I pace around the small enclosure, like a wild animal trapped in a pen. I circle the small area again and again, run my hands along the earthen walls.

Then, a glint. Something dark on the ground, but not dirt or a rock. I'm grinning before I even bend down to scoop it up. My phone. I've never been so happy to see it.

I tap the screen to turn it on and the NO SERVICE tag glares at me. *Nonononono*. I hit the emergency dial button anyway, because I think sometimes that still works, but nothing happens. The call doesn't go through. I hit the button to disconnect and try again. I walk around the perimeter of the hole with the phone to see if I can get reception anywhere. I can't. I try holding the phone high up in the air, in case that helps. It doesn't. I remember looking at my phone a few times out on the trail, and even there the reception was spotty. I'm fucked. The phone isn't going to work down here.

"Help!" My voice sounds tentative at first. I'm not used to yelling, and it feels unnatural. Barbaric, even. It's a strange dichotomy, to want to be polite even when you're in dire need of help. Shouldn't my primitive instincts take over? But maybe it's because the whole situation doesn't yet feel dire; it feels, to be honest, completely absurd.

I force myself to yell again, louder this time. I put my whole aching diaphragm into it. "Help! Somebody, help me!"

From above, King whines. He's never heard me yell before, not like this. He can tell that something's wrong. Not a game anymore. He peers down at me, his chocolate brown eyes narrowed in concern.

"Help! Please help! I'm stuck! Anyone!" There has to be someone on the trail by now, or there will be soon. According to my phone it's almost eight o'clock, and by mid-morning, the trail tends to get a bit busy. Well, busi*er*. Hikers and trail riders and birdwatchers and what have you. But will they be able to hear me from all the way out here? How far did King and I travel? It felt like I was chasing him forever, but it couldn't have been more than a couple of minutes, right? If I yell loud enough, someone will hear me.

"Help! Help me, please!" I put more volume into it because I'm starting to really get scared. I'm trapped in a hole, with no phone and no idea how I'm going to get out. This is actually a thing that's happening. To me. It's ridiculous and absurd and completely fucking terrifying. What am I going to do?

"HELP ME!" I bellow. My lungs thunder with the vibration. I try to yell again but I can't take another breath. I gasp, trying to suck in air. Gulping at it, but not getting anything into my lungs.

Oh no. Not a panic attack.

As if on cue, my heart starts to race. My veins aren't veins anymore but racetracks, and blood rushes through me so fast it's as if my skin has whiplash. My chest tenses, my hands curl up into a set of claw-like pincers.

Definitely a panic attack.

The walls of the hole close around me. The space, which was already small, grows smaller. There's not enough oxygen down here. Does oxygen rise? Is it like heat? What if I breathe it all up? What if I've already breathed it all up? I imagine what would happen to my lungs if there wasn't enough air, how they would constrict and close in on themselves. Fear surges.

The panic attacks are a new thing for me. No, that's not true. I had them a long time ago, when my life looked very different than it does now. But eventually those panic attacks went away. I thought I was cured. Six months ago, when everything in my life imploded, they started back up again. That was when I started seeing Dr. Monica, my therapist, again. She isn't an actual doctor. She has a doctorate in philosophy, of all things, and gets people to call her Dr. Monica because of this. I'm not sure it's entirely ethical, but otherwise, I like her, so I keep seeing her, questionable ethics aside.

Sitting in her dimly lit office, with the brightly patterned sari draped over the table lamp, as if we were in some college dorm room cum opium den, Dr. Monica had talked me through how to handle the panic. I try to recall the things she said. That I won't die. That the best thing to do is not fight it but lean into it. Let it come and let it do its worst while I focus on breathing, and counting, and counting my breathing.

It all sounded so useful, so easy, when we were in her office. But down here, at the bottom of a hole in the middle of the forest, it's a completely different story. I have no coach, no books, no distractions. I reach for my phone, because at least that will help preoccupy me. The bright glow of it is comforting, even if it's not functional. I scroll through and count my apps — sixty-three — then count the number of apps with blue icons — seventeen — then count the number of games — nine. I give myself stupid little things to do to take my mind off the panic that's coursing through me. Distraction has always been the best way for me to ward off a panic attack — or get through one. This time it doesn't have the same effect. It's the walls around me, or the lack of fresh air, or maybe it's the sound of all those damn birds chirping high above me, but the sense of drowning doesn't abate. The panic is poured concrete, filling the space around me until there's nothing left.

King whines again. I look up and he paws at the ground. His brow is furrowed, his eyes worried. Seeing him loosens something in me, just a little. Enough to get half a breath in and I leverage that to get another half. I don't look away from King, but force myself to keep staring into his wide, compassionate eyes. The thing inside me loosens another turn.

It's a slow process, coming down. The way landing an airplane takes way longer than getting up in the air in the first place. The breath comes slowly, in jagged stuttering pockets, and my heart unclenches like a fist unfurling. I try to match my breathing to King's, and I never look away from him and he absorbs all my mania and terror and somehow sets it right.

I can breathe again.

Once I'm not struggling for air, the space feels just a bit bigger, a touch more manageable. This is a stupid situation, but it's not like I'm going to die down here. Eventually someone is going to find me, and get me out. I just need to wait.

And I can do that. I've always been patient. I have many, many flaws — I'm emotional, disagreeable, and I hold a grudge like no one else, to name a few — but a lack of patience isn't one of them.

TWO
SIX MONTHS AGO

James pulls the chair out and Lily slips into it.

"Is this okay?" he asks as he pushes the chair back into place with her in it.

"It's perfect." She smiles. It *is* perfect.

It's Valentine's Day, their first together, and James has outdone himself. He's always been fond of surprising her, and in the year they've been together, he's gone out of his way to bestow her with jewelry, flowers, countless little luxuries. Now he's planned an entire trip from Seattle to San Francisco without telling her, surprised her this morning with roses and an envelope with airline tickets. They're staying at a trendy boutique hotel with a gas fireplace in the room and a jacuzzi bathtub big enough for two. He'd made dinner reservations at an intimate little French restaurant, and even though the place is full because of the holiday, it's laid out in such a way that their table still feels cozy and private. Lily sets her napkin on her lap while James takes his seat across from her.

A server arrives and, with a flourish, presents them with a bottle of champagne. Obviously another point that James has thought ahead on. She swoons a little. He's always five steps ahead of everyone else, and it's one of the things she respects about him. Loves about him. It's a quality she's worked hard to cultivate in herself, too.

When their drinks have been poured and the server has receded into the dim interior of the restaurant, James lifts his glass.

"To you," he says. "The woman who makes me happier than I ever thought possible."

Lily flushes with pleasure. "I love you," she says as she clinks her glass against his. "And you make me just as happy."

"Good," he says, pleased.

In the flickering candlelight, his eyes are dark, and the way his hair flops down over his forehead is both boyish and handsome. She sips her champagne and feels the bubbles pop and fizz all the way down her throat.

When the waiter returns, James orders for them. Something with beef and red wine, and some sort of asparagus tart. More champagne. They talk and laugh the same way they always do, but halfway through dinner Lily starts to notice that James seems distracted. His eyes drift over her shoulder, above her head. She turns around a couple of times to see what's got his attention, but there's nothing of interest, just other diners and a swinging steel door where the waiters come and go to the kitchen.

"Are you okay?" she asks, swallowing a bite of beef so tender it hardly even needs chewing.

"Huh? I'm fine. Great, actually." He smiles, and it's so open that she relaxes.

Maybe he's just distracted by the peek into the kitchen every time the steel doors swing open. He's always been fascinated by those restaurant reality shows. They're one of his guilty pleasures. He told her once that if he hadn't become an architect, he would have liked working in a restaurant. At home he does most of the cooking, and is far better at it than she is, though that's not saying much. Cooking isn't her strong suit. Before she met James, she ate take-out almost every night of the week. Cooking reminds her of her mother, and that's an association she doesn't relish.

When they finish eating, more champagne arrives. She starts to feel tipsy and tries to slow down, because she doesn't know what else James has planned for the evening and she doesn't want to be too drunk to enjoy it. She takes small sips, letting the bubbles pop on her tongue.

James sneaks a glance over her head again, and this time he makes a gesture at someone. She turns around, but there's only a waiter returning to the kitchen, his back disappearing behind the metal doors. She idly wonders how they keep the stainless steel from being covered in fingerprints.

When she turns back to James, he's sweating. Her brow wrinkles in concern.

"Are you sure you're okay? You're not feeling sick, are you?" She doesn't want to have to cut their night short, not after he's gone to so much trouble.

Instead of answering, he gives her a wan smile. His face is pale and his lips thin. His eyes keep flicking to something over her shoulder.

There's a commotion behind her. No, not a commotion exactly, but a collective intake of breath, a couple of delighted laughs. Their server appears beside their table, and this time he sets down a plate with a piece of chocolate torte on it. In the torte are three sparklers. Lit and crackling. Lily can smell the faint char over the rich scent of chocolate. She smiles at James, who is studying her intently.

"Did you order this?" she asks.

He nods and tips his chin at the plate. She looks down. The sparklers are burning out and another sparkling thing catches her eye. A ring.

"Oh my God." She looks from the dessert over to James and back down. "Oh my God," she says again.

"Lily." He gets out of his chair and goes down on one knee. The people sitting around them gasp and there are more breathless, anticipatory laughs. "I love you. This is fast, I know, but being with you has made me realize that there's no one else in this world I'd rather be with — and I want to be with you forever. Will you do me the honor of being my wife?"

"Oh my God," she says again. She's dumb with the shock of it. She's considered the idea of marrying James. Of course she has. But it seemed like an impossible dream. Good things happened to other people, not to Lily. And here was the best thing of all, happening right in front of her. Happening *to* her.

James gazes up at her with a grim expression and she realizes she hasn't actually said yes yet. She slides off the chair and onto her knees in front of him, and she takes his face in her hands and kisses him, murmuring the word *yes* into his mouth, over and over. She hears applause. She's self-conscious, suddenly. Too aware of the people around them, of all those eyes. On her. She prefers to stay inconspicuous, although dating James has made that difficult. He draws attention wherever he goes, with his dark hair and his striking green eyes and his chiseled romance-cover-worthy jaw. A flush of anxiety covers her, distracts her from the kiss. Over James' shoulder she opens one eye a crack and gazes around the restaurant, but everyone has already gone back to eating.

BACK AT THE HOTEL, James opens another bottle of champagne, which had magically appeared in their room before their arrival. He binds her wrists with his silk tie, which is not unusual, but then he pushes her face down on the bed, which is. He takes her from behind. She doesn't struggle, but she hates that she can't see his face, and two tears pool in the corners of her eyes. She reminds herself that he loves her, that he wants to marry her, but still a slither of something dark runs through her. A memory, the pressure of the pillow against her mouth, choking off her breath. She pushes it aside, where it can't trouble her. She's so good at that now. So good it almost scares her.

Afterward, Lily lies awake. James is beside her, sound asleep. She's tired, too, but adrenalin keeps her from settling. She can't believe any of this is really happening. She examines her ring in the glow of the pale moonlight that filters through the blinds. It's a *rock*. A rock and a half, one might say. He did good. She wonders if he enlisted a sales clerk to help him pick it out, but that isn't his style. He prides himself on knowing her tastes. On knowing what's best for her. It's why he likes to surprise her with trips like this, why he orders for her at restaurants. Sometimes, she thinks he has a secret file on her somewhere, where he catalogues her likes and dislikes in minute detail. Her favorite deodorant, her brand of tampons, the fact that she likes her Diet Coke to always have ice and her salads to always have bacon. Maybe some women would be disturbed by how well he seems to know her, but she welcomes it. It shows he cares. She sees herself reflected in his eyes and it's the only time she truly likes — and believes — what she sees.

She wishes for a second that there was someone she could call or text, someone to celebrate their news with. She has no girlfriends — too risky. A few coworkers she likes well enough, but there aren't any that she'd share her happy news with tonight. For a second, she lets herself imagine that she comes from a normal family; that she could call up her mother and squeal into the phone with her. But it'll never be that way, and there's no point in wishing it were so. James isn't close with his parents, either, and she doubts he's bothered to tell them.

So, it will be just them for now, and there will be colleagues on Monday. They'll be happy for her, even though some of them will tease her by saying *"That's pretty quick, isn't it?"* Or some variation thereof. It *is* pretty quick, but she doesn't mind. She's been waiting a lifetime for this. For her own happy ending. But she'd have waited forever if she had to, because deep down she always knew that eventually her patience would be rewarded. She's a patient woman. Always has been.

THREE
PRESENT DAY

Eight hours have passed. I've checked the time on my phone every five minutes or so. Each time, I'd been convinced that at least an hour must have passed, and each time, I was discouraged to discover that it had been mere minutes since I last looked.

My throat is raw from yelling. Late morning to early afternoon is when this trail is the busiest, and I'd figured that was my best chance to get someone to hear me. I'd yelled myself hoarse, but to no avail. I'm not sure my voice even carried that far. I'd stopped yelling a few times to listen for signs of life. For any sign at all that humans ventured out this far into the forest. Voices, traffic, some of the dirt bikes or four-wheelers that sometimes come out here. There was nothing like that. Just the damn birds. Capitol State Forest has so much untraveled land, and I conclude that I'm too deep in it to be heard.

King is still here. He lays in the grass above the hole, his paws slightly over the edge and his chin resting on top of them. He alternates between dozing and watching me with a guarded expression. I've tried telling him to go to the trail, to get help, but his commands aren't that good. He knows sit, stay, roll over, play dead. Lassie, he isn't.

I sit on the ground of the hole and lean against its earthy, rocky side. My clothes are stiff with filth already, and there's dirt in my ponytail from where I keep leaning my head against the wall. I want a shower and a bowl of soup.

I keep myself busy by repeatedly going over the inventory of things that made it into the hole with me. My phone. My FitBit. My windbreaker. The sneakers, leggings, t-shirt, and sports bra I'm wearing. The half-empty sports bottle of water. The can of bear spray. My car keys. And King's leash, which was looped around my waist. I keep thinking I can do something with that, but so far I haven't figured out what. It's long enough that if I toss it, the end will reach outside of the hole, but what can I do beyond that? I can't see anything outside the hole to catch it on, so I can't exactly use it to pull myself up and out of the hole. But I'm glad to have it, even if I can't yet figure out what to do with it.

Tomorrow is Monday. That's the thought I keep coming back to, the thought that helps ward off the panic. I'm not the type to miss work, so someone will notice. They'll probably even dispatch the police to my apartment. It happened before, when a guy from the development team didn't show up one morning. The HR department called the police and the police went to his house and found him dead in his bathroom, sitting on the can with his pants around his ankles. Massive heart attack. If they sent the cops out for him, they'll send them out for me, too.

I try to think through what the police will find when they show up at my apartment to do a wellness check. They'll spot

King's food and water bowls in the kitchen, so they'll know I have a dog. They'll deduce that I've gone somewhere with him. They'll check my space in my apartment building's parking garage, maybe, and realize that I've taken the car. If they ask around at the office, someone might remember that I walk out here with him on the weekends. Daphne, I think, with a happy lurch. She'll remember because of the black flies.

The police will come out here, once they put all that together. They'll find the Explorer on the side of the road. And when they come in looking for me, they won't stay on the path, they'll realize that if something happened to me, it's probably because I strayed into the woods. They'll be out here looking for me before long. These woods will be teeming with people, and maybe search and rescue dogs. Once I hear them, I'll get King to bark. They'll find us. They'll find us.

They have to find us.

But a wave of pessimism hits me. The police won't want to go to my apartment to begin with. They'll think it's a waste of their time, that I'm just playing hooky from work. If they come into my apartment at all, they won't notice anything amiss. I keep it tidy, and there won't be any real reason for them to suspect that anything's happened to me. If they notice King's dishes, they'll assume I took him with me for a day of adventuring. They'll be on to the next call after barely more than a cursory glance around, and that's if they even make it inside the unit, which is doubtful since it'll mean tracking down the landlord and getting him to open it up, which he'll bitch and moan about.

But my coworkers will notice. I come back to that because it's the only thing that grounds me. Maybe they'll buy that I took one day off without telling anyone, but eventually their concern will mount. How long will that take? Two days? Three? Four? Will it be next Monday before they really sound the alarm?

I won't last until next Monday. I only have half a bottle of water. I might be able to make it without food, but I can't go that long without water. If it rains, I can try to fill the bottle, maybe spread my windbreaker out and collect water in that, too. But that's only if it rains. Is rainwater even safe to drink? I have no idea.

I crack my knuckles and try to get off this train of thought, because it's one that threatens to loosen the panic that's right below the surface, bubbling away like a pot of potatoes, waiting to boil over. I'm not going to have to collect rainwater in my windbreaker, because it's not going to come to that. Someone's going to find me. It's probably only a matter of hours. I can't imagine still being here when the sun goes down and the sky gets dark. I'll be home long before then, showered and souped and cuddling on the couch with King, watching old episodes of *Mad Men*. I can almost feel my feet sliding into my fuzzy Angora slippers.

I look at my phone. Another five minutes have passed. My battery is down to forty percent.

A low moan fills my ears, and I realize it's me. I bang the back of my head against the wall and let the defeated moan get louder, until it's the only thing I can hear. A higher pitched sound joins it. King, above me, whining. I stop moaning. I feel bad for making him worry, which is ridiculous. I'm stuck in a hole, and I feel bad for my dog.

"Sorry, buddy," I tell him, anyway.

He pants and paws at the ground. The sun perches high in the sky now, and although it's pretty cool down here in the hole, he must be baking up there in the grass. He doesn't have water, either. Another thing to worry about. I think there are streams out here somewhere. Little creeks, at least. Puddles. Is he smart enough to go find them and drink something when he needs to? Or will he stay here with me?

The thought of King dying because I was stupid enough to fall into a goddamn hole fills me with impotent rage. I scream and beat my fists against the dirt floor. I beat them until my hands are throbbing.

I look at my phone. Four minutes this time.

The phone will be dead within a couple of hours. Especially if I don't stop waking it up every few minutes just to look at the clock and realize that virtually no time at all has passed. I remember my FitBit and tell myself that I'll only use that to check the time from now on. The FitBit battery will last a lot longer, probably four days or so. Certainly, long enough for me to get the hell out of here.

What about using the FitBit to communicate? I know it has GPS in it, but I'm not sure how anyone else can access it. The police might be able to, but they'd probably have to get a subpoena first. How long does something like that take? A few days? And that's assuming they ever reach the point where they start to think something bad has actually happened to me. How long will that be? Another week?

I'm back where I started. I can't last a week down here. Not without food or water. And neither can King. I have to find a way to get us out of here.

FOUR
SIX MONTHS AGO

Lily and James take a cab home from the airport. When James unlocks the door to their apartment, Lily bursts in ahead of him. She's needed to pee since they deplaned and she lurches toward the bathroom while James wrestles with their luggage.

She screams. On the floor of the living room is something big and black. A bird. She hates birds under the best of circumstances, and inside their apartment is *not* the best of circumstances.

James is at her side and she wordlessly points.

"Jesus Christ," he says.

The bird lies at an unnatural angle. Flat on its side, head cocked. Lily doesn't think she's ever seen a bird lay like that, and she realizes that it's dead. Her stomach turns over. She doesn't know if a dead bird is better or worse than a live one.

"How the fuck did that get in here?" James says.

Lily shakes her head. She doesn't trust her voice. She looks around for an open window, but her eyes zero in on the bird shit. Everywhere. White piles on the window sill, the bamboo floors, the arm of the white leather sofa. The bird must have been in here the entire time they were away. Desperately trying to find its way back out and eventually, she supposes, starving to death. Her throat clenches and she tries not to gag.

"Get me some gloves, babe." James has dropped the luggage and is taking charge, which is what he always does and one of the reasons she loves him. Without a word, she goes to the coat closet and grabs a pair of black leather gloves and hands them to him.

He stares down at them and then at her. "Not my fucking good driving gloves," he snaps. "Work gloves. Dish gloves. Something."

"Right. Of course. Sorry." Her cheeks flame but she goes to the kitchen and gets the yellow dishwashing gloves from under the sink. She's forgotten all about her need to pee. She hands the gloves to James.

"And a plastic bag and some newspaper," he barks. He yanks on the yellow gloves, pulls them up over the sleeves of his crisp white shirt.

She fetches the supplies and hands over the newspaper. Her hands are shaking. He instructs her to hold the bag open for him, which she does, although she keeps her head turned while she does it. She doesn't want to see the bird. She's afraid she'll have to look into its beady little eyes. It's a crow, or maybe a raven. Are those common around here? Probably a crow. She closes her eyes and wretches when the weight of the dead bird falls into the plastic bag she's holding.

James takes the bag and kisses her forehead. "I'll go throw this out."

"Thank you." Lily swoons with gratitude. She's not usually a weak person, or at least she doesn't like to think she is.

Something about the sight of the dead crow really threw her, though. How did it get into the apartment?

While James is out, she grabs a spare pair of dishwashing gloves and some cleaning supplies and starts wiping up the bird shit. That damn thing got it everywhere. She finds small stains on the sill of the bedroom window, in the marble shower stall, a splat of it right in the middle of the oversized kitchen island. Only James' office was spared, since he keeps the door closed. She sprays everything down with Lysol, but it still feels tainted. Dirty. This weekend started out so perfectly and now everything's ruined.

No, she tells herself. Nothing is ruined. James is still wonderful and they're still getting married, and everything's working out exactly as she wanted. This is just a weird freak thing that happened. It doesn't mean anything. It doesn't mean anything at all.

———

ON MONDAY MORNING, she's exhausted. She barely slept at all last night, and when she did, she had strange and disturbing dreams about crows who smiled with human teeth.

"Anyone home?" James snaps his fingers and Lily jolts. They're in James' car, parked outside her office building, where he drops her off every weekday morning on his way to work.

"Sorry." She tries to smile. James leans over and she kisses his cheek, which has been freshly shaven. She likes him best with a thin layer of scruff, but he prefers a clean look. "See you tonight."

"I love you, Lily," he says as she gets out of the car. His fingers wrap lightly around her wrist. "Remember that."

"Love you, too." She tries to tug her arm away but he tightens his grip, until she smiles and adds, "I'll remember."

She goes inside the broad glass doors of the office tower and rides the elevator up to the seventeenth floor. Lily works for an advertising firm called DigitaLuster. They're one of those hip and young and nauseatingly innovative companies. The kind that tries to mirror themselves after some Silicon Valley start-up. Despite the fact that her office is in a soulless glass tower in downtown Seattle, it's been tricked out with arcade games, life-sized clear lucite animal sculptures — there's a rather terrifying ostrich outside Lily's office that she's christened Betsy — and Jetsons-esque furniture in retina-searing colors.

Despite this, Lily loves her job. Advertising wasn't her first choice, but she's come to find that she's good at it. She knows how to keep even the toughest clients happy, and she likes being someone the firm can count on. It's stabilizing, the routine and the predictability of it, especially after all the years she spent adrift.

She says hello to Daphne, the perky blonde at the front reception desk, and walks past her, into her own semi-open-concept glass-walled office. She wishes she had a door to close, but DigitaLuster doesn't believe in doors. Something about walling off creativity. Most days it doesn't bother her — she already has more than enough carefully constructed walls in her life. But today she'd like the privacy.

She and James haven't spoken about the bird since he got back to the apartment after depositing it down the garbage chute at the end of their hallway. It's like he's forgotten about it entirely. Lily can't forget. She's confronted with the dark shape of it every time she closes her eyes. She twists her mind over and over, chewing on the question of how it got into the apartment. Last night, while James was in the shower, she inspected every window and found all of them locked up tight, the way she knew they'd left them. She even inspected the dryer vent, but the grate was secure, and anyway, she isn't sure the vent even goes all the way outside. The only possibility is that it somehow flew in the apartment door when they were leaving on Friday. But how was that possible? The bird would have to have been in the hallway, and how would it get there? And wouldn't they have noticed it scooting into their apartment? But that morning had been a flurry of activity — thinking she was getting ready for work only for James to produce the plane tickets and announce that he was whisking her away for the weekend, that he'd already cleared it with her boss, that she should pack the backless black dress he loves her in. They'd left the apartment in such a hurry that maybe they'd failed to notice a bird fluttering past them.

Yet the explanation seems unlikely.

Maybe, she thinks as she slips down behind her white lacquered desk and onto her hot pink chair, the property managers let themselves in. James owns the apartment but the building itself is managed by a third party, a property management company responsible for maintaining the common areas and the overall integrity of the building. If there'd been a gas leak or something, the property manager might have had to go around and open all the windows to vent the building. The bird got in that way, unnoticed. That has to be it. Or some variation, anyway.

Without even taking off her coat, she looks up the number

of the property management company and dials it from her desk phone. It rings twice and then is answered with a brusque, "Yeah? Leaside Property Management."

"Oh, hi. My name is ..." She stumbles. She isn't sure they'll talk to her, since she isn't listed as an owner. She's only been living there a few months. She changes track. "I'm calling on behalf of James Russel, regarding his unit at 498 Beckham Avenue. Unit 1412."

"Right. What can I do for you?"

"I was just wondering if someone entered our — *his* — unit over the weekend. Maybe someone went in and opened a window?"

"Did *we*? Is that what you're asking?"

"Yes."

"No, ma'am. If someone opened a window, it wasn't us."

"No, there were no windows open. It's just that, we — *he* — found this bird in the apartment..."

"Birds?" His gruff voice turns sharp. "No pets allowed on the premises."

"No, it wasn't a pet. It was just this bird that got into the apartment somehow, and it died, and ..." She doesn't know how to finish the sentence because she still doesn't understand exactly what happened. Or, to be honest, why it's unsettled her so much.

"You got dead birds in your apartment, maybe you want to call the Department of Health or something. I don't know."

"No, it was just the one. Just the one dead bird. All I'm doing is trying to figure out how it got there."

"My guess is it's because someone left the window open." He says it like she's a child who doesn't grasp that two plus two equals four.

"No," she starts to protest, but decides it isn't worth it. "Thanks for your time."

"You need the number for the Department of Health?"

"No, no, that's alright."

Lily hangs up the phone and sits there staring at it. She's starting to sweat so she strips off her coat, unwinds her scarf. There's a battery acid taste in the back of her throat, and she wants water.

A knock comes from the front of her office. She may not have an office door, but generally people here are pretty respectful about knocking before they enter. She looks up and finds Damian Herschmann leaning against the glass and staring down at his phone. He's one of the firm's creative directors, the one she works with most often. She's normally quite fond of him, but today she suppresses a groan. She's not in the mood for chitchat. She plasters on a smile and says, "Good morning."

He saunters in and perches on the edge of her desk. Damian is exactly the kind of guy she'd expect to find working at a company like DigitaLuster. He wears an argyle sweater vest and a pair of Converse sneakers, an expensive pair of black-rimmed round Prada glasses. His cologne smells like pine trees, though she doubts he's ever set foot in a forest in his life. He leans over and peers at her hand. "Whoa! What a rock. So, your man popped the question."

"Oh." Lily looks down at her finger, where the diamond solitaire sparkles under the fluorescent office lights. She's surprised he noticed. She hopes the ring isn't too conspicuous. She's not used to drawing so much attention to herself. "Yes, he did."

"That was fast." He shakes his head, chuckling. "You must've been determined to lock this one in."

Lily makes a non-committal noise and offers him an equally non-committal smile. She turns on her computer, hoping he'll take it as a sign that she wants to get to work.

Instead, he waves at someone passing by her office. "Aurora, get in here. Look at this."

Aurora Watts, a red-headed wisp of a woman that Lily also works with frequently, sticks her head in the entryway. A familiar scent of orange rinds drifts in after her.

"Show her," Damian nudges Lily.

She holds up her hand, ring facing out. Aurora grimaces but manages to turn it into a smile. "Congratulations," she says. "I guess you got what you wanted."

Lily knows a backhanded compliment when she gets one, but she just smiles back and instead imagines Betsy the giant lucite ostrich toppling over and squashing Aurora like a bug. It's not so much that she and Aurora dislike each other personally, it's just that their roles in the company are almost always at odds. Aurora is a project manager, and Lily is an account manager. Lily works directly with the clients. Schmoozing them up, keeping them happy, making them unreasonable promises. Aurora manages the development team, which means it's her job to deliver on those unreasonable promises. Lily has to reluctantly admit that she's just squirrely and neurotic enough to be good at it.

Neither woman says anything else, so Damian smooths things over, as he often does. "So, when's the big day? Do you have a date yet?"

"Um." For the first time, Lily considers the practical realities of getting married. The guests that will need to be invited, the pictures that will be taken. Her stomach clenches. Her tongue thickens and refuses to shape any words. The silence stretches out uncomfortably.

"Come on," Damian says eventually, when the break in conversation has gone on too long. "Let's go downstairs. Coffee's on me."

Lily goes downstairs with him and Aurora. She doesn't want to, but she tells herself the distraction might be healthy. She won't have to think about the wedding *or* the dead bird.

And it is. For twenty whole minutes, she only thinks about the bird once, when her ring catches the light and it reminds her, momentarily, of the beady eye of a crow.

FIVE
PRESENT DAY

Another four hours have passed. It's almost eight in the evening. Above ground, there'd still be sunlight, but down here in the hole, it's getting dark.

I'm hungry. Thirsty. Scared. Tired. The earlier adrenalin has burned away and left me queasy and cold.

I've finished half of my water already. A mistake, probably. I didn't think I'd still be here. I thought for sure someone would hear me screaming this afternoon, but I must be further into the woods than I realized. No one has come. There doesn't even seem to be the hope of anyone coming. My best chance is tomorrow morning, when I don't show up for work, but even then I don't know. I don't know.

I try to doze a little to make the time go by faster, but I keep jolting awake every time I start to nod off. The scent of dirt is in my nostrils and I keep imagining worms or ants or beetles slithering or scuttling across me when I sleep. I keep scratching at my skin, which stretches too tight. Panic throbs inside me, lurking right below the surface.

King is still here. He's above me, laying in the grass just at the edge of the top of the hole. A few times, he's gotten up and wandered away for a couple of minutes. I hold out hope that he's going to the trail to find someone, or at least that he's gone to look for water for himself, but he always returns a moment or two later. Probably just going to pee.

Speaking of going to pee. My bladder aches. I've been putting off going, but after twelve hours down here, I can't wait anymore. I have a strong bladder — mostly because I despise public toilets — but it's not *that* strong. I stand up and stretch out my legs. My tailbone is stiff from sitting on the ground for so long, and there's a chill in the lower half of my body. I stamp my feet as I walk from one end of the hole to the other, trying to find a place to 'go.' King watches me with curiosity from above.

"You wouldn't have this problem, I know." I look up at him. "You go wherever you want."

King grins at me, though it's more at the sound of my voice than my words. The sight of his face perks me up, and I thank God that he's here with me. The fact that he's the entire reason I'm in this mess doesn't factor into it. He was just doing his own thing. I was the idiot who ran right over a hole. I was the idiot who let him off the leash in the first place.

The walls of the hole are all essentially the same, so I pick the point that's farthest away from where I've been sitting. I yank down my leggings and underwear, press my back against the wall, and hold myself in a squat. Even with how badly my bladder is aching, it takes a minute for the signal to make it from my brain to my body.

"Come on, come on," I mutter, trying to picture running faucets, waterfalls, garden hoses. Finally, an eruption. A long stream of piss pours out of me, and I slump against the wall with both relief and disgust.

It isn't peeing outside that bothers me. Not really. I'm not a fan of camping or any kind of rugged outdoor lifestyle stuff, but being something of an amateur hiker means I've peed in the woods on occasion, when necessary. It's peeing in such close quarters that turns my stomach. This puddle will be here with me for as long as I'm in here, stinking and reminding me of what I've done, how dirty I am.

The lack of toilet paper also doesn't help the situation. I hold the squat position until my thighs are burning, trying to squeeze out any remaining drips, and yank my leggings back on.

As I stand, I get a whiff of urine. The scent of it brings back a memory, something I haven't thought of in ages. Something I've worked hard not to think about. A closet. A locked door. The starchy smell of pressed shirts, of shoe polish, of leather belts with teeth marks in them. And, when I couldn't take it anymore, when I was aching with it, the acrid scent of my own urine. My hot flush of shame. And still the door didn't open. The smell made the insides of my nostrils burn.

I push away the memory. I can't afford to go there. Not now. Not when I'm stuck down here and the odor of urine and the air of claustrophobia are so similar. I can't. I mustn't.

Above me, King whines. I wonder if he can sense my distress. Dogs are smart like that, aren't they? Intuitive. That's what the woman at the shelter told me, anyway, and even in my six months of being a dog owner, I've found it to be true. King has an uncanny way of sensing my moods, of knowing when I need a cuddle or a silly game of tug-of-war or to get my ass out of the apartment for some fresh air.

"It's okay," I tell him. "I'm okay." It's a lie. I don't feel okay. But I don't want him to worry. I know how absurd that sounds. What I want most right now is to climb up out of here and bury my face in his fur. That way we'll both feel better.

As soon as the idea occurs to me, I realize how simple it could be. How stupid I've been to not consider it earlier. These walls are just dirt. Someone dug this hole. So maybe I can somehow dig or climb my way out of it. The walls are sheer, but I could try to gouge out handholds, footholds. There are already a few spots in the bottom half that have rock outcroppings, and around the top half there are bits of root from trees that perhaps once stood above this very spot.

I start to get excited. This might actually work. It's getting dark, and it'll be hard to see, but I don't want to wait until morning to at least try. I could kick myself for not thinking of this sooner. I blame the shock of the fall, the dumbness of the adrenalin.

I gaze around the hole, evaluating which section of the wall has the most natural outcroppings. There's one area, a couple of feet from my new bathroom, where the rock juts out and there's a sturdy-looking tree root about two-thirds of the way up. If I could get my foot on that, if it holds my weight, I could almost reach the top of the hole from there.

Now that I have a plan, I'm ready to go. I pulse with it. This is going to work. I don't have anything to dig with, but I use the toe of my sneaker to start grinding away at a chunk of the wall a foot and a half above the ground.

It doesn't go as easy as I thought. The dirt is hard packed, more rock than rubble, and my sneaker is too wide. I manage to scrape away some of the earth, but not enough to get a toehold. It just looks like I've dented the wall. Not something I can get purchase on. I'd need a tool of some kind, something to hack away at the rock with. I crouch down and use my hands to claw at the dirt. It's difficult and before long, my fingers ache and bleed.

But it works. Sort of. I gouge out enough dirt that I think I can get the toe of my shoe in there. I stand up, wiping my hands on my pants. I brace my upper body against the wall and hoist up my leg. It's tight, but I can almost wedge the toe of my shoe in. I claw out more dirt and try again. My toe goes in. I test the weight and yes, God, this is working. I heft myself up, grabbing on to the tree root. My leg shakes and slips and the root tears and then my foot is slipping for real, the earth is giving way, and then I'm sliding to the ground. I bang my knee, hard, and let out a frustrated sob.

The toehold I'd carved out is gone, the rock crumbled away under my weight. My knee throbs but I force myself back up. There has to be a way to make this work. There just has to be.

I start again, clawing out a new toehold, even though my fingers are aching. I dig until they're bloody, my skin raw, my nails starting to rip away from the beds. I get another toehold carved out and that one collapses, too. A third one does the same. I can't even get enough purchase to reach up and grab that tree root.

I slump down onto the ground again. The daylight is almost gone and the hole is dark and I can barely see anymore. I'll try again tomorrow, but I'm no longer as optimistic about my chances.

I find myself wondering again about how this hole got here

in the first place. Someone, at some point, dug it. I'm sure of that much. And judging by some of the sharp scrape marks along the side — from a shovel or a machine of some sort — I don't think it was all that long ago. Otherwise the marks would have eroded or faded away, wouldn't they? With rain and snow and the passing of time.

Also, I realize with a start, there aren't many dead leaves down here. The hole itself is in a bit of a clearing but it's surrounded by trees. Lots of evergreens, but there are also plenty of oak and maple and birch and God knows what else out here. Trees like that produce lots of leaves. If this hole had been here longer, wouldn't there be moldering leaves down here? So if I had to guess, I'd say this hole hasn't even been here a year. It hasn't gone through an autumn yet.

Sometime in the last year, someone — or multiple someones — dug this hole. But for what purpose?

The forest is state-owned land, as far as I know. A few of the trails are groomed in the winter. I've never thought to wonder by whom. There's no real parking lot, at least not where I hike, but at the shoulder of the road where cars park, there are trashcans that get emptied and trail signs that sometimes get updated. The state must do that, or maybe the local parks department.

But what would they dig this hole for? It's not big enough to be the foundation of any kind of building, and I can't think of how it might be connected to the logging that goes on here. The idea I keep coming back to is a well, but why build it all the way out here, when the public areas are so far away? I must be at least an hour's walk from the road.

I think of something that cheers me. My car. It's parked on the side of the road, up near the trailhead. My Discover Pass is right on the dash. Someone will see it. Maybe not tonight, but after a day or two, someone will notice this silver Ford Explorer that hasn't moved. Someone will call the police. That's what people do.

I sit and lean against the rock wall, a couple of feet away from my failed toeholds. Things are happening. My bones hum with it. Tomorrow my colleagues — Damian and Daphne and our trusty HR department — will notice my absence. Someone from the state will find my car. Somewhere, a good detective will put two and two together. They'll find me.

They have to. Because the alternative is unthinkable.

SIX
SIX MONTHS AGO

Lily walks home from work, as she always does, stopping at Pike Place Market for lamb chops and asparagus and tarragon. James is the cook in the relationship, but she's the shopper. It's a game they like to play — she surprises him with a couple of different ingredients and he concocts something special out of them. Lily is pretty sure she's getting the better end of the deal on that one.

She arrives on Beckham Avenue with her bags in tow. James won't be home for another hour or so, which will give her a bit of time to maybe sneak in a nap. She stands outside the building and fishes in her handbag for her keys. She keeps them tucked in the small pocket at the front, but they aren't there. Her skin flushes as her heart skips a quick beat. She's been so careful with her keys. James made such a production of it when he first gave her a copy, as if he was bestowing nuclear codes on her instead of just the key to his apartment. She fishes around her purse again. There are two pockets stitched into the soft purple lining; one she uses for her phone, and the other for her keys. She checks both of them and paws around the bottom of the bag, because sometimes they spill out of the pocket. They aren't there, either. She checks the pockets of her coat, in case she stuffed them there without thinking but no, there's nothing.

She stands there, outside the building door, trying to remember the last time she saw the stupid things. It would have been Thursday. Friday was the day James whisked her off to San Francisco. Yesterday and today, they'd used his keys. So the last time she'd touched her own must have been when she'd come home from the market on Thursday. She doesn't even really remember last Thursday, at least not in any specific detail, but that must have been when it was.

"Fuck," she mutters to herself. The keys are probably in the apartment somewhere. She hopes so, anyway, because otherwise they're lost somewhere between here and San Fran.

Another tenant approaches, a man in a charcoal overcoat and a gleaming briefcase. He brandishes his own keys, opening the front door of the building and holding it open for her. Lily slips in behind him. Normally, she hates it when people let strangers into the building all willynilly, but today she nods her gratitude. Out of habit, she rides the elevator up to the fourteenth floor and stands in front of her apartment door. She still can't get in, but at least she's out of the cold.

She digs through her bag again, in case this time the keys magically appear. She yanks out handfuls of stuff and lets it fall onto the floor around her feet. Tissues, lip gloss, a half a pack of lemon and honey flavored cough drops, a half a pack of berry flavored antacids, breath mints, her eReader, hair ties, napkins, safety pins, bobby pins, a nearly-empty stick of deodorant, a take-out menu from the Thai restaurant down the street, leftover from when they'd handed it to her last time she picked up an order.

Still no keys. Everything *but* keys.

She considers trying to pick the lock with the bobby pins, but she has no idea how to do that. No, she'll have to call James. Dread pools in her stomach.

She scoops everything off the floor and back into her bag — with an internal promise that she'll organize and purge the thing soon — and leans against the wall next to the door and phones James. It takes him forever to answer.

"Hello?" He sounds out of breath.

"It's me."

"I have caller ID," he snaps.

So he's in a bad mood. Great. This should be fun. "I'm sorry. I just realized I don't have my keys."

"Where are they?"

Not *are you okay?* "I don't know. Probably in the apartment somewhere. I got home about five minutes ago but I can't get in. I have lamb," she adds, hoping that will buy her some goodwill.

"I can't leave now."

"It's okay," she says hastily. She doesn't want to pick a fight, not when everything's been so pleasant between them. Better than pleasant, really. She realizes she's running her thumb over the solitaire diamond on her ring.

"I need another twenty minutes here."

"That's totally fine. I'll be fine. The lamb will keep."

"Alright. I'll see you then."

Lily goes back down to the lobby to wait for James, because at least there are guest chairs down there and she can rest her feet. She hates wearing stilettos, but James loves them and so do her clients at work so she considers them part of the price of both love and success. But, God, do they kill her feet. She sets the shopping bag on the floor and crosses one long leg over the other and waits.

JAMES ARRIVES HOME NEARLY an hour later. Lily's happy to see him but cranky about having to wait for so long. She follows him wordlessly into the mirrored elevator and they ride back up to the fourteenth floor. He unlocks the door with a flourish, dangling his keys in front of her as if to point out how easy it was, letting yourself into your apartment, when you came prepared. She smiles wanly. She wants to tell him that if he'd just upgrade to one of those smart locks, they wouldn't have this issue, but James is anti-technology. You wouldn't think it, because he's very modern in most regards. But the one thing he truly cares about, that he goes batshit over, is his privacy. And he's convinced that smart technology is too vulnerable to hacking. When she dared suggest they get one of those Nest thermostats so she could turn the heat on in the winter before she got home from work, he'd nearly blown a gasket. She'd never dare suggest a smart lock, even if it means sitting down in the lobby and waiting for him to take his sweet time getting home.

While James starts dinner, she changes into a pair of jeans and a cozy turtleneck and starts to hunt for her keys. She'd hoped that she would find them in the glass dish in the foyer, or maybe on top of her bedroom dresser or even on the floor of the coat closet, where perhaps they'd spilled out of her purse. She doesn't find them anywhere.

James emerges from the kitchen carrying two glasses of wine. "Any luck?" He hands her one with a smile, and she accepts the conciliatory gesture.

"No." She gnaws at her lip. "I hope I didn't lose them at the airport."

"When did you last have them?"

"Thursday night. When I got home from work, I let myself in."

"No, you didn't."

"Sorry?"

"Thursday night I picked you up at the office and we went to dinner with Duncan and Cora. Remember? I let us in because you were practically falling asleep on my shoulder."

"That's right, I was, wasn't I?" She remembers now. She's no great fan of Duncan — James' business partner — or his vapid wife Cora, who only ever wants to talk about when James and Lily will be joining the country club, a prospect that Lily finds abhorrent on so many levels. Lily had consumed one glass of wine too many just to get through the evening. James hated when she drank too much, so he'd been peevish and irascible most of the evening, barely speaking to her in the cab. She'd pretended to fall asleep. Easier that way.

"So, they could be at work," James offers. "Or at the restaurant."

"Or anywhere," she says glumly. If she'd noticed right away that they were missing, she might have been able to retrace her steps. Now it's likely a lost cause.

"I bet you left them at work," he says easily. "Tomorrow morning, you'll find them on your desk somewhere. Or under it."

Lily doesn't think so, but she smiles anyway. She's

surprised he's being so easy-going about it. She'd expected him to blow a fuse. He's usually quick to blow when things like this happen; it's because he's always under so much stress from his job. She sips her wine while James goes to the kitchen to put the finishing touches on the lamb. The meal is delicious, and for a while she forgets about the missing keys.

After they've finished eating and she's loaded the dishwasher, she pours them the last of the wine and goes to find James. He stands in the middle of the living room, facing her. With excruciating slowness, he undoes the cufflink on his left sleeve, and then the one on his right. The starched fabric of his shirt is crisp and white and she swallows at the expression in his dark green eyes. She's tired tonight, drained, really, but she'll go along with this anyway, because James is her everything, and this is what it takes to be his. And besides, he was so understanding about the key thing. She drops to her knees in front of him and winces as his fist winds through her hair. She stares at the spot on the floor where they'd found the dead bird. The bamboo is as pristine as the day they had it installed, but Lily swears she sees a stain.

———

THE NEXT MORNING, James drops her off at the office with a kiss and a take-away coffee. When she rides the elevator, she inspects herself surreptitiously in the mirror, trying to ensure the bruises aren't visible over the collar of her shirt. Her eyes look dark and smudged, but if she puts on a tired-but-happy-smile, everyone will think she and James were just up late, celebrating their engagement. Which, she supposes, is what they were doing. In a way.

Despite her absolute certainty that her keys wouldn't be found at the office, and that they'd been lost somewhere between here and California, Lily pulls open the bottom drawer of her desk ... and finds them. Just like that. Just sitting there. Right where she always stows her handbag. James was right, she thinks, pulling out the keys and fingering the daisy keychain he gave her when she moved in. He'd been right.

But then, he so often is.

Holding the keys doesn't bring her the sense of relief that she expected. Instead, she feels unsettled, the same way she did after James finally disposed of the dead bird. As if something's changed, but she has no idea what.

SEVEN
PRESENT DAY

Morning. The sun came up a couple of hours ago, but it took a little longer for the light to drip down to the bottom of the hole. I stretch out my legs miserably. I'm stiff and sore and so cold that even my bones ache. I slept a little last night but not much. Most of my time was spent worrying and trying to stave off a panic attack. Throw in a heaping dose of self-pity and concern for King, and my mind whirred like a hive of busy, fearful bees.

I stand and stretch. My tailbone screams in pain. I twist my neck around until I hear that satisfying crack. People hate when I do that — they always wince at the sound — but God, it feels good.

My hunger has returned. Yesterday, around the dinner hour, it had roared up, but eventually faded into a sort of nauseated stasis. Now it's awake again. I imagine a heaping stack of pancakes, limp with butter and syrup. A coffee with extra cream. An orange. An orange would be so good right now. I can practically taste that bright citrus burst on my tongue. I moan.

Above me, King whines. My hunger is forgotten. He's been there all night, I'm almost sure of it. I dozed off a few times, but I never lost my awareness of his presence. He hasn't eaten or drank anything since yesterday. My heart aches. I feel like it's my fault. It *is* my fault.

I grab my water bottle off the ground. It's down to about a quarter. I uncap it and take a small sip. I've been trying to conserve it, but it still isn't going to last much longer. I look up at King and he licks his lips. Guilt fills me. Even though it's the last of my water, I'd still share it with him if I could think of a way to get it up to him. I can't throw it up there with the cap on because there'd be no way for him to get to the water inside — and I can't throw it up *without* the cap because everything would just spill out. Even if a little bit managed to stay in the bottom of the bottle, he'd have no idea how to get it out. King drinks out of bowls and occasionally hoses, not bottles.

"I'm sorry, buddy," I tell him. "Go find water. Go." I make a shooing motion with my hand, but he whines again, lying down and resting his chin on his big paws.

I check the time on my FitBit. Almost eight o'clock. In another hour, I'm supposed to be at work. People will notice I'm not there. Damian. Damian will notice. Damian knows I don't skip work without telling anyone. He thinks I'm weird and neurotic and twitchy — all true — but I'm not irresponsible. He'll sound the alarm.

But what then? Even once Damian alerts HR, even once HR sends the police to check on me, how will they ever figure out that I'm here? And even if — *even if* — they track me as far as Capitol Forest, what are the odds they'll ever find me out here? I'm in a fucking hole in the middle of the fucking forest.

Don't think like that. I breathe. *You can't think like that because then you'll have no hope, and hope is literally the only thing you have going for you right now. You lose that and you'll really have nothing.*

Eight o'clock turns into nine and then into ten. If I was at work, I'd be going for my second coffee, ducking down to the tiny cafe on the ground floor of the building or, if there's time and the weather's good, outside to the Starbucks down on the corner. I'd be ordering my coffee and hemming and hawing over whether or not I should also treat myself to a pastry. I should have got the damn pastry. All those times I could have had the pastry and I didn't take it. I'd give my left arm for a pastry right about now.

I look down at my arm. I have a sudden vision of one of those survival movies where the main character has to chop off their own arm to free themselves from their predicament. At least my own circumstances aren't quite that dire. So, I have two things going for me — hope and the use of both of my arms. The thought does little to cheer me up. I go back to dreaming about the pastries. Danishes with gummy raspberry filling and tart cream cheese. Almond croissants, white with powdered sugar. Mini cinnamon buns with the vanilla glaze. Big ass cinnamon buns with the mound of icing. Now I really *am* ready to gnaw my own arm off.

I get up and pace. Better to keep my legs stretched, even though I don't want to expend too much energy. If there's one thing to be grateful for, it's that I haven't had to pee again, probably since I've barely consumed any fluids. My mess from yesterday gives off a faint acrid smell, but it's not nearly as bad as it could be. Still, I avoid that end of the hole as much as possible.

I've been in here over twenty-four hours. The realization

sobers me. More than an entire day. Will I still be here tomorrow at this time? What about two days from now? Will I stand here next Monday and think, "I've been in here a week now'? Probably not. Probably by next Monday I'll be dead.

I have to get out of here. I have to.

I drop to my knees and start clawing at the dirt. There has to be a way to dig myself out of here. It's just dirt. I'll tear down this whole wall if I have to.

I work haphazardly, with no plan. My fingers still ache from yesterday. The caked and dried blood under my nails starts to bleed fresh again. My hands ring out with pain, but I keep working away at the rock and the earth. I dig out a hole that looks big enough for my foot, and when I put my sneaker on it ... it holds.

It holds.

Jubilation fills me. I can do this. I can do this. It's working. I start clawing out another hole, this one a foot and a half higher and about ten inches to the right. This one is harder. There's dirt, but there's rock shard, too. I try to dig around it, thinking I can dig it right out. It would make a perfect sized hole, and then maybe I can even use the sharp edge of the rock to dig out further cuts.

But I can't budge it. I try to go above it, below it, over a few more inches. It's solid rock. I claw until my fingers are torn to shreds, but I can't make any more headway.

I stand, my knees and back stiff, my hands a mess of raw hamburger. Maybe I can still climb it. I've got one foothold carved out, and maybe the rock is out enough that I can get my other foot on it. That would give me enough height to maybe grab onto those tree roots. Then it's only another four feet or so to the top of the hole.

It seems so simple when I look at it that way. I can do this.

I jam my foot in the hold at the bottom and try to brace most of my weight against the wall itself while I drag my other leg up. I run my foot all over the wall, trying to find anything that I can get even the smallest bit of purchase on, but the rock is too flat and the dirt crumbles away too easily. My hands start to slip and when I try to dig my fingers in to hold on, they scream in agony. My lower foot starts to slip again, slowly at first and then all at once, and I'm on the ground again. The toehold is gone, given way to crumbled earth, just like all the ones from yesterday.

For the first time, I cry. I mean *really* cry. Hot, salty tears of frustration stream down my face, dripping off my chin, onto my chest, slipping down and joining the sweat between my breasts. It's the kind of wretched crying that only toddlers do, where you'd swear their world must be ending. Only mine really is. I actually might die down here. It's not hyperbole but reality.

Something makes me stop. At first I'm not sure what it is. Certainly not some inner fortitude. All my resolve is about as crumbled as the piles of dirt around me.

I realize what it was: a sound. A branch cracking from somewhere above me.

I look up. There's King, still lying in his spot at the top of the hole, only this time he's not looking at me but back over his shoulder. I can't see what he sees, but I hear the low growl that comes from the middle of his chest.

King is protective. It's half the reason I chose him. He'd been a guard dog at an auto body shop, but they'd replaced him after they found him 'too soft'. But he wasn't too soft at all, he just didn't give a shit about rusted-out car parts. When it came to his people, he was the fiercest defender you could ask for. And I was his people now.

"What is it, boy?" I'm afraid to speak too loudly. I picture a big moose or, worse, a black bear. There are all kinds of animals in these woods. There might even be wolves. Probably not many, but I can't be sure. I imagine the helplessness I'd feel down here if King came face to face with something stronger and wilder than him.

I hear something else. Something that changes everything.

"Hey there. Who's a good boy?"

A voice. Oh, God, a human voice. Thank you, God. Thank you, Jesus. Thank you, Obama.

"Help me! Oh, help me, please! I'm stuck down here!"

There's no more sound. I listen as hard as I can, but nothing. King has stood up and turned, and I can't see more than his tail, which isn't quite tucked between his legs but is held low. Cautious.

Maybe I scared the guy away, I think. *Or imagined him,* a more nasty voice offers.

"Help me!" I yell again. "I fell in a hole. Be careful," I add. The only thing worse than being stuck down here is if my would-be rescuer fell down here, too. Wouldn't that be a treat.

There's another beat of silence, and I hear, "Who's a good boy? Yes, that's a good boy."

Maybe he can't hear me. Sound might not travel that well from down here. But how come I can hear him just fine?

"Help me!" I shriek as loud as my hoarse voice will allow. "Hey! I need help!"

There's more silence. I can't see or hear King, and I can't see or hear this man. I know it's a man by the timbre of his voice. It's deep, almost unnaturally so. I picture a heavy-set man, barrel-shaped to go with his baritone inflection.

"Help me!" I scream again. I pound against the side of the hole, as if that'll help get his attention, even though all it does is reignite the pain in my hands. "Help me!"

"Shut-up."

The words take me so by surprise that I do shut-up. My mouth clamps shut, jarring my poor tongue again. My eyes start to water.

I didn't really hear that, did I? That man didn't just tell me to shut-up? Maybe he's talking to a companion. I didn't hear anyone else's voice, but that doesn't mean there isn't anyone there.

"Help!" I yell again. "I need help. I fell in this hole and I—"

Something hits the edge of the hole and tumbles down, landing on the earthen floor with a thud. I stare at it for a minute, disbelieving.

It's a bottle of water. One of those kinds you buy in a huge flat at Costco. Oh thank God. I crawl toward it and untwist the cap, which is still sealed. I drink half of it in one giant, grateful gulp. Liquid streams down my chin; I can't even swallow fast enough to keep up with the flow, but it's so delicious and life-giving that I can't stop.

When I'm forced to pause for a breath, I wipe the back of my hand across my mouth. "Thank you," I call up. "I've been stuck here since yesterday. I thought no one was ever going to find me and I was going to die down here." I sound crazy and manic but I don't care. I *feel* crazy and manic.

Something else lands in the hole. I stare down at it again. This time, when I reach out to pick it up, it's with trembling hands. It's a square package, wrapped in wax paper and then clear plastic. A sandwich. No, two sandwiches.

"Thank you," I call again. "But really, could you help me get out of here?"

Something about this situation gives me a boggy sensation in my stomach. Why haven't I seen him yet? Shouldn't he have leaned over to check on me? I could have been lying here with a head injury and he just blindly threw a water bottle down on top of me. Who does that?

Someone who isn't planning to help you.

I ignore the voice because it's too absurd. Of course he'll help me. I might be a pessimist, but even I have enough faith in humanity that I can't believe anyone would leave me here, stuck in a hole in the middle of the woods.

Unless …

A thought occurs to me that's too horrible to contemplate. I stare down at the sandwich, at the bottle of water. At these signs of life. These signs of … preparation.

I close my mind to it, but the thought is still there. Like an itch. Like a bad smell, the reek of urine from yesterday's mess.

Someone dug this hole. And I haven't been able to come up with any ideas for its purpose. But what if its purpose is … this?

What if this isn't a hole but a trap?

"Help me," I yell again. "Oh, please, oh please, help me. Let me out."

There's silence from above me. No, not silence. He's murmuring softly to King, calling him a good boy, a handsome boy. Panic is foaming inside me, so corrosive that I'm eaten away by it.

"Let me out," I scream again. My voice lodges in my

throat; my tongue sticks to the roof of the mouth. I'm barreling down a rollercoaster track without my feet ever leaving the ground.

I'm being crazy. This is crazy. I'm losing my mind after being down here, and reading dark motivations into situations that don't warrant it.

That's what I try to tell myself, while I wait for the man on the ground above to say something. Anything.

He doesn't. I don't even hear him talking to King anymore. Has he gone? Or is he still up there, listening to me? Waiting for something?"

"Help me!" I scream. I belt out the words over and over until I'm hoarse. Until my throat feels like a burnt out firecracker. There's still no answer. King pads back over to the edge of the hole and settles himself above me again. Thank God he's still here.

But is the man? I listen for ages, but I don't hear him again, and I conclude he must be gone.

Gone to get help, I tell myself. To the police or at least to get a ladder or a rope or something.

But there's a part of me that already knows that isn't true. There won't be anyone coming to my rescue.

I'm stuck here.

No, not stuck. *Trapped.*

EIGHT
SIX MONTHS AGO

As the calendar flips over to March, Seattle turns frigid. The air takes on a dampness that seeps into Lily's bones. She arrives home one evening after another stop at the market — beef medallions, shiitake mushrooms, pearl onions — so cold that all she can think about is stripping off her clothes and climbing into a hot shower.

Standing in front of the apartment door, she fumbles for her keys. For a moment, she's sure she's lost them again, but then there they are, in the same pocket where they're supposed to be. It must be her cold hands. Her fingers are like frozen fish sticks, and about as useful. She manages to slide the key into the lock, turns it to the left. There's no resistance, no satisfying click. Strange. She turns the key back and twists it again, but of course there's no way to tell. Was the door already unlocked? Or did she imagine it?

She pushes the door open cautiously and scans the apartment. It looks the same as it always does. White, clean, orderly. Almost everything in here belongs to James, reflects his tastes, his preferences. She has a closet in the bedroom, half the bathroom vanity, a cabinet in the kitchen where she keeps her peppermint tea, her vitamins — A for her hair and nails, B for energy, D because she can't name one person in Seattle who actually gets enough sunlight — and the salt and vinegar potato chips that are her secret guilty pleasure.

Everything else is pure James. The white Italian leather sofa, the quartz coffee table with an organic shape that's always struck her as vaguely obscene, and the garish modern art that he 'collects', not because he loves it but because rich people make it a habit to collect things that make them richer. To be fair, James once invited her to come to an art auction with him, saying that he wanted to pick out something she would like, too, since he wanted her to feel at home. She laughed and told him to get whatever he wanted because she knew she'd love it. What a joke. She hates this art. She's pretty sure she could paint the same thing with some red paint, her toes, and a tab of LSD. Lily knows a lot about art, but that's a part of herself she won't ever share with James.

She looks around the apartment, ignoring the garish art and the obscene coffee table and the sofa she's terrified of sitting on lest she spill something. She's looking instead for any sign that anything is amiss. Her ears are tuned to every single sound. The hum of the climate control, the whir of the refrigerator — another overpriced Italian import — and the faint buzz of electricity that always exists in the apartment. For a second she thinks she can hear something else in there

(breathing)

but then again, maybe it's her mind playing tricks on her, because the sound doesn't come again.

The apartment, otherwise, is exactly the same as it always

is. She moves from room to room, inspecting each one, even the ones she barely ever ventures into. James has a four bedroom apartment. Besides their master suite, there's a guest bedroom for guests they never entertain; another that's been converted to James' office, and one that's become a de facto storage room. Mostly, it holds James' old sports equipment. Skis, a surf board, an old lacrosse stick. Things he hasn't touched in the entire time Lily's known him but with which he swears he can't part.

She finishes her tour, but there's nothing in the apartment that causes her any concern. Everything looks exactly as it did when she and James left for work this morning. She must have only been imagining the thing with the lock. Or maybe they'd simply forgotten to lock it when they left. It doesn't mean anyone's been here. This is a safe building. They could probably leave their apartment door wide open and one of their neighbors would simply close it for them, or alert the front desk. No, no one has been in the apartment.

But as she walks back out toward the living room, she catches a whiff of something. She realizes it's not a sound that was nagging at her, but a smell. Nothing she can pinpoint, nothing that strong, but there's a whiff of ... something. She cranes her neck to breathe in the scent of her coat, in case it's her own self that she's smelling, maybe she walked through something on the way home, but it isn't. She picks up the market bag and breathes that in, thinking maybe it's the shiitake mushrooms, but it isn't that either. She breathes deeply and there it is again, fainter now, and by the time she inhales again, it's gone or faded so far into the background that she can no longer detect it.

She stands in the middle of the living room, still wearing

her coat, her boots, the Burberry scarf James had bought her for Christmas, and looks around. Everything looks the same, but everything feels different.

The main door of the apartment rattles and Lily has a moment of panic. *Did I remember to lock it when I came in?* But seconds later, a key turns in the lock and James enters the apartment. It's funny, she thinks, how she knows it's him before he's even said a word.

"Babe?" he calls.

"In here."

He comes into the living room and finds her standing there in her coat, her scarf. He frowns. "What's going on? Are you okay?"

"I'm fine." She forces herself to smile. She holds up the shopping bag. "Shiitake mushrooms."

James hesitates a minute, still studying her. "I could use a cocktail; what about you?"

She nods. She doesn't want to admit how much the idea of a cocktail appeals to her right now. Something to take her mind off this uncomfortable feeling of paranoia, of not-rightness. Surely, she's imagining it all. Surely, she just needs to unwind a little.

James makes them both gin martinis, extra dry. Just the way he likes them, and the way she's learning to like them. She drinks it faster than she means to, and by the time James is glazing the mushrooms, she feels almost normal again, and she laughs at his jokes as if they're the funniest thing she's ever heard in her life.

THE ELATION DOESN'T LAST. She outpaces James with the cocktails, and when they sit down to eat, he makes a point of setting a giant glass of water in front of her. This leads her to pick a fight with him, because she's had too much already but wants to keep going, and because the alcohol has dulled her sense of self-preservation and she forgets that she shouldn't be pissing James off. He grits his teeth all through dinner, sawing into his beef medallions with the vigor of a lumberjack felling trees. When she goes into the kitchen and returns with another drink — just gin and ice this time, who can be bothered making an entire martini? — he loses it.

He stands up from the table and knocks the glass out of her hand. Ice and gin go flying; the glass shatters on the wood floor. She'd taken off her shoes and socks earlier, and her bare feet are surrounded by broken glass.

She doesn't say anything for a minute. She stares down at the mess, at her empty hand. She swallows. "Can you get me the broom, please?"

"No." James stands a few feet away from her, his arms folded across his broad chest.

She looks around her. There isn't as much glass behind her, so she could take a big step backward, make it into the kitchen where there are rags she could use to clean up this mess. But James sees her looking, deduces her plan.

"Come here," he says. He points to the area right in front of him.

Lily looks at the place he's pointing, and at the broken glass that's between here and there. She doesn't move.

James doesn't move either. He simply stands there, his eyes boring into hers.

"Lily, come here," he says again. His tone brooks no

argument. She wouldn't argue even if it did. She would never, could never, defy him.

She had never expected to find herself in a relationship like this. One so fraught and demanding. Being with James is like walking on the blade of a very sharp knife. At one time, the idea of his proclivities might have repelled her, but at one time, the idea of being with *any* man repelled her. Instead, she'd found herself coming alive under his touch. Blossoming under his strict hand. She'd heard the expression once, 'bloom where you're planted.' This is where she'd been planted, at the intersection of sex and violence and fear.

In this moment, she knows she has a choice. She could take a very big step toward him, get her foot over most if not all of the broken glass, but that isn't what he wants. He wants to know that she is willing to endure this. For him.

So she takes a small step forward, the glass grinding into the bottom of her bare foot. The first step isn't too bad. The shards are small and mostly lay flat, and at first it doesn't feel much worse than walking over gravel or sharp beach sand. She takes a second step, and a shard pierces her heel. She wants to wince but she forces her face to remain neutral. She takes another step and another. The glass slices into her skin. Blood starts to trickle from her foot. Pain ribbons up her leg. She keeps walking. She's cleared the glass now, but the shards still cling to the soles of her feet, so as she walks toward James, they grind further into her skin. But she's steady as a rock. Cool as a carrot in a snowman's face, like her daddy used to say.

When she reaches James, he tips her chin up so he can look into her eyes. He doesn't say anything for a minute, and she can tell he's searching for signs that she's learned her lesson. She tries to look as contrite as possible without actually changing her facial expression.

Finally, James nods. "Wait here," he says.

She doesn't answer. She simply waits. She doesn't know how long he's going to make her stand there. It could be hours. She tries not to think of the glass piercing her skin or the blood seeping onto the bamboo floor, mixing with the gin and melting ice. She tries not to think of anything at all.

James reappears a couple of minutes later, bringing with him their first aid kit. He swoops her into his arms, carries her to the couch. When he lays her down he takes her feet into his lap.

He's more tender and gentle than any doctor. He lovingly removes every shard of glass, using a penlight and a magnifying glass to make sure he gets them all. He goes to the linen closet and gets towels, rubbing alcohol, bandages. He washes the blood from her feet, cleans them, treats them, wraps them. He loves on her like a father tending to a child. When he's finished, he carries her to the bedroom, helps her get out of her jeans, tucks her under the covers.

The gin martinis wore off long ago, and Lily finds herself unbearably tired. She's content to let James put her to bed, to tuck her in like a doll. He kisses her forehead, and she thinks she'll be dead asleep in minutes.

She gazes around the room as she snuggles down under the covers. Her eyes catch on something on her nightstand. It takes her a second to figure out why, but when she does, she sits straight up on the bed. She reaches out and snatches up the picture frame that always sits on her nightstand, the last thing she sees before she closes her eyes at night. A picture of her and James, taken early on in their relationship, at a fundraiser for cancer or Alzheimer's or some other disease; she can't remember. She's always loved how wild her eyes look in that photo, how intense James is. It's her favorite picture of them.

Only the picture's gone. Inside the frame is a picture of a body of water. A lake, maybe. Mist rises off it, and in the background, a mountain looms, its snow-capped peaks covered by a layer of wispy clouds. For a second, she sees Bryson City, North Carolina. She sees Fontana Lake, the Great Smoky Mountains. She sees *home.* It makes her shudder.

It's also impossible. No one here knows about her life in North Carolina, not even James. She made damn sure she put that well behind her when she moved to Seattle. New hair, new wardrobe, new name. New start. There's no way anyone knows. No way.

But that doesn't stop the bile from clawing its way up her throat. She stares down at the photo, half expecting the mist to drift or the lake to lap at the edges of the shot. It's not Fontana Lake, she can see that now. The mountain in the background is too tall, too isolated. It's some other lake, some other snowy peak. She bolts out of bed, intent on storming down the hall to ask James what the hell's going on.

As soon as her feet hit the floor, a bolt of pain courses through her. The soles of her feet scream in agony. Her aggressive storming becomes a hobble. She tries to put as much weight as she can on the outside of her foot, which isn't as badly cut, but still every step is agony.

She finds James in his office, in front of his laptop and with the pale glow of the lamp casting shadows over his face. He looks up when he hears her.

"Yes?"

"What is this?" She waves the picture at him.

"I don't know; you tell me."

"It's a picture, but it's different." She thrusts it into his hands, waits for him to be as horrified as she is.

"It's a picture of Puget Sound," he says after a beat. He is frustratingly calm.

"Yes," she says, realizing he's most likely right. She experiences a breath of relief, but it's only temporary. It still doesn't explain what happened to the old picture. She explains to James, "It used to be a picture of you and me. It's the one from my nightstand."

"Alright," James says. He still doesn't grasp what's happening.

"Someone changed the picture. It wasn't me."

"Someone …?" His forehead wrinkles. "Are you sure? That seems …"

"Of course, I'm sure." Lily wants to scream, but screaming at James is a surefire ticket to more punishment. "It was a picture of you and me. And now it's something else." Her voice is level, practically serene.

"And who exactly do you think changed it?" His voice is even calmer than hers, a fact which never fails to drive her absolutely insane.

"I don't know." She loses some of her rage as she contemplates the question.

"You think I did it?"

"I don't know." *Does* she think James did it? She remembers the feeling when she got home from work, that someone had been in the apartment. But does she really think someone broke in here just to swap out a photo? For what purpose?

"Are you sure you didn't change it?" James looks at the picture again. "This is Puget Sound. Where we went sailing that time. Look, this is Mount Rainier. Almost the exact view we had from that little B&B."

Lily realizes he's right. This is one of the pictures she took that day, or at least something very close. But she'd remember if she'd swapped out the pictures … wouldn't she?

"Why don't you get some sleep?" James says, as gentle as when he'd been picking glass from the soles of her feet. "We can talk about it in the morning. You probably changed it and forgot."

She sighs. "Maybe." Her head is starting to hurt and her feet are really aching. She wants to take the pressure off them. She hobbles back to the bedroom and climbs under the covers. She sets the photo on the nightstand and stares hard at it. When was the last time she really looked at that photo? It could have been days ago. Weeks, even. *Had* she changed it?

When James comes to bed, she's still awake, but she pretends not to be as he slides under the sheets next to her. He drifts off with his hand on her hip while she lies there, staring into the darkness.

NINE
PRESENT DAY

I don't sleep. Not that night.

I try to tell myself I must be wrong. That this man, the one who threw me the bottle of water and the two sandwiches that remain untouched beside me, will come back. Of course he will. Maybe he was just scared; maybe he thought the whole thing was some kind of trap. That's it. I was the lure and when he came too close to the hole, someone else would ambush him, maybe take his money or worse. That's what he thought. But he'll report it, still. Whether he believes me or not, he'll find a ranger or a cop or someone and he'll tell them about me. They'll come.

But no one comes. The sun sets and the air grows dark and cold and no one comes.

I try to tell myself I imagined the whole thing. That there was no man, I'd only dreamed him up. A hallucination. Understandable, really, after being down here by myself for almost two full days. But the water bottle beside me, those wrapped sandwiches, reeking of corned beef, are real. Definitely not hallucinations.

I come back to the same conclusion, again and again. That it wasn't an accident that I fell in here. That this hole was dug for a purpose, and that purpose was to trap someone. The lingering question that haunts me is: was I the target? Or just the unlucky soul who happened upon it?

And which is worse?

I pace the hole, unable to settle. Since I've had more water, I need to pee, but I can't bear the thought of pissing down here again, now that the smell has abated. I'll have to eventually, but for now it gives me a small sense of control to be able to hold it. My hunger, which had settled into a dull sense of nausea, roars up again every time I get a whiff of that corned beef. I don't want to eat them — that desire for control again — but I know I'm going to. I'm weak that way.

Just like he always said.

I stop pacing, dead in my tracks. Him. Just the thought of him is enough to make my blood run ice cold, to make my bladder want to release, to make my toes curl up in misery. Him. He wouldn't have anything to do with this. This isn't his style. Forests, dirt, nature. No. He's too clean for this. Too urbane.

Besides, he doesn't know where I am. He doesn't know about my apartment on Flagstaff. He doesn't know about King or that I like to walk him out here in the forest. He'd never know to look for me out here, and even if he did, we're an hour and a half outside his comfort zone. He'd never do it like this.

But he'd do something. If he knew about me, about what I did. That knowledge has haunted me for months. It's the reason for my panic disorder. It's the reason I got a dog. It's the reason I come out here and hike and try to clear my mind, because when I'm in the city, he's there with me, noxious as a gas.

The panic wells up. I lean against the side of the hole, but it's already seizing my lungs, squeezing them, wringing out my throat so it's closed tight as a vice. I beat my fists against the earth wall, as if that will do something, but all it does is hurt the sides of my hands. I slump down onto the ground, desperate to breathe, clawing at the earth and so sure my heart is going to explode right out of my ribcage. I curl up onto my side and pull my knees as close to my chest as I can.

"Please," I say to no one. To anyone. "Please, I just want to go home."

No one answers. Of course they don't. King is still lying there above me, looking at me with concerned brown eyes, but he doesn't answer. Even Dr. Monica's voice has gone silent. I rock myself into a kind of dull stupor and lie there for hours.

I don't sleep, but somehow I dream. All night, crazy dreams of earthworms slithering out of the walls of my prison, of ants clambering over my prone body and feasting on my flesh, of roaches skittering past me with their glossy exoskeletons and their fetid guts. I dream of *him*, following me on the trail as I walk with King, furtive as a cartoon bandit and tiptoeing behind tree trunks every time I turn around. I start to run but he runs after me, invisible and terrifying. I dream of King growling at something I can't see. Growling. Growling.

Still growling.

It isn't a dream. I sit up straight, blinking. The hole is dark and my eyes aren't adjusting. Above me, there's a faint slant of moonlight, and I can make out the dim silhouette of King's arched back. He's growling at something, but it's beyond my line of sight. Please let it be rescuers, I think. But I already know it isn't.

Since I don't have my vision, I have to rely on my hearing. I hold my breath and listen as hard as I can to the surrounding woods. The nocturnal sounds of the forest are loud and eerie. The chirrup of crickets, croaking frogs, and somewhere, the hoot of an owl. And then the rhythmic crunch and crackle of footsteps. Heavy footsteps.

"King," I hiss. "Be good." What I mean is *don't do anything stupid.* Don't be a hero. I should be excited to hear footsteps, to think that someone might be coming to rescue me, but in the middle of the night like this, I only feel afraid. I'm afraid that the man has come back, or that someone else who means me harm has come. I'm not thinking of rescuers; I'm thinking of tormentors.

As it turns out, both counts are wrong. I hear a low growl and it's not coming from King. Whatever's out there, it's some kind of animal. A big one, judging by the sound of it.

Bear. I know it suddenly, without seeing it or even hearing anything else. Maybe it's the smell, the dusty brackish odor of black bears. A scent I never would have thought I knew until it was right there in front of me.

My heart hammers in my chest and I can't tear my eyes away from King's shadow form. I want to tell him to stand down, to slink away, but I'm afraid to speak in case it lures the bear closer to us. Of course, if King keeps growling, it's going to come anyway. Or will it? Will a bear attack a dog? I have no idea. I have pepper spray in my holster, but it's no good to either of us down here.

Frustrated tears fall down my cheeks. I can't lose King. I

can't. He's such a good boy, such a brave boy. He growls again, a snarling, mean, scared sound.

"King, stop," I plead. "Let him go on his way. Just let him go."

King ignores me. A dog that's bent on protecting you is a wonderful thing, until it's not. I listen and try to discern whether the sound of those footsteps is coming closer, but I can't tell. Then they stop altogether.

I imagine King staring down the bear. I imagine the two of them standing off in the darkness. King so much smaller, but with something to protect. The bear so much larger, but with nothing to lose. I want to weep.

"King," I hiss again. "King, no." I try to sound commanding, but I doubt he even hears me. All his senses are focused on the animal in front of him.

Branches crunch again. I hold my breath. I almost believe I can make out every ambling footstep. They seem to be … receding. Are they? I listen harder. Yes, they sound softer now. And King's growl, too, is not as ferocious.

I wipe at the tears that are drying in salty trails on my cheeks. Thank God. Thank God. I don't have much to be thankful for right now, trapped in a pit for who knows what reason, but I can be thankful for this.

King doesn't settle down right away. He paces around the hole, patrolling the area the way I imagine he used to patrol the empty auto body shop after hours. He's a good dog. Such a good dog. Eventually, he stops. He's still wary, but he lays down, watching. His tail swishes back and forth slowly, the way it does when he's tense.

I slump back down onto the ground. I know I won't sleep.

According to my FitBit, it's almost five, anyway. The sun will be up soon enough. The sandwiches sit on the ground beside me, and I pick up the bundle. A sticker is applied over the seam where the ends of the plastic wrap meet. Zigman's. One of my favorite delis. What does that mean? It could mean that whoever brought the sandwiches, whoever that man was, knows that I like Zigman's. Or it could mean that lots of people like Zigman's. They've got three locations in the city and are very popular. Lots of people go there. An easy coincidence. Right?

I unwrap the sandwiches to inspect them. Corned beef, as I'd guessed from the smell. Sauerkraut. Relish. My mouth waters. The smell is even stronger with the paper off. My stomach clenches with need.

Above me, King whines. He's looking at down at me. Or more specifically, at my sandwich. His tongue darts out and rolls over his lips.

I take a desperate bite of the sandwich. Flavors explode in my mouth. I love a corned beef sandwich, but this tastes like the best thing I've ever eaten in my life. Better than anything from those fancy steakhouses I used to go to once upon a time, better than the four-hundred-dollar-an-ounce sashimi we once feasted on at a tiny little Japanese place. This sandwich tastes like heaven.

King whines again. I take the second half of my sandwich and throw it up to him. I can't tell where it lands, but I see him go for it, and a second later, I hear the sounds of him inhaling it. Oh God, that sound makes me happy. Finally, something I can do for him. I finish my half of the sandwich and rewrap the remaining sandwich in the wax paper and set it aside. I want to keep eating, but I have no idea when I'll get more food, and it's probably a good idea to conserve what I have.

Will that man come back? He might. He might not. I don't know. And I don't know which I'm more afraid of.

TEN
SIX MONTHS AGO

Lily doesn't sleep a wink. At one point she takes the picture and sets it face down on the nightstand, deciding that if she can't see it, she won't obsess over it so much. It doesn't work. It's still the first thing on her mind at six in the morning when the alarm goes off.

While James is in the shower, she pads around the apartment. Her feet ache. They aren't as raw as last night, but she still moves slowly and deliberately through the apartment. She's looking for anything out of place. That feels *off*. She'd walked through the space yesterday when she got home from work, but clearly she hadn't looked closely enough. What else did she miss?

But she finds nothing, and she forces herself to stop when James emerges from the bathroom. She doesn't want him to know that she's still thinking about this. He made it clear last night that he didn't believe her about the photo, and unless she finds something else, there's no point in letting him know what she's thinking.

Soon, she's distracted by their morning routine; James

makes coffee and eggs and she changes into a pencil skirt, a pale pink silk blouse. She digs out a pair of ballet flats from the closet and carries them toward the front door. James frowns.

"What are those?"

"Flats. For work."

"Wear the heels," he says.

"But..."

"I like you in heels."

She stares at him for a minute. "Alright." She returns the flats to the closet and slips on a pair of stilettos. The pain in her feet is exquisite.

———

LILY GROANS when she crosses the building lobby. A crowd waits in front of the elevator bank. The building only has two elevators, which is ridiculous, given how many people work here. During rush hours, the elevators are busier than the freeways. She joins the throng and prepares to wait. She pulls out her phone and checks her inbox, firing off a syrupy sweet email to one of her clients and a much more terse one to Aurora, who claims to need yet another extension on the craft beer project her team's been working on.

The elevator doors ping open and Lily waits in the thick of bodies as the people coming down stream out of the elevator and push past them into the lobby. She doesn't pay any attention to them; they're just anonymous faces. A sea of eyes, hair, coffee breath, polyester. Until she hears something.

"Stacey?"

The voice barely registers in Lily's ears, yet the sound of

that name pierces her consciousness. She holds her head steady, not making eye contact. They're probably not talking to her. *Stacey* isn't exactly an uncommon name.

"Stacey Kincaid? My God, is that really you?"

Lily swallows hard. She risks a glance over, and the dark, scruff-covered face is right there. She recognizes him immediately. Connor Franklin. From Bryson City, North Carolina.

Lily blinks and looks right past him. She starts to follow the crowd into the elevator. But she underestimates Connor's persistence. He grabs her arm, throwing her off balance.

"Sorry," he says earnestly. "But Stacey, it's me, Connor. From Bryson City."

"I'm sorry," she murmurs. "You must be confused." She keeps one hand on the elevator door to keep it from closing. Most of the people inside look irritated that she's holding up the elevator, but a couple of them — women, mostly — wrinkle their foreheads in curious concern. Wondering if she's being harassed. Wondering if they should step in and what they'd be risking if they did.

"You're not Stacey?" he says, incredulous. "For real?"

"For real," she says, the sarcasm obvious.

"God." He shakes his head. "You could be her twin. Except for the different hair color. Unbelievable." He shakes his head again, clearing it the way a dog shakes off water.

Lily wants — *needs* — to get away. She presses herself into the elevator and hits the button for her floor, even though it's already lit up. She hits it a few more times for good measure. She wants the doors to slide closed so she won't have to look at Connor anymore. Connor, who's still standing there, staring at her like he really can't believe it's not her.

Finally, the doors glide shut. She's sweating, but at least the pain in her feet is momentarily forgotten. A woman with curly hair and a bright pink suit catches her eye and flashes her a smile that's as tight as her curls. "They've always got some line, haven't they?"

"Always," Lily says and laughs. But in her head all she can see is Connor, and all she can hear is her name — her *real* name — on his lips.

This is not good.

FOR THE REST of the day, Lily is uneasy. What were the odds of running into someone from back home right in her own office building? And why, of all people, did it have to be Connor Franklin? Connor had gone to her high school. Had played football with her brothers, in fact. She'd given him a blow job once, when he'd crashed on their couch, drunk out of his mind. He'd cornered her on her way to the bathroom, pushed her down on the floor in front of him. She remembers how cold the tile was under her knees, how she'd shivered in her nightie. Thank God it was over quick. A drunk teen guy was easy enough to handle; in comparison to the rest of her existence back then, Connor was barely a blip on her radar. She hopes that's all he is now, too.

Several hours later, when she makes her way down the hall to the DigitaLuster boardroom for a meeting, she finds her legs are still shaking, and she's relieved when she slips into one of the neon orange shell chairs. She barely watches as the room fills with people; all she can think about is Connor. She tells herself that he'll let this go. He'll convince himself he's wrong, that she isn't Stacey. He hasn't seen her since the last day of high school, and that was over ten years ago. She looks completely different now — her blonde hair dyed a dark brown, her long layers cut into a blunt, fringed bob. She's not the same person she was back then, not at all. She's changed. Not just the outside, either. She's a different person. A better one.

And if she needs it, there's always the storage locker in Interbay. An escape route. It won't come to that, she tells herself, but a ready voice whispers, *just in case*.

"What do you think? Can you make it happen? Lily?"

Lily blinks to attention. She hasn't been listening, and now everyone's staring at her. She smiles at Peter Serrano, the Vice President of the Green Acres Golf Club. A tomato of a man with a comb-over and a suit that most definitely came from the 'extended sizes' section of Brooks Brothers. "Of course. Not a problem."

Damian makes a slashing motion across his neck, but she ignores him. She wonders what she just agreed to, but it doesn't matter. Her entire job depends on keeping the client happy, so if Peter Serrano wants something, she's going to bend over backward to make sure he gets it.

"Good. Excellent." Peter Serrano looks pleased, and she knows she made the right call.

She's irritated at herself for not paying attention — for letting that asshole Connor Franklin throw off her game like this — but she'll survive. Lily is good at her job. *Really* good. She knows how to keep rich, powerful men happy. Just ask James. She fights back a tiny smile and rubs her thumb over her diamond, which, after two weeks, still brings her a spark of pleasure whenever she looks down.

Peter and his posse of stuffed shirts stand, and Lily shakes their hands. Damian does, too, but Lily can see that he's sweating. She's pretty sure she agreed to something insane. She doesn't care.

When the golf club guys have left the building, Damian leans against the conference room table. "What were you thinking?"

"I was thinking that if we want to keep them as a client, we better do what they want."

"Aurora is going to bite your head off."

"I don't answer to Aurora."

Damian chuckles. "She would say the same about you."

She knows what Aurora will say. The timelines are too tight, her team is already strapped. She'll argue that the quality of the work will be compromised if they rush, that they still have the craft beer project to finish up. She'll tell Lily she's being unreasonable.

Lily's heard it all a thousand times. Aurora doesn't know the first thing about satisfying a client. Nor, Lily thinks uncharitably, does she probably know how to satisfy a man. Lily thinks of herself as an expert in both.

"You really think you can meet their timelines?" Damian sports a sardonic grin. Lily suspects he's realized she wasn't paying attention. She holds her chin out.

"I'll find a way to make it happen."

"Glad to hear it," he says, starting out the door. "But I want to be there when you tell Aurora."

THEY FIND AURORA IN 'THE POD', where all the programmers and technical artists work. She leans against the slick white desk of a Java developer named Bao and fiddles with some sort of *Star Wars* or *Star Trek* or video game action figure, probably from Bao's desk. Lily doesn't understand the people who work in the pod. It's why they call it 'the pod' to begin with. They're a species unto themselves.

Aurora glances up when she sees them coming. "Is the meeting over already?"

Damian snorts. "Don't need a long meeting when you agree to everything they ask for."

Aurora gapes at them. "You didn't." She says it accusingly, and her ire is directed straight at Lily.

Lily purses her lips. "They're the client."

"And we're the ones who have to do the work." She sets the plastic figurine back down on the desk.

"And you do it so well."

Aurora isn't placated, of course. She folds her arms. Bao looks away. It makes the developers uncomfortable to watch the project managers and the account managers duke it out. They probably start yapping about her as soon as she leaves. She doesn't care. She has one focus at work and one focus only.

"What exactly did you agree to?" Aurora asks.

Lily's neck flushes. The truth is, she still isn't entirely sure. She was too busy thinking about Connor Franklin. Goddamn Connor. Why did he have to show up now? She doesn't answer Aurora, and Damian jumps in.

"The entire app needs to be finished and live by the end of the month."

Lily almost chokes. She's used to unreasonable demands from clients, but the Green Acres Golf Club app is a 3D golfing simulation that uses real renders of their golf course. It was a project she'd been estimating at least four months for, possibly as many as six. She doesn't want to admit her concern, so she paints on an expression that reads as decidedly nonplussed.

Aurora, on the other hand, is pissed-with-a-capital-P. She leaps away from Bao's desk and toward Lily who, despite her resolve, takes a step backward. "That's impossible!" Her voice is thin and reedy and disturbingly high-pitched at the best of times. Now it's almost unbearable.

"We'll find a way to make it happen," Lily says evenly.

"*We.*" Aurora purses her thin lips. "You mean 'we'." She circles her finger around the pod, including herself and her team but clearly not Lily or Damian.

Bao and the rest of the developers are trying to pretend they aren't watching, but Lily can tell that they, too, are annoyed by this new timeline. Well, they can just suck it up and deal with it. Green Acres is a big account. That's the reality.

Lily and Aurora stare each other down. Aurora, who's slim and pale-faced, with shocking red hair and a dusting of freckles that Lily has to admit are rather charming, is trembling with anger.

"Look," Lily says. "It is what it is."

"*It is what it is* because you have no backbone," Aurora spits. "Though I guess I shouldn't be surprised." She says that last part under her breath, but Lily hears it anyway.

"What's that supposed to mean?"

Aurora doesn't answer but folds her arms over her narrow chest.

"Alright," Damian says calmly. He takes off his glasses and wipes them on the hem of his chambray shirt. "Let's take the rest of the day and start plotting out a timeline. Aurora, be realistic but don't exaggerate. What would you need to make this happen? Maybe we can bring in some outside resources if we have to. We'll regroup tomorrow and see where we're at."

"Fine." Aurora actually likes Damian, so of course she agrees to his suggestion, though Lily has to admit, it's reasonable enough. But knowing Aurora, she'll still exaggerate and make it sound as if Lily is asking her to build the Great Wall of China out of toothpicks and glue.

Lily and Damian walk back to the front of the building, where the offices are walled in glass and it doesn't smell like sweat or artificial cheese powder. She breathes deeply.

"You okay?" Damian asks, before she can escape into the sanctity of her office.

"I'm fine."

"You seem distracted lately."

"I'm fine," she repeats.

His eyes drift down to her hand, and she realizes he's looking at her ring. She hurriedly covers it with her other hand. He frowns.

"Just don't turn into one of those women who are so busy dreaming about white dresses and screaming at caterers that they can't get anything done."

"Damian, you know me," she says. "When have I ever been that person?"

"I'm just saying, don't turn into her."

"I'm not turning into anyone."

"Alright," he says, hands up in the air. "Alright."

Once Damian leaves, Lily sinks into her pink chair and throws herself into her work. She doesn't want to give him — or Aurora, for that matter — any reason to think she's off her game. She's come so far. She can't afford to slip now.

ELEVEN
PRESENT DAY

Monday night passes, finally, and Tuesday comes. Tuesday is the same as Monday, it turns out, except I have both more and less hope. Or maybe I should say that the logical part of me holds out hope — after two days of being absent from work, surely Damian or someone else would have sounded the alarm. Maybe the police will visit my apartment today, or maybe today will be the day one of the park employees or a state trooper will notice that my car's been sitting on the side of the road since Sunday morning. There are so many options, so many opportunities for aide to come to me.

But the core of me doesn't believe. The core of me, the hard walnut of my soul, knows no one is coming. Except maybe him. The man. He remains a mystery to me. His motivations are unfathomable. Or maybe I just don't want to fathom them. Won't let myself.

Tuesday passes. The remaining sandwich is eaten, split between me and King. I should save it for myself, since I don't know when or even *if* I'll be getting more food, but to me it isn't even a question. I can't sit down here and watch King starve.

My water is almost gone, too. Something else I should have conserved. Fear has made me reckless.

I go through my inventory again. Water bottle, now empty. Cell phone, now dead. Bear spray, useless down here. Dog leash, the only thing that seems potentially useful, even if I haven't quite figured out what to do with it yet. My FitBit's still ticking along, but I don't know for how much longer. I can't remember the last time I charged it, but I estimate it has maybe one or two days of life left in it, at most. After that I'll have nothing to mark the passing of the time except the setting sun, and I'm afraid of that because it'll mean marking time in days instead of hours. It'll be a kind of giving up.

Maybe I'm already starting to give up. Maybe that's why I drank almost all the water, why I gave half of my sandwich to a dog. Maybe that's why this morning, when I woke up, I went to my pee corner and squatted without batting an eye. Even the smell doesn't bother me anymore. I expect I'll have to do more than pee soon, especially after eating that sandwich, but the thought doesn't fill me with the disgust it did even twenty-four hours ago. Times have changed.

Tuesday night. Again, I don't sleep. This time my fear is worse, because I'm waiting to see if the bear will return. King, too, is on edge. At random intervals, he emits a low, throaty growl. At least, I think they're random intervals. Perhaps he's responding to something in the air, a smell or a sound that doesn't register on my puny human senses. But nothing comes near us.

By dawn, I have to use the bathroom. I shit in the corner like an animal. I don't even care.

Wednesday. Another day for Damian or anyone else to raise concerns about my absence. I hope their concerns would be significant by now. Three days no-show from someone who was always, I like to think, known for being reliable and dependable. Another day for the police to go to my apartment, to find my dog and my car gone.

I'm hungry again, but the sandwiches are nothing but a memory and a sour taste in the back of my throat. I sip water from the bottle that was thrown down to me. It's not enough to slake my thirst. It's barely enough to lubricate my dry throat. I think about King up there, with nothing. Has he found his own source of water yet? Has he found a creek or a stream somewhere to drink from? I don't think so, but I still hope. I have enough hope left for that.

Wednesday rolls into evening. I doze a bit during the day, tired from my night of sitting bear vigil. No insect dreams this time. Instead, I dream my tongue has been infected where I bit down on it during my fall. I dream that it swells with pus that slowly leaks down the back of my throat until it chokes me. I wake up coughing, gagging.

The light is lower. Not dark yet, but coming on twilight. Maybe seven, seven-thirty. I look at my FitBit and it says seven-twenty. I'm getting good at this, reading the light. A new skill to add to my resume. If I ever get out of here.

Above me, King growls, and I tense. Is it the bear? Do bears come out in the evening? What about coyotes? I listen hard, waiting to learn what's come upon us.

Instead of animal noises, a voice rips through the dimming light. *His* voice. I think so, anyway.

"There's a good boy. Hi, boy. Hi, good boy."

I picture King leaning in for a scratch and a pat. My

stomach churns. I want to scream but my lungs have seized up. The dream comes to me again, the sensation of my airways filling with rotten pus. I try not to gag.

A bottle of water comes sailing over the top of the hole and lands across from me, not far from my pee corner. I scramble for it, twisting the cap off and drinking half of it in two long swallows.

"Hey!" I yell, when I have my voice back. "Hey, please let me out. Please. I won't tell anyone about this, just let me out. I don't care who you are, I won't even look at you. I just want to go home."

My words had been coming out in a mad, frantic tumble, but at the word *home*, my voice cracks and breaks. I fall to my knees, drop the water bottle.

Instead of an answer, another package thumps onto the earthen floor. Two more sandwiches, by the looks of it. I snatch them up, as if they might disappear if I don't.

"Thank you," I say, thinking appreciation might buy me some goodwill. "Thank you. But I really just want to go home. Please. Please let me go home. Please let me go home."

There's no answer. He's still murmuring something up there, but I think he's talking to King.

"Please," I shriek. "Please, oh God, please. What do you want? What do you want?"

He doesn't answer. Will he ever speak to me? What is the point of this? Why keep me down here? Is he waiting for something? Or is he taking some kind of perverse pleasure in my helplessness? I read an article once about people — mostly men — who have a fetish for women trapped in quicksand. Maybe this guy's got some version of that. Maybe he goes back to his car and jerks off. Let him, I think. Let him do whatever he wants as long as he doesn't hurt me or King.

From the sounds of crackling branches above, I can tell he's starting to move away from the hole. So he's finished here already. That's it. Throw me some water and food and leave. He came Monday and he came again on Wednesday. Maybe that's a pattern. Does that mean he'll come on Friday, too?

"Hey!" I yell, while I hope he's still in earshot. "Hey, next time can you bring some water for my dog? Please. He really needs food and water."

There's no answer. Of course there isn't. I don't even know if he heard me, and even if he did, I have no reason to believe he'll honor my request. Why would he? He's holding all the cards here. I don't know who he is or what he wants or what the hell is going to happen to me.

I slump back down onto the ground, unpeel the wax from around the sandwiches, and take a giant bite. Pastrami this time. Spicy mustard. It's delicious. I cry while I'm eating it. I throw King half the sandwich, but this time I take two big bites out of it before I toss it up. I sob the entire time.

TWELVE
SIX MONTHS AGO

It's Thursday, the day Lily's been waiting all week for. On Thursdays, James plays racquetball with his business partner. Duncan Wexler is the other half of Wexler & Russel, husband to the vapid Cora, and the best reason Lily knows to never join the Rosewood Country Club, mostly due to the fact that Duncan's head is as large as his wife's is empty. But he has plenty of contacts, especially foreign ones, and James swears he's an integral part of the business. Their Thursday night tradition means James won't be home until at least ten, because after their game they'll go for dinner and probably drink a few too many expensive glasses of scotch while they talk shop.

That gives her plenty of time alone in the apartment. She's tried, during the times when James is in the shower or busy in the kitchen, to inspect the place for signs of an intruder, but those stolen moments haven't afforded her the opportunity to be as thorough as she'd like. Now, alone, she can go over this place with a fine-tooth comb. She doesn't know what she'll find, but the anticipation of it makes her toes curl inside her stilettos.

She stops at the market on the way home, but instead of buying fancy ingredients for one of James' elaborate dinners, she buys a protein bar and a peach. Dinner of champions. She hurries home, her head tucked low into her jacket, fighting the frigid early March temps.

At home, she shrugs off the jacket and is biting into the protein bar before she can even make it to the bedroom to change. Jeans, a sweater, her squishiest slippers. The bottoms of her feet are still tender, but they're getting better. They hurt the worst after a shower, when the skin gets soft and stretchy, but now, after wearing her stilettos all day, they're tough and hardened, and with the slippers on, there isn't too much pain. She finishes the protein bar, bites into the peach, and decides to start in the kitchen and work her way down through the apartment.

She works with precision and thoroughness. She doesn't know what she's looking for, so she simply looks at everything. She opens drawers and cabinets, runs her hands over the tops of moldings, shakes out the curtains, swipes her fingers around the inside of lampshades. She doesn't find anything. Not even dust. The apartment is exactly as clean and organized as it always is. Of course. James wouldn't have it any other way.

The only room she doesn't thoroughly inspect is James' office. He'd notice if she moved something, and though she's certainly allowed in the room if she needs to get something — a pen, say, or the set of tiny screwdrivers he keeps in his desk drawer — she isn't sure how he'd react to her pawing through everything. She can't blame him, either. A man is entitled to his privacy.

She finishes the search down in the master bedroom. She's disappointed to have not found anything in the rest of the house, but hopeful, too. The bedroom was where the photograph was swapped out; maybe something else will turn up. She pulls open her closet and rifles through all the clothes — so many expensive dresses, things James has bought her for special occasions and which she's worn once and never again. Gowns from designers she's never heard of, in fabrics and colorways she can't pronounce, with price tags beyond her wildest reckonings. It's extravagant, and she loves it.

Nothing appears off in the closet. Everything is hung neatly, her shoes in perfect order. She turns next to James' closet. It is, if possible, more fastidiously organized than her own. She's spent a great deal of time in here, so she knows the order of the starched shirts, the crisp tailored suits, the gleaming Oxfords as well as she knows the contents of her own closet. She rifles through them lightly, breathing in James' scent as it wafts up to her.

James' closet looks as it should. She stares at it for a long moment before closing the door and moving around the rest of the bedroom. She leaves the nightstand for last. The picture is still there, still face down. She hasn't been able to bring herself to move it since she discovered it. She picks it up now and turns it over. The new photo is still in place, the one of Puget Sound. She doesn't know how she didn't recognize it before James pointed it out, because it's so obvious. The waves, the fog, the soaring mountain in the distance. She'd been so happy that day, her first boat cruise. Holding on to James' hand as they were sprayed with seafoam, mist.

She turns the photo over again and claws at the back of the frame. She wants to hold the picture in her hand. The back of the frame pries off easily, and she pulls the photo out, knocking the glass onto the bed.

The photo is just that: a photo. Now that she holds it in her hand, she sees there's nothing special to it. It's only a piece of paper with a series of inks spread out in a pleasing palette. The other photo is nowhere to be found. The picture that used to be in there, the one of her and James at the miscellaneous disease gala. Where is it? If she changed out this photo, or if James did, where did the original one go? She paws through the nightstand drawer, but there are only the usual items — a sleep mask, ear plugs, a bottle of Advil, a book of Sylvia Plath poetry, and a tube of personal lubricant, unscented. No photo.

Lily paces the bedroom. The act of searching the house should have calmed her, or at least brought her some assurance. Instead, her head buzzes with unanswered questions. She knows she didn't change that picture. But who would have? And why? To what end? James and their cleaning woman, Mathilde, are the only other people who have access to the room, as far as she knows, but she can't fathom why either one of them would have done something like that. And what about the dead bird? What about her missing keys? Had someone really been in the apartment?

She doesn't know, and that's what scares her the most. She can't see her way around this problem, and she isn't used to that. Doesn't like the feeling. Lily has always been very good at thinking two steps ahead — she had to be, with everything she'd been through in her life. It was the only way to survive, and she'd been surviving ever since she moved to Seattle. Surviving's what she does.

Frustrated, she goes back out to the kitchen. She finishes the peach and pours herself a glass of wine. She thinks about whether she should talk to James about this and decides she will. They might need to change the locks, after all. He won't be happy with her, but it'll be better if he knows. Better for both of them. With the locks changed, she can relax.

She drinks two glasses of wine before James gets home and cuts herself off at that. She doesn't want a repeat of the other night, when she'd drank too much gin and made James mad. She drinks a glass of water and takes a shower and by the time she gets out, he's home.

"Hello," she says, brushing out her hair with her fingers. It leaves wet splotches on the shoulders of her silk robe.

James comes over and kisses her cheek, breathing in deeply at the scent of her. "Hello, beautiful."

She smiles. He's imbibed in a few cocktails of his own, which means he's in a good mood. An amorous mood. It's the perfect time to talk to him.

"I've been thinking," she says, running her fingertips along the collar of his jacket.

"Oh?" he says with a sardonic grin. "Should I be worried?"

She laughs lightly. "I was thinking about how I lost my keys the other day."

"You didn't really lose them, though, did you?" James frowns. "They were at your office. Exactly where I told you they'd be."

"Right." She knows he added that last bit on purpose, probably couldn't help himself. He was right, and she was wrong. Just how he likes it. "But they were still missing for a while. I mean, I didn't have them in my possession. And it seems like a strange coincidence, don't you think, that the dead bird got in? And that the picture got changed?"

James sighs. He's visibly irritated now. Not amorous anymore. "I thought we talked about that. You probably changed out the picture yourself and forgot about it."

She wants to say she didn't, but she'll just sound petulant. "What about the bird, then? I certainly didn't let a bird into our apartment."

"A fluke incident." He shrugs. "It probably came in through one of the windows and couldn't find its way back out again."

"But what window?" She doesn't care about sounding petulant this time. Why is James so set on ignoring the presence of the bird? A *dead* bird. In their locked, sealed apartment. For a second, she entertains the thought that James put the bird there himself. Her stomach curdles. "There weren't any open."

"I don't know." He shrugs. "Maybe the property managers came in and opened the windows for some reason."

"They didn't," she says triumphantly. "I called them. No one entered our apartment. They would have had to tell us, anyway."

"You called the property management company?" James' face is stormy.

"Yes." She holds her chin out in defiance. Fine, it *is* James' apartment, technically, but she has a right to ask questions if she needs to. She's going to be his wife, after all. Her dark voice wonders if his anger is more proof that he's hiding something, but she pushes the thought away.

James doesn't say anything. He stalks off into the kitchen.

She realizes she's holding her breath and lets it out in one huge exhale. She waits for him to come back, waits to see if he's going to punish her, but when he returns it's with a glass of scotch and an exhausted expression.

"Are you alright?" he asks. To her surprise, he hands her the glass. She takes it warily.

"I'm fine. I just think something strange has been going on."

"Maybe it's the stress," he says gently. "Ever since we got back from San Francisco, you've been acting a little…"

"What?"

"A little off."

"I'm not off."

"Maybe it's the stress of the wedding," he suggests.

"It's not. Why would I be stressed about that?" The last thing she wants is for him to think she isn't grateful for everything he's given her. "We haven't even set a date yet."

"Exactly," he points out. "Most women would have a date picked out and half the arrangements made already. You haven't even, I don't know, brought home one of those magazines with all the dresses."

"A bridal magazine? That's your reasoning? So I'm not a bridal magazine kind of person. Did you expect me to change who I am, just because we're getting married?"

"Is this about your parents?"

This startles her. But of course, he'd be thinking about her parents. Her *dead* parents. She thinks of all the lies she's told James over the last year, of the way he so willingly bought every word that spilled out of her pretty little mouth. How can she suspect him of this kind of treachery when she's the one with blood on her hands? "You're right," she says. Contrite. "Maybe it's the stress."

And maybe it really is. Ten years of lies would surely take a toll on one's mental health, wouldn't it? Is it possible that she's losing details, moments? *Could* she have changed the picture and not remembered?

"Maybe you should go to bed," James says. He takes the glass of scotch, untouched, from her hands.

"You're right," she says, nodding. "That's what I'll do. I'll go to bed." She turns and starts to walk toward the bedroom. Her feet, still soft from the shower, scream in agony, but she refuses to limp.

THIRTEEN
PRESENT DAY

It isn't the lack of food or water that will kill me; it isn't even the fear. It's the boredom. Thursday passes. In excruciating slowness. Minute by minute by minute by minute. Somehow. I try to pass as much time as I can by sleeping, but I can't get into a deep sleep, so I only doze in that way that actually makes the time seem longer. If that's even possible.

With all that time on my hands, I do nothing but think. Memories bubble up to the surface, one after another. Things I haven't thought about in years. Things like:

Christmas morning. Stealing a sip of champagne and orange juice from my Nana's glass. The bitter bubbles on my tongue. The slap on the back of my hand when she caught me. Nana wore eyeglasses that were pink on the outside and orange on the inside, and she had grey hair that was wild and curly and in retrospect I think she looked kind of cool but at the time I just thought she looked old. She didn't even die of anything age-related; she got hit by a drunk driver on her way home from Christmas dinner. The last time I saw her was the day she smacked my hand and I called her a bitch.

Another memory: John Kubrick-Kent asking me to prom, and telling him no, and watching him go off with that hang-dog expression. I should have said yes. I always wonder how my life might have been different if I'd said yes. But John Kubrick-Kent didn't play football, and to my teenaged self, that meant he wasn't worthy of going to prom with. Teenagers are assholes. I was, anyway.

Another memory: that day. That horrible day. When everything went so wrong. How did it go so wrong?

That's the memory that plays on eternal repeat in my mind. Like a looping gif. A horrible meme that I can't unsee. The two of us, standing there, staring each other down. The pain, the rage. The fall.

I try to think about happier things. Like the first time I saw King's sweet brown eyes gazing up at me from the shelter kennel. The moment the shelter volunteer opened his cage and I crouched down to pet him and he shoved his snout into my armpit and shook with happiness. That first night at home, when he hopped into bed with me, taking up his rightful place as the little spoon.

All my good memories seem to involve King. I try to remember other ones, ones that don't involve my dog, but they're in short supply right now. It becomes a challenge, coming up with one good memory. One bit of lightness down here in the dark.

I remember: a birthday. I must have been six or seven. My best friend, a little girl named Lisa who lived down the street from me, wrapped her favorite doll up in a blanket and gave it to me as a gift. The doll's name was Izzy. Lisa cried when her mom came to get her, because it had suddenly dawned on her that Izzy wouldn't be going home with her. I tried to give the doll back, but despite her tears, Lisa was resolute. She wouldn't take it. I waited until it was her birthday and wrapped it up and gave it back to her. It became a running joke between us — we gifted that doll back and forth for years, until her hair was falling out and her blinking eyes were stuck in a suspicious half-lidded gaze. It probably would have gone on even longer, except Lisa's family moved to Chicago when her father got a new job. I never saw her again.

I hold onto that. I fall asleep holding onto it, but in the dream it morphs so that it isn't Lisa, but a faceless man, with big mean hands. He rips the doll — Izzy, he rips Izzy — limb from limb. I wake up sweating and crying, the night sky above me so black that I can't see a thing.

FRIDAY. I cling to the fact that maybe the man will come tonight. Even though I hate him, even though I'm terrified, I also crave his presence. I crave any human presence. In a strange way, I've become resigned to this hole. It's amazing how quickly the human spirit can acclimate to things, even the most terrible circumstances. Instead of being afraid of him, I count down the hours until he might come.

I finished the last half of the sandwich yesterday around lunch time, and the water this morning — I tried to hold off for as long as I could, but in the end, the boredom drove me to it — and now I'm starving again. I try not to think about how King is doing. He moves around a lot less now, preferring to sleep in the shade to the side of the hole. Thank God the bear hasn't come back. Maybe it'll stay away now that it knows we're here. Maybe, maybe.

Around five, I start to get antsy. Will he come? Won't he? What if the two-day pattern wasn't really a thing? What if he's planning to come at random intervals? What if he's never planning to come again?

I torture myself with these thoughts. Then I think about what I'm going to do when my FitBit dies, which I'm pretty sure is going to be any time now. What will I do when I can no longer mark the hours? Will time move faster or slower?

More hours pass. He doesn't come. My FitBit finally dies. The sky darkens. I weep. Bitter, angry, fearful tears. My hunger fades to a dull ache. Sleep.

MORNING. I awaken to the sound of birds. I no longer fear them. They're welcome now, a sign of life in what feels like a dead place. There's another sound, too, something achingly familiar that I can't quite place. I strain my ears. Try to recall what that sound is — wet, rhythmic, almost like waves on a beach but faster.

It's King. It's the sound of King lapping from a big bowl of water. But what water? How can that be?

"King?" I call carefully.

The voice comes again. "Good boy. That's a good boy. Drink up."

Relief sags through me. The man has come back. He's come back and he's brought water for King. At least … I hope it's water. What if it's actually something else?

"Hey," I call up. "Is that water? Are you giving him water?"

There's no response. Did I really expect one? Three trips now and he hasn't said one word to me since he first told me to shut-up. Only to King, and only to tell him he's a good boy. Not that I can argue with that. I tell myself that someone who's good to animals can't be all bad, but I know that's not true. It's easier to love animals, in some ways, because their motivations and desires are so simple. It's easy to love someone who will never hurt you, who will never think less of you, who's never had a single hate-filled thought darken the inside of their heart.

I wait, eager, for him to finish with King and to toss over my water and sandwiches. Like a good dog, I already know my routine. Be good, get food.

Only nothing comes this time. The man moves around, crunching through the dry grasses. I realize it hasn't rained since I got stuck in here. Almost a week now. My God, almost a week.

"Hey!" I yell. Terror is clawing at my throat. "Please. Help me. Please. You have to let me out. I can't stay down here. Just tell me what you want. Anything. Anything you want."

Just like that, he appears. His face leans over the edge of the hole. He's wearing a mask. Nothing fancy; a ski mask. The only visible features are his eyes and his lips. They look familiar but I tell myself that I'm grasping. Reaching for any sense of humanity, of knowability.

"I want you to think about what you did," he says. His words send a bead of cold sweat down my spine. "I want you to think about it long and hard."

"No." My voice is barely a whisper. I can't manage more than that because I can't wrap my head around what's happening. This is — what? Some bizarre type of punishment?

The man holds a sandwich and a water bottle, hanging down at his sides, one in each hand. He lifts them and my eyes automatically follow, my lips parted. Desperate for them, despite the fear. The lips behind the mask stretch into a mirthless smile. "Maybe another day without this will help with your thinking," he says. There's a note of cruelty in his voice. More than a note — a whole chord.

I slump down onto the dirt floor. My heart is thudding against my chest. Not just at the thought of going without food and water, not just at the terror of his words.

I can no longer deny that I am here on purpose. Intentionally. Someone knows what I did, and someone wants to make me pay.

FOURTEEN
SIX MONTHS AGO

The frigid March temperatures have made their way into Lily and James' apartment. Though she isn't quite sure she would call things between them 'icy', they have noticeably cooled. She and James have barely spoken since the other night, and James hasn't once reached for her in his usual way. It makes her feel like a stranger in their apartment. It makes her want to cry.

She decides she'll try to put it out of her mind. The whole thing — the dead bird, the changed photograph, the lost and found keys. Nothing else has happened since then and she's starting to wonder if maybe James is right. Maybe she did change the picture and forgot about it. Maybe the stress of their upcoming nuptials *is* getting to her.

Work is no better. Aurora's giving her the cold shoulder, and Damian's taken a hands-off approach, telling her it's her job to make sure the project goes smoothly, and that means managing the team. She brings in donuts for everyone, but when she presents them at the creative briefing, Aurora yawns and uses her pen to push them away.

In the back of her mind is also the looming concern about Connor. Every day when she arrives at work, she tenses. She expects to run into him on the street, to see him follow her into the building. She starts keeping her pepper spray in her pocket instead of her purse, even just for the short walk from James' car to the building's front door. She tells herself the odds of running into him again are slim-to-none — she looked him up on Facebook and, at least according to his profile, he works at a real estate firm halfway across town, which means he was probably only here for a meeting — but it doesn't take away that band of tension that runs from her shoulders to her temples. It's all exhausting. Too exhausting. She doesn't want to tiptoe through her own life like this. She's had enough of that. She decides she'll apologize to James. Not Aurora, though. Aurora can suck it.

At the market after work, she picks up a huge fillet of salmon, fresh dill, a bottle of capers. Salmon is one of James' favorite foods, but Lily always complains about the way it makes the house smell. So it'll be a peace offering. James can't stay mad at her forever, right?

As she makes her way home from the market, the back of her neck prickles. She scans her surroundings. The streets of the market neighborhood are teeming with people, so it's not exactly odd to feel that someone is looking at her, but this is more than that. She feels ... followed. She looks quickly back over her shoulder, but there's only the usual crowds of pedestrians, shoppers, single people on their way out to the pub, families on their way home to cook dinner and vegetate in front of the television. Everything is perfectly ordinary.

Except she can't shake the feeling. She keeps walking, but it follows her, like a lost puppy. She sneaks another glance behind her but again sees nothing. *It's all in my head,* she tells herself. It's the stress. Still, she picks up her pace.

She's almost home now. She debates going around the block a time or two, just in case there *is* someone following her. It's stupid to lead them straight to her door, isn't it? But she dismisses the idea as soon as it occurs to her. She's vowed to put all this paranoid nonsense behind her. She's stressed about the wedding; just like James said. Nothing more.

But as she approaches the entryway of the building, she looks furtively behind her. She whips her keys out of her bag and jams them into the front door in one fast, fluid motion, and then she's slipping into the building and hurrying toward the elevator. She hears the door click closed, and too late, she realizes she should have stayed to push it closed, to make sure no one slipped in behind her. A rookie mistake.

She stabs the elevator call button and waits for one of the cars to arrive. She hears footsteps behind her, footsteps striding over the marble floors, footsteps coming closer, nearing the corner turn-off for the elevators.

She punches the button again, and again, as if that will make it come faster. She's terrified, suddenly, of seeing someone round that corner. She doesn't know who she's going to see — or *what*. What kind of creature might be lurking. A crazy thought. Insane. She's going insane.

The elevator arrives and she practically leaps inside. Relief floods her, especially as the doors start to glide closed.

Then, a hand. It thrusts inside, barring the door from closing. Lily shrieks. She presses her back against the mirrored wall at the rear of the elevator and reaches into her pocket. Panic surges through her, turning her stiff and spastic. It's an instinct, grabbing the can of pepper spray.

Unlocking the safety and hitting the push nozzle in one fluid motion.

A fog of capsicum shoots forth from her fingertips.

She recognizes the face too late. She drops the can, but not before the damage has been done.

"Jesus, Lily, what the hell did you do?" James is there, bent over, clawing at his face, rubbing his Armani scarf over his skin.

"Oh my God, James. I'm sorry, I didn't—"

"Hit the button, for fuck's sake. Get me to the apartment."

"I—" Shock has made her numb. She hits the button for the fourteenth floor and the doors glide closed, pushing James into the interior with her. He's still hunched over. She puts a hand on his shoulder but he shrugs it off. "Are you okay? I'm so sorry."

He doesn't answer. He's breathing in and out slowly, trying to keep calm. She tries to imagine the pain he must be experiencing. Pepper coats her own tongue and her throat, sears the membranes of her eyes. She's never used the pepper spray before, but the guy at the sporting goods store had assured her it would get the job done if she ever needed it. Now she wishes he hadn't been so right.

They get to the fourteenth floor and she trails James down the hallway until they get to their apartment. He waits for her to unlock the door and swears loudly when she fumbles with the keys. When they're finally inside, he rushes to the bathroom. She tries to follow him in, but he slams the door in her face.

Inside the bathroom, the shower runs. James stays in there for what seems like hours. Lily rinses out her own eyes in the powder room, then paces the apartment. Eventually she remembers the salmon, the dill, the capers. She takes the bag down the hallway and shoves it into the garbage chute. It disappears with a whoosh. So much for her peace offering.

When she gets back to the apartment, the bathroom door is open, steam pouring out into the hallway. James isn't anywhere to be seen, but his office door is closed. She hesitates before knocking, but she can't stand not knowing how he's doing.

When he doesn't answer, she pushes it open a crack. "James?"

"What?"

She pushes it open further, enough to wedge her head in. "I wanted to see if you're alright. To tell you again how sorry—"

"I'm fine."

In the dim light from his desk lamp, his face is still a screaming red. His eyes gleam with unshed tears.

"Maybe we should go to the hospital."

He gazes up at her from behind his desk. "The hospital," he spits. "And how do you think that would look? Having to tell them my fiancee pepper-sprayed me. How do you think that would go over?"

"I'll tell them it was an accident."

"Right. Because they've never heard that before."

"I'll make them believe me."

James shakes his head. His lips are stretched into a rueful grin. "And what do you think we'll do if some nosy nurse decides she needs to go to the police? I know I certainly don't want that. And I can only assume you *really* don't want that."

Lily freezes. James regards her but she can't read the

expression on his face. What does he mean by that, that *she* really wouldn't want the police getting involved?

He doesn't know, she tells herself. It's impossible. There's no way he would have found out. She covered her tracks. She knows she did.

James sighs. "Anyway, I feel fine. My eyes are still watering a bit, but I should be fine by the morning."

He turns back to his laptop, which signals to Lily that he considers the conversation to be over.

Lily goes to bed, but she can't stop turning James' words over in her mind. Surely, he just meant that the police would push her harder, that they would want her to admit that James was abusing her or some crazy nonsense like that. Surely, that's all he meant. Surely.

She doesn't fall asleep for hours, and James stays in his office even longer.

———

IN THE MORNING, James is silent. His eyes have stopped watering, but the sclera is still red. It makes him look a little like a stoner, and Lily almost cracks a smile, picturing him sporting a beanie and chowing down on a bag of Doritos. She can't think of an image that's less like James.

She catches him watching her and bites back the smile. They ride to work without saying a word.

———

ON THE WAY HOME, she stops at the market and tries again

with the salmon, the dill, the capers. When James gets home, his eyes are considerably less red.

"How are you? You look better." She tries to touch his face, but he jerks away. She flushes.

"I'm fine."

"I bought salmon."

"Great." He doesn't sound enthusiastic, but he cooks the salmon and they eat it. Instead of proving to be a peace offering, it festers between them. The apartment stinks. It makes her throat close. James watches her obsessively.

After dinner, after she's loaded the dishwasher and taken the trash down the hall to the chute, she returns to find James in his office.

"I'm going to lie down for a bit," she says, but he stops her.

"Come here."

She stands at the door of his office for a minute. She recognizes that tone in his voice, that note of commanding. She wants to say no. She isn't in the mood to play. But James points to the wingback chair across from his desk and she finds herself walking wordlessly toward it, falling into it with a defeated thump.

She expects him to stand, come to her, already unbuttoning his shirt or unfastening his cufflinks. Instead, he reaches into his desk and pulls out a bottle. A little plastic prescription bottle. He hands it to her.

"I want you to start taking these," he says.

She reaches out to take it from him, operating on autopilot. She scans the label. Xanax, 1mg. And the prescription is made out to her. She wonders how he managed that little bit of trickery, but she knows better than to question his means.

She shakes the bottle. There are probably fifty or sixty pills in there.

"I don't want to," she says. She sets the pills down on his desk.

"Lily," he says. He sighs, speaking slowly, as if she were a child. "I really think you should take them. I think it could be good for you."

She wants to tell him that he's wrong, that it wouldn't be good for her at all, but she doesn't bother. There's no point arguing with James. Not when he gets set on something like this. And besides, what could she say? She pepper sprayed him yesterday. She doesn't have a leg to stand on. She nods once and picks up the pills. She starts to take them out of the room.

"No," he says. He points to the chair again. "Take them here."

She stares at him, wide-eyed but, frankly, unsurprised. She flips the cap open, pops one of the little blue tablets into her mouth, swallows. Opens her mouth to show him that it's gone.

"Good," he says. He nods. He looks like a proud parent, a dog-owner who just got their pup to shake a paw. "Very good. Thank you, Lily."

She can't even speak, she's too mad. She gets up, pockets the bottle, and goes to the kitchen. When she's sure James hasn't followed her in, she quietly spits the pill into the sink and washes it away with a stream of hot water.

FIFTEEN
PRESENT DAY

I haven't stopped shaking since he left. The man. The man who's keeping me here. The man who wants to punish me.

I know who it is now. Or I think so. The voice isn't right and the eyes don't look the way I remember, but who else can it be? It's true that being out in a forest and digging a hole isn't exactly his style, but the menace of it is. He has a twisted soul — I know that better than anyone. He loves to psychologically dominate. It's the only thing that gets him off. The only thing he lives for.

And now here I am. Trapped. A plaything for him, a helpless mouse before the big cat.

But at least he gave King water. That's the only thing I can cling to. That there's at least a little bit of humanity left in him. I'd worried that maybe he was poisoning him, but he left hours ago, and King appears fine. Better than fine, really. He's got a spring in his step again. His eyes are bright and clear. He's my good boy, back to his usual self. Thank God. If he'd hurt King, I would have found a way to kill him. It wouldn't even matter that I was stuck down here in this pit. I would have found a way to do it.

He didn't leave me anything this time. My stomach is too knotted for food, but I'm almost delirious with thirst. How much longer can I go without drinking? A day? Maybe two?

He'll come back, I tell myself. He has to. He'll want to, surely. He's got me here to torture me, for some sick reason, and what good is torturing someone if you aren't there to enjoy their suffering?

The sun has set, and the hole is dark. I can't even see my hands in front of my face. In the blackness, the delirium worsens. I imagine my body crumbling into dust, my brain shriveling like a hardened bit of snot. I wonder for a moment if I might actually go crazy down here.

Wouldn't he love that?

I decide I won't give him the satisfaction. I won't. I bring myself down to earth by breathing and counting my breaths. In for four, hold for two, out for six. Over and over, until finally my heart no longer threatens to thunder right out of my chest.

Maybe things will look better in the morning.

THINGS DON'T LOOK BETTER in the morning.

If anything, my outlook is even more bleak. I could blame it on the hunger or the thirst, but I know that it's not. Or at least not entirely. Knowing who's behind all this, the lengths that he went to trap me down here ... I know he means to kill me. He knows what I did, and he's going to kill me for it.

There's no doubt in my mind. This whole hole thing is just his fucked up way of doing it. Drawing it out.

I have to do whatever I can to get away. It's my only hope. If I even still have a hope left.

When the sun has come up, I get to my feet and try to do some jumping jacks, some push-ups. Anything to get my blood pumping. I don't want to exhaust myself too much, but I'm worried about how much strength I might have lost over the last week.

Oh God. I've been here a week now. That's right. It's Sunday today, I'm pretty sure, and that means it was exactly a week ago that I fell down here. Has anyone at work gone to the police yet? Maybe there's still hope someone might come.

I brush the tears away. I can't let him win. He may think he has the upper hand, but he doesn't. He underestimates my will to live, my desire to get away from him once and for all.

If it's a fight he wants, he's got one. I refuse to be afraid any longer.

SIXTEEN
SIX MONTHS AGO

The morning is tense. James and Lily ride to work together, as they always do, but even in James' small little Miata, she senses the distance between them. She doesn't like it, but she doesn't know what to do about it. He made her take another pill this morning, and she held it under her tongue until he left the room, but that took so long that the pill started to dissolve anyway, and now there's a haziness to everything. The worst part is, the pill doesn't even do what it's meant to, because the haziness makes her more anxious instead of less. When James lets her off in front of her building, her foot misses the curb and she goes tumbling onto the sidewalk.

Get it together, she tells herself. James' frozen expression says the same. She offers him a curt smile and strides into her building, trying to fake a confidence she doesn't really possess. She imagines she sees Connor out the side of her eye, but when she turns to look closer, it's a blonde woman in a mohair jacket. Not even close. She's clearly losing her mind.

She rides the elevator up to the seventeenth floor, fully

intending to immerse herself in projects for the rest of the day.

It doesn't work. When she gets to her office, she slumps down in her pink chair and spins around to look out the window. The sky is mottled in grey. It might actually snow. She hates when it snows. Even a few flurries, and Seattle drivers lose their damn minds. Sometimes she wonders what it would be like to live in a part of the country with real winters. Minnesota, maybe. She wonders if her life would be different if she'd ended up somewhere other than Seattle. Maybe she'd have settled down with a nice man, the kind of man who wore plaid flannel and knew his way around a handsaw. They'd cut down their own Christmas tree every year, and she'd drive an SUV, an all-wheel drive. Maybe she'd have taken up cross-country skiing. Or snow-shoeing. Now there's a winter hobby.

But there's no point in thinking like that. She hates looking backward. She chose Seattle. She chose James. And every day she chooses to stay the course.

When her desk phone rings, it startles her out of her daydream. For a few seconds, she has no idea what's happening. She spins around and grabs the phone, registering the word RECEPTION on the phone's display. Daphne, then.

"There's a Connor Franklin here to see you."

Lily freezes in her seat. Her insides turn to ice. No. How did Connor find her? She'd been imagining it all week, yet part of her felt confident it would never happen. She wasn't going by the name Stacey anymore, and no one here knew that's who she used to be. If Connor had come asking for someone named Stacey, then Daphne would have told him that there was no one here by that name. He'd have gone away disappointed, maybe, but would have eventually assumed she didn't work here and had only been on the premises for a meeting or whatever.

So how come Daphne is calling her and telling her that he's here?

Daphne must be able to sense there's something wrong, because a second later, a chat window pops up on Lily's computer screen. It's Daphne, and she types, "Should I tell him to fuck off?"

Lily breathes a sigh of relief and types "YES please."

Daphne speaks smoothly into the phone, as if Lily had spoken out loud. "No problem, I'll let him know you're unavailable."

She feels guilty for fobbing Connor off on Daphne, but she can't see him. She can't. She doesn't know what he wants, or how he figured out who she was, the name she was going by now, but she knows it's bad. Really bad.

She thinks again of the locker in Interbay. The escape hatch. If she was smart, she'd go now. Withdraw everything and run. But why should she have to give up everything she's worked for? Why can't Connor just leave her alone? Doesn't he know that would be the polite thing to do?

But Connor isn't known for his politeness. At least not the Connor she remembers. She remembers arrogance, entitlement, an insatiable appetite for sex, and an odd fascination with feet. Nothing there about politeness.

After ten minutes have passed, she rings Daphne again. "I'm sorry to do that to you. Is he gone?"

"He's gone, alright," she says. "But he says he'll be back. He seemed pretty insistent."

"Ugh," Lily says. It's not quite a word so much as a sound. "When he came in, did he ask for me by name?"

"No," Daphne says, surprised. "He described you, but I knew right away who he was talking about. He said he met you at a coffee shop but didn't get your name. He seems sweet." She pauses, maybe sensing Lily's anxiousness. "Oh God. I fucked up, didn't I? What is he, like, some kind of stalker?"

"Something like that." She hangs up.

Does Connor reach the level of stalker? She thinks probably he's just a nuisance, but she doesn't like the way he's shown up here out of the blue, and it makes her nervous to think that he knows her name and where she works. She considers the possible outcomes. One is that he knows about what she did, about the warrant. In which case, he'll probably try to blackmail her. She can deal with that if it happens. The second, and actually more worrying scenario, is that he doesn't know about the warrant and that he'll mention offhand to her brothers — or someone else from back home — that he ran into her.

She decides this possibility, though concerning, is unlikely. There probably isn't a single soul in all of North Carolina who doesn't know about Stacey Kincaid and what she did.

The most worrying possibility of all is that Connor will go straight to James. She couldn't bear it if he ever found out the truth about who she is, what she's done.

James thinks he knows her, but he doesn't really. The woman he loves is an illusion, a persona concocted to escape a past that threatened to drown her. Lily Castleman isn't real, but sometimes she can barely believe that Stacey Kincaid is real, either. That life feels as fleeting and unreal as the fog that mists up off of dry ice — here and gone, just like that. Is it really a lie, then? If Stacey Kincaid is dead and gone, surely it's not a lie to say that she's Lily Castleman now?

But James will never see it that way. He would never understand what she went through, what she had to do. She loves him, but he doesn't understand shades of grey. He sees the world in black and white.

James believes she's an orphan, the middle-class daughter of an artist and an English teacher who were killed by a drunk driver. He likes that idea of her. Little Orphan Lily. The theme song practically writes itself.

The truth is, her mother, at least, is very much alive. She has two brothers. Also alive. They're all, as far as she knows, still living in Bryson City. She checks on her brothers' Facebook profiles once in a while. They're fat and balding; it makes her believe in karma. One works at a car dealership and the other's a maintenance worker, which is the polite way of saying he pushes a mop around the same dump where they went to high school.

Once upon a time, her brothers had been football gods. Just a year between the two of them, Dale had played quarterback and Ray was the school's best tight end in years. They'd dominated on the field and, in her opinion, nowhere else. That didn't matter in Bryson City. They were the great white hope. They were also far too busy — or too blind or too willfully oblivious — to see what was happening to her. But oh, how she wanted them to. They were *her* great white hope, too. At school, she followed them around like an injured street cat, hoping for a scrap of whatever magic it was they possessed.

Even then there was a darkness inside her, a vile and

slithering snake, a black hole. It'd started when she was seven. Her daddy, Eldon Kincaid, sneaking into her bedroom at night. Making her play his little games, pushing her nightie up over her pale thighs. She learned how to bury things so deep she never had to feel them. She learned how to let the world believe she was anything they wanted her to be.

Her only solace was art. In between her father's lecherous gaze and her mother's baleful moonfaced stare and her brothers' self-imposed blindness, there was art. It was her secret solace, her soul soother. Someday, she'd move to New York and become an artist and put everything about Bryson City behind her.

She almost made it, too. She was awarded a full scholarship to Columbia University, where she planned to study visual arts. And then —

Panic bubbles up inside her again. It's as real, as visceral, as it was that day. She hadn't known who to turn to, but in the end, it was art that saved her again, this time in the form of her high school art teacher, Mr. Winthrop. She'd never exactly confided in him before, but she knew — or maybe hoped — that her art put words to things she couldn't. She'd often catch Mr. Winthrop watching her with his owlish gaze, rubbing his spectacles mindlessly on the hem of his paint-stained plaid shirt, a look of profound sadness on his small face.

She hadn't chosen the name Lily Castleman. That came courtesy of Mr. Winthrop and whatever mysterious connections he had. She liked it. It sounded both exotic and powerful, two things she'd always wanted to be and never felt even close to. He'd given her some leeway in choosing her city, as long as it wasn't New York. She had to let New

York go, he said. Everyone would know to look for her there.

She'd picked Seattle because … well, she still isn't sure why. She ruled out Los Angeles right away — no interest in fake boobs, fake hair, fake tans. Not to mention all that sun. She considered Atlanta, Boston, Chicago, but it was Seattle that called to her. Maybe it was the fact that no one from her high school had ever expressed any interest in it. Maybe it was just the gloomy weather. She'd have moved to London, if she could.

It took her over four weeks to get here, riding buses and trains on tickets paid for in cash, leaving a trail that snaked across the country. Looking back, she wonders how she had the fortitude for it. She must have been running on pure adrenalin. Once in Seattle, she'd dyed her mousy blonde hair a deep chestnut brown. She'd cut a dramatic fringe of bangs, her hands shaking as she stood in that grotty little bedsit bathroom and stared at her waxen face in the medicine chest mirror. She found a job working the nightshift at a 24-hour coffee place, where she could sleep through the day and travel by night, more like the tatty raccoons she'd find ranging around the coffee shop's Dumpsters than like a person. It was terrifying at first. Riding the Metro buses. Buying groceries. Smiling at people while she handed over donuts and coffee in exchange for grubby coins and trying not to look over her shoulder every five seconds.

But years passed. The natural order of things took over, and Lily, in her early twenties by then, started to want more. Mr. Winthrop had told her to stay away from art, because someone could recognize her that way, too. Advertising felt like the closest she could come. She found an unpaid internship at a small digital firm. She liked it. Loved it, actually. She started wearing red lipstick, black pencil skirts. She kept the coffee shop job to pay the bills, but the internship is where she truly came alive. And she busted her ass. So much so that they offered her a paid position. She quit the coffee shop. She stopped looking over her shoulder so often. She forgot. Stacey Kincaid was dead and gone, and she was Lily Castleman. It wasn't the life she'd once dreamed of, but it was still a good one, and she was grateful for it.

And then she met James.

James. Just thinking about him makes her stomach clench. James brought a light to her life that she hadn't even realized was missing. She never let herself pick up a paint brush, but being with James felt as close as she could get to the art and the passion she'd been forced to leave behind. Losing him would be unbearable. He can't know any of this. She has to preserve his image of her. His precious Lily.

Maybe she should meet with Connor after all and explain the situation to him — well, at least the highlights — and ask for his cooperation. Maybe appealing to his humanity will be enough. If that doesn't work, there's always money, but that's a slippery slope. She tries to reassure herself: though she remembers Connor's arrogance and entitlement, there was never any cruelty in him.

There's a knock outside her office and Lily looks up, startled. For a second she expects to see Connor standing there. In her mind, it isn't the Connor she saw the other day in the lobby, in the moderately-priced suit and the fine layer of scruff. It's Connor from ten years ago, with his football jersey and his six-pack of Coors. Connor with his empurpled erection and his sparse pubes.

But it's not Connor at her office. Of course it's not. It's only Damian, leaning against the glass wall and staring down at his iPhone.

"Peter Serrano says he's been trying to get ahold of you," he says without looking up.

"Who?"

Damian raises his eyebrows, finally drawing his attention away from his phone, which Lily's pretty sure is melded to his hand. "Peter Serrano? Green Acres? He says he's sent you about six emails and you haven't responded to any of them. It's not good when they have to call me, Lil'. I don't like it, and they don't like it."

"Right. Sorry. I was going to get back to him." She looks at her computer monitor, which is black. She hasn't even turned it on yet. And she's been sitting here for, what? At least two hours. Thank God her screen faces away from the door and Damian can't see it.

"Well, do, please. That guy gives me the creeps."

Lily bites back a laugh. "Why?"

"It doesn't bother you the way he looks at people? The way he looks at you?"

"How does he look at me?"

"Like he wants to eat you," Damian snorts. "Or fuck you. Or both."

"Oh. God. Really?" She pretends to sound surprised, but of course she's noticed. She encourages it. A little wiggle of the hips here, a suggestive raise of the eyebrows here. A perfectly-timed lick of the lips. It's how she's got everything she's ever wanted. And men like Peter Serrano are easy; it's the more complicated ones like James who take real work.

"Well, let me know if he ever starts to give you any real trouble."

"I will," she promises. She wants to ask what Damian will do if she does; fire him?

"And you'll get back to him?"

"I will."

She waits for him to leave. She doesn't want him to see her reach for the power button on her monitor.

SHE ARRIVES HOME that night with more goodies from the market. Scallops, baby potatoes, a bottle of rose. She checks three times to make sure the door locks behind her. She wants to have a glass of wine and unwind from her day, but it's more important to keep her mind sharp. Her thoughts have been racing all day. She kept expecting Connor to appear again, but he never did. She also never managed to call Peter Serrano back. Damian will be pissed if he finds out. She promises herself she'll do it tomorrow.

She changes into a pair of jeans and decides to sweep the floor. James hates when he catches her cleaning the house — they pay someone to do that, and he says it makes her look cheap — but she finds something meditative about passing the broom around the wide open floors. She finishes the kitchen, the living room, the hallway, and then tackles the bedroom.

She sweeps in long, even strokes. There's barely a speck of dirt to be found. Mathilde, their cleaning woman, is worth her weight in gold, even accounting for her considerable weight. Lily passes the broom around the bedroom and swipes it under the bed. When she pulls it out, there's something black stuck to the bristles. She bends, then recoils.

A feather.

Lily stares at it and almost feels as if it's staring back at her. How the hell did a feather get in here?

She thinks straight away of the dead bird. It had flown around the apartment for two days — surely it isn't unreasonable to imagine that it could have lost a feather or two along the way.

But isn't it also equally reasonable to expect that Mathilde would have captured any stray feathers last time she cleaned? There wasn't a speck of dust under the bed — Mathilde is nothing if not thorough — so how did she miss the feather?

Unless the feather had ended up there more recently. Mathilde comes on Thursdays, which means she's been here since the bird incident. And, Lily realizes, she herself checked under the bed just yesterday, when she'd been searching the apartment for signs of an intruder. She would have found the feather then. Wouldn't she?

Her hand is shaking as she bends to pluck the feather up from the bottom of the broom. It's black, like the bird they found the other day, with a pointy tip sharp enough to pierce her skin. On a whim, she holds it to her nose. It smells dusty and dry.

The sound of the apartment door opening makes her jump. She catches her breath. James. It's only James.

She looks down at the feather and decides she won't tell him about it. He already has her on Xanax. And besides, she doesn't know what she'd say. *I found a feather under the bed?* If he didn't believe her about the photo, he certainly isn't going to give a shit about a stray feather. He'll probably say one of them tracked it in on a shoe, or that Mathilde missed it when she was cleaning.

She pulls open the drawer of the nightstand and drops the feather in, then eases it closed. She goes out to greet James, plastering a wide and placid smile on her face. It surprises her, actually, how normal she's able to act when inside, her stomach is a whitewater raft.

SEVENTEEN

PRESENT DAY

On Sunday, he doesn't come.

On Monday, he still doesn't come. I wanted to fight, but how can I when the bastard won't even give me a chance?

I've been here over a week. Eight days that I've been stuck down this godforsaken hole. In that time, I've had three bottles of water. A little less than three sandwiches. Technically four, but I gave one and a bit to King. That's it.

I know it's not enough. The stretchy running leggings I'd been wearing when I set out for my hike last weekend are starting to hang off me. *Need to lose ten pounds? Try the Hole Diet! It's the latest Hollywood craze.* I promise myself that if I ever get out of here, if I make it out alive, I'll never complain about feeling fat again. I'll welcome and embrace every extra pound, every roll of skin. I'll eat every damn pastry or bit of fabulous cheese or glass of wine that's offered to me. Right now my skin feels stretched and dry and weird, a fact I contribute to the dehydration. I imagine myself shriveling like a dead plant, growing brittle and brown. I've got plenty of experience with dead plants — I'm many things, but a green thumb isn't one — and once they go past a certain point, there's no reviving them. There's no bringing them back.

For the first time, I'm truly afraid I'm going to die down here. I've known all along that it was a possibility, but knowing it and feeling it are two very different things. Now I actually feel the closeness of death. Not just that I'm going to die, but that I'm already starting to. My body is getting weaker. Fading. So is my hope. At some point my muscles will atrophy. My organs will shut down. I'll probably go into a coma. I hope it will be like going to sleep, that I won't be aware of anything except the feeling of passing into peace. But I doubt I'll be that lucky. I'll probably be aware of every last gasping, dying breath. That's the only way he'd want it.

I hope King won't stay with my body. That he'll have enough sense to find the trail again, to find kind people who will take care of him, bring him to a vet or a shelter. I don't want to think of him wasting away out here, or tangling with bears, or growing wild and feral.

By Tuesday, my thoughts have become unbearable. I think of Dr. Monica, how she always used to tell me, 'act the way you want to feel.' I have to do something. It's do or die, as they say. Shit or get off the pot. Get out of the hole or die trying.

But how? I've exhausted all avenues. I can't climb out. Can't jump out. Can't yell loud enough for anyone to hear me. Can't get King to go for help. I'm out of options.

I try to open my mind. Let my subconscious go to work, the way we used to do in brainstorming sessions at work. The rule was always: There are no bad ideas. Everything is on the table.

I lean back against the wall of the hole, my ass cold from the ground beneath. All of me is numb with cold. I don't have the energy to pace anymore, and even if I did, I'm at the point of conserving every iota of strength I can. So I lean, and I look up at those twelve foot walls, and at the shock of blue sky above.

I think: what would be the opposite of what I want to do? I want to go up and out. The opposite would be down and in. I could dig further down into the hole. No. That wouldn't get me anywhere. But maybe I could dig sideways. Tunnel up on the diagonal.

Or, even simpler, dig away at the walls until they aren't walls anymore. Turn one side into a gentle incline that I can climb right up and over.

And, for that matter, if I could dig into the walls or the floor enough, eventually there'd be so much dirt that I could mound it up, turn it into a little incline or a stair step, something so I could reach higher up the walls, maybe pull myself over the side.

I start to get excited. It seems logical, doesn't it? Dirt is my prison, but what is dirt but a very basic building material?

But then I consider how much digging that would involve. The effort required. Maybe I could have pulled it off when I first fell down here, but I'm weaker now. Exhausted.

But what choice do I have? In the face of defeat, the only thing I have left is ... myself. Be your own hero; that's another thing Dr. Monica used to say.

I look down at my hands. They're still sore from my last digging attempt. Prying at the rock walls left my fingers bruised and bloody, at least two nails ripped away and another couple ruined beyond measure. But my fingers still work. I can still bend them.

I survey the other things down here with me, wondering if there's anything else I can use to dig. My sneakers, my dead cellphone, a couple of empty water bottles. My eyes light on King's dog leash. I'd been wracking my brain to try to come up with a way I could somehow use it to pull myself up and out of here, but I'd neglected to consider the metal clip on the end, the part that attaches to his collar. It's not big and not overly sturdy, but it's hard, and maybe I could use it to chip away at some of the rock, or to gouge in places my fingers can't get purchase. I could use it to loosen some of the dirt, then use my hands to dig it and pile it up.

Excited, I crawl over to the leash. I close my fingers around the clip and say a silent prayer. I start to scrape at the earth on the bottom of the hole.

It works. Not amazingly, but it works. I scratch at the tightly packed dirt, and eventually it becomes less tightly packed. I scoop and push and claw and pack. I make a little step. Not a big one, but about six inches high. Why didn't I start doing this earlier? I could already be out of here. This whole nightmare could have been over.

But when I try to put my weight on the earth, it crumbles. I'm only maybe two or three inches off the ground now, the earth compacting beneath my foot. It's still something, but at this rate, I'll need to dig up so much dirt that I'll never be able to make it work.

But what other choice do I have? I crouch down and pile the dirt again, harder this time, really packing it in there. Then I dig up more.

I dig until the clasp on the leash breaks. It doesn't matter.

Even with the latch part broken, I can still use the metal hook to scrape at the earth. My hands throb, and my fingers scream, and now my lower back is joining the party, but still I dig.

When I've doubled the amount of earth, I try again. I get maybe six inches of lift this time. It's heartening. For the first time all week, I allow a sliver of hope. That hope might be dangerous, of course — just a blade to slice open my veins with — but for now, I'll take it.

I keep digging. I stumble over myself and my vision keeps going black, but this is my only chance. Finally, I get almost a foot of height. Only ten or so more to go.

I take a break. Just a short one. I need to rest my arms, my back.

I end up falling asleep. Maybe it's the physical exertion, but for the first time in days, I sleep soundly. When I wake up, the light has changed. It must be coming on twilight.

I'm hungrier than ever now, and my throat is coated in a fine layer of dust. I try to stand and my back and arms scream in agony. I sit back down. I need to rest for a moment. Just for a moment.

While I sit there, I study the walls of the hole, the levels of formation in the earth. Grass and dirt and tree roots in the top third, the craggier rock sections below. I wonder again how he managed to find this place. The idea of him digging it himself is almost inconceivable — he hated to get dirty. I remember that much. But then again, he may have taken a sick sort of pleasure in doing the work. He probably pictured my face with every shovelful of earth, with every rock dug out, every tree root unearthed.

The tree roots. I look up again at my earthen enclave. The roots up there aren't just trees, there are all sorts of little shrubbery roots, and above that, the smaller network of grass roots. A hierarchy of plant life lives in those layers.

But what catches my attention is one of the thick tree roots. It juts out of the wall slightly, as if it had been hacked away at but not carefully. It's about two thirds of the way up the wall, maybe around the eight or nine feet mark. Maybe even a little higher. Too high to reach from down here, but if I could build up this dirt mound enough, maybe I could grab onto it, somehow pull myself over the top.

It reignites my drive. I have no idea how exactly I'd get myself over the top if I managed to grab hold of that thing, but it's the only idea I have, so I start working. The light is getting dimmer, but I don't want to stop working. Maybe I could even be out of here by morning. The thought makes me laugh, and the sound is strange and shocking as it bounces off the dull walls.

I dig some more, building up the dirt another half a foot. There's a big hole in the middle of the floor now, because that's where the dirt is the easiest to dig. I scrape with the dog leash clasp, and, when I have enough scraped loose to make a couple of handfuls, I carry it over and press it into the mound I've started against the wall. It's an exhausting and back-breaking system, but it's all I've got.

I stop for another break. I've got about a foot and a half now, maybe more. I might be able to make it a bit narrower, scrape some dirt from the edges and use it to build up the center part instead. Yes, that's what I'll do. I only need enough space for one foot, just enough to reach up there and grab that root.

As I sit, I scrape dirt off the clasp of the dog leash. It's starting to fray where it connects to the actual leash part, but

I'll still be able to use it once it comes apart. It might be a little harder to hold — right now I'm wrapping the leash around my hand a couple of times so I can keep my grip on the clasp — but I'll manage.

That stupid leash should have been useful down here. That's how people normally get out of holes, right? Ropes. But there's no way to attach it to anything outside the hole. There was nothing I could do to make it work.

But as I sit there, I think about the leash, and an idea comes to me. I might not be able to attach it to anything outside the hole, but what if I could attach it to something *inside* the hole? If I could toss it up and get it to loop around that root, I could hold onto the ends and use it to pull myself up. It probably would have been too short before, but if I can build the dirt up another few inches, I bet I can get enough height that I'll be able to reach the ends of the leash, even with it wrapped around that tree root.

The thought is enough to get me on my feet again, even when my knees and my back scream in agony as I do. I eyeball the root, the leash, the dirt. Yes, math-wise, at least, it works out. Whether I'll have the strength to pull myself up is another story, and what I'll do when I actually get myself up there is yet another story, but I feel energized. Motivated.

I resume my digging. I'm getting out of here tonight. I can feel it in my bones.

EIGHTEEN
SIX MONTHS AGO

The smell of James' cologne lingers in the apartment long after he's left for work. Lily's called in sick. It's the first time in three years that she's done it, and the last time was because she wrenched her neck on an ill-advised trip to a rock climbing gym, part of a stupid team-building exercise at work. This is why she doesn't support team building — that shit can be hazardous to your health.

Today's sick day is even more well-deserved. She's afraid of facing Damian and Peter Serrano. The things that never used to bother her — dealing with pissy clients or irritating coworkers — feel harder and more fraught. And she's afraid of running into Connor again. She's let it go too far now. The thought of Interbay beats like a drum in the back of her mind. It would be the smart thing to do. The prudent thing. Her storage locker contains a brand new identity, one she'd finagled from a shady connection that started with a vague Craigslist ad and ended in the alley behind a pet grooming salon. She'd handed over two grand in exchange for an ID and a social security card, all to the haunting sounds of a lowing bloodhound being bathed. The name on the ID was Giana Rossi. A redhead, this time. Lily has no idea if the ID will even work, but she knew she needed a back-up plan, in case she ever felt them closing in. She's also got extra clothes in there, a pre-paid credit card, and as much cash as she's been able to sock away. She used to go once a year to top up the funds, but she hasn't gone lately. Not since she met James.

James. James is the reason she hasn't already gone down there, emptied out the stash, and escaped into the mists of Puget Sound. She can't leave him. She loves him, of course, but there's also a tiny part of her that's afraid of him. If she left, he'd look for her. She knows he would. James has money, and money gives him means. If he wanted to find her, she thinks he probably could.

So she won't leave. Not yet. She has another idea.

She's sure, now, that someone is coming into the apartment when they aren't home. That dead bird didn't get in here on its own, and neither did that feather. Someone came in and deliberately left them, the same someone who swapped out the photo on Lily's nightstand. She doesn't understand why, but she knows it's happening. She feels it right down to her bones.

She also knows James doesn't believe her. He thinks it's wedding stress, that she should just take a Xanax and chill. He won't listen if she asks him to change the locks, and she can't do it herself without having to give him a new key and watch him implode with fury.

But there's one thing she can do. She can get proof. Once she has proof that someone's entering their apartment, she can present it to James. With no emotion, just the solid evidence that someone is coming and going, he'll have no choice but to believe her and to change the locks. Maybe pull whatever other strings he has in order to keep her safe.

For James, the only possible proof will be if he sees it with his own eyes. It's not enough to hear her tell it. It's not enough to show him the strange leavings, the inexplicable artifacts. He needs to witness someone enter the apartment.

That means cameras. They're the only solution. They'll make his head implode nearly as much as new locks would — James is insane about privacy — but at least once he sees the truth, he'll have no choice but to believe her. That's the thought that she clings to. It's the thought that carries her down out of the apartment, into the taxi, all the way up to the nightmare hellscape that is Walmart, where electronics are cheap and plentiful, and where no one cares who you are or if you pay cash.

———

ONCE SHE'S MADE the purchase, she takes another cab home. Being out of the apartment for this long — nearly two hours, thanks to traffic — has made her anxious. When she gets back to the condo building, she can't help but look over her shoulder. She still has the sense of being followed, but she tries to tell herself she's just on edge as a result of her errand this morning. James won't like it, and the thought of pissing him off makes her almost unbearably nervous. But her paranoia is stronger. She's more afraid of a stranger breaking into their home than she is of James, who has a mind and an appetite that at least she understands.

She slips into the building, feeling furtive even though she lives there, and is relieved to see that no one else is in the lobby, no one has followed her in. She rides the elevator up to the fourteenth floor alone.

Standing outside their apartment, she's walloped by another wave of nerves. What if there's someone in the apartment right now?

She remains in the hallway, silent and listening. Is that movement behind the door? She presses her ear up against the cold steel and holds her breath. Yes, there's definitely a noise coming from inside the apartment.

Lily's body tenses with equal parts adrenalin and fear. Maybe she won't even need the cameras. If she can catch the intruder, she can put a stop to this entire thing.

Except she's afraid to open the door. She has no idea what she's going to find on the other side, and she's not so sure she wants to find out. She remembers one of the weird sex clubs James brought her to, earlier in their relationship. She wasn't keen on the whole thing from the start, but she'd said yes because she'd say yes to anything James asked. The whole thing revolted her. All those women with their desperate eyes, the men greased up like pigs. Some of them wore costumes, masks, and one man in particular stood out to her.

He was tall, probably six foot four, and so he towered over most of the others in the playroom. He wore an executioner's mask, black and solid, with only holes for his eyes. Lily hated him on sight, and yet her gaze was continually drawn to him. She eventually lost track of him as James led her around the room from one playmate to another. But at one point during the night, she saw him again. He still wore the mask, but now a line of blood dripped down his naked chest. The sight of that blood made her dizzy. Who did it belong to? Had he just got a bloody nose or bit down too hard on his own lip? Or did the blood belong to someone else? She never forgot that image, and sometimes, the sight of him would strike her right as she was falling asleep, jolting her into a sudden and miserable alertness.

It's him that she thinks of now, standing outside her apartment with her keys between her fingers like a weapon. It's absurd, she knows, but for some reason she envisions opening the door and finding him in there, the tall man in the mask with the line of blood.

Stop being ridiculous. But still she gets out her phone, pre-dials a nine and a one. Just in case.

She slips the key into the lock and turns it as softly as she can. The lock clicks open and she holds her breath, hoping whoever is inside the apartment hasn't heard anything. She eases the door open.

Inside, the apartment appears exactly as she left it. But there's something — a smell. She breathes in. Something citrusy and floral. Lemon, maybe.

A noise comes from the bedroom, and her heart hammers against her chest. *I knew it,* she thinks. There *is* someone here. Her phone is at the ready, her keys tucked between her fingers. She debates going into the kitchen — at the opposite end of the apartment — to get a knife, but before she can decide, the noise comes again. Her heart is really thundering now.

The bedroom door swings open and Lily screams. The person coming out of the room screams. Lily brandishes her keys. She tries to dial the final one on her phone but she ends up dropping it by mistake. Her fingers are covered in sweat.

"Miss Lily! You frightened me."

Mathilde, their cleaning woman, stands in front of her.

Yellow cleaning gloves grow from her fingertips up to her elbows, and she carries a plastic bucket in one hand, a rag in the other.

Lily bends to pick up her phone, mortified. "I'm so sorry," she says. "I didn't realize you were here today."

"Thursday, Miss Lily." Mathilde's been working for James for longer than Lily's known him. Lily tries to like her but if she's being honest, she's always been a bit intimidated by her. Mathilde is an enormous woman, not just heavy but tall — at well over six feet, she towers over Lily — and her dark eyes are most often unreadable.

"I know. I just … forgot."

"You aren't at work today?"

"I wasn't feeling well." Lily tries to hide the shopping bag in her hand. Not that she cares if the maid thinks she's playing hooky from work in order to go shopping. It's more that she's concerned Mathilde could mention something to James, and she doesn't want to have to come up with an excuse for why she left the house when she's supposed to be so under the weather. But Mathilde isn't even looking down at the plastic shopping bag.

"You want me to go?" She glances around the apartment, clearly not fond of the idea. "I have a few things left to do, but I could finish them quietly if you like. I'm done in the bedroom if you want to lay down."

"Thank you," Lily says. "That should be fine."

She goes into the bedroom and closes the door, then sits down on the bed and starts to go through her purchases. Two wireless cameras that automatically upload their footage to the cloud in real time. They weren't cheap, but she wanted to get something reliable, and something that was small enough that James wouldn't notice. She's already decided she's going to put one near the front door, and another one in the bedroom. She doesn't like the idea of a camera in the bedroom, but she can always delete any footage that turns x-rated. And hopefully she's going to catch a lot more than that.

The cameras are easy enough to set up, and she uses her laptop to register an account where she can retrieve the footage whenever she needs to. There's an app that can go on her phone, too, but she decides not to download it in case James finds it. She'll still be able to log into the website to see the live feed, but at least she can erase her browser history when she's done.

She doesn't like sneaking around behind James' back, but he hasn't given her much choice. He's still pushing the pills on her, still insisting that she relax, and every time he says it, she wants to spit on the floor and stamp her feet like a child. Why can't he see what she sees? This isn't her imagination. Someone has been in their apartment.

She realizes there's one other person who might know what's going on — Mathilde. In the main part of the house, the vacuum is still whirring away, so she leaps from the bed and goes to find the housekeeper.

"Mathilde," she says, over the whir of the appliance. "Can I talk to you for a second?"

Mathilde doesn't turn. She's humming something, rocking her hips back and forth as she pushes the nozzle of the Dyson along the over-priced Persian carpet in James' office. Lily has to bite back a smile. It's unusual for her to catch the woman in such an unguarded moment, and for a second she doesn't feel any intimidation at all. Only a brief burst of affection.

"Mathilde!" Lily says, louder this time.

Mathilde jumps and spins around. "Oh, Miss Lily! You scared me! Again." She smiles as the vacuum silences.

"Sorry," Lily says. "But I wanted to ask you something."

"Of course, Miss Lily. Anything. Am I being too loud?"

"No, no, nothing like that. I just wondered if …" she trails off, not quite sure how to finish now that she's here.

"Yes?" Mathilde is watching her curiously, her eyebrows raised, her dark eyes once again unreadable.

"I guess … some strange things have been happening here, and I wondered if you've noticed anything out of the ordinary."

"Strange things? Like what?"

Lily isn't sure whether she should tell her or not. She doesn't want Mathilde to think she's crazy, too. But she wonders if Mathilde might not have a perfectly reasonable explanation for what happened. Like, oh, maybe she let the bird in while they were away, she switched the photo out because she thought Lily might need a change. In the end, it's this desperate hope that leads Lily to tell her everything.

Mathilde's expression grows more and more concerned as Lily talks. She starts to shake her head furiously. "No, no, Miss Lily. I don't know anything about that. Goodness. I would have told you or Mister James if I'd seen anything at all."

"Of course," Lily says. "I just wondered." She's disappointed but not surprised. It was a long shot. "Please, finish your cleaning. I'm going to go lie down."

This time she actually does go lie down, tucking the cameras back into the bag and hiding them in the drawer of the nightstand on the off chance that James decides to surprise her by showing up and checking on her. She manages to sleep a little, and when she wakes up, the apartment is silent. Mathilde is gone, and Lily has the place to herself.

She checks the time and realizes it's almost five o'clock. She panics for a second, thinking that means James will be home pretty soon, but then she remembers it's Thursday and he has his standing racquetball game with Duncan. She has time. She digs the cameras out again and goes out into the living room, peering up at the wall adjacent to the foyer.

She decides to stick the first camera behind the wall-mounted television. If she angles it right, it will capture most of the front hallway, but won't be noticeable from the rest of the room. Plus, the black plastic body will be easily camouflaged against the edge of the television. It's the best option she's got out here — James' minimalist style doesn't leave a lot of places to hide things.

In the bedroom, she decides the second camera will go on her nightstand, facing the door. She camouflages it by placing it in her glass jewelry bowl and draping a heavy beaded necklace on top of it. The arrangement looks bulky to her eye, but James won't notice. At least she hopes not.

She's just stashing the empty boxes back into the plastic Walmart bag when the front door opens. She freezes. An intruder?

"Lily? I'm home."

James. Instead of feeling relieved, her panic intensifies. She looks down at the shopping bag in her hands. She dives down onto the floor and stuffs it beneath the bed.

"Lily? Are you okay?" James comes into the bedroom and finds her on her knees beside the bed. "My God, did you fall?"

"No, I'm fine." She stands quickly, spreading her hands

wide as if to demonstrate just how fine she is. "I dropped a tissue."

"Oh." James looks at her hands, which are, of course, not holding a tissue.

"I thought I did, anyway."

"I brought you some soup." He holds up a bag, and the smell of thyme and chicken broth tickles her nose.

"That's so sweet. But how come you aren't out with Duncan?"

"I cancelled. I wanted to make sure you were okay."

"How kind." The handle of the Walmart bag is still protruding out from under the bed. She pushes it back with her heel and steps quickly toward James, hoping he won't notice. She puts her hands on his shoulder. "I'd kiss you," she says. "But I don't want you to catch what I have."

"I'm willing to risk it."

When he lets her go, she leads him into the living room. She doesn't want him in the bedroom until she can get rid of that bag. But once there, she remains on alert. Even though she's done a pretty good job of hiding that camera behind the television, she's somehow sure James will notice it anyway. That he'll be drawn to it automatically, or that he'll sense her guilt and start poking around.

But he doesn't. He takes out the chicken soup — from Zigman's deli, her favorite — and a bottle of ginger ale, and turns on the television. Lily tenses when he does that — what if the camera somehow interferes with the reception, or what if she knocked the plug out somehow and he has to go look behind the television? But nothing of the sort happens. The television turns on as fast as it always does and James puts on *Friends*, her favorite comedy and the only way she allows herself to indulge her old fantasy of a glamorous New York life. He pats the sofa next to him, where she goes to snuggle up. She starts to relax as she eats the soup. She even starts to get sleepy.

This will work, she thinks. She'll get her proof, and James will have to believe her.

NINETEEN
PRESENT DAY

I can't believe it. It's working. It's actually working.

I've built up my stump of earth enough that I can get almost two feet off the ground. Just that two feet gives me a wondrous sense of optimism. If I stand on it and stretch my arms all the way up, I can almost reach the root on my own. From there, it's only another two feet to the top. I start to wonder if maybe I could make it just by jumping, but ten minutes of effort disabuses me of that notion.

Still. I have the leash. The leash and the root might be enough leverage to pull myself up and then … what? Maybe I'll be able to wrangle myself up further somehow. There's a rock cropping that might serve as a toehold part way up, and if that root is as sturdy as it looks, I might be able to use it to actually stand on. That would easily put me over the top.

I can't believe it. I'm so close. I can taste the freedom.

It's getting dark, but I don't want to wait until tomorrow. Even another night in here is going to sap my strength, what little I have left. No. It has to be now.

I grab the dog leash and climb back on my make-shift step.

I try to toss the end of the leash up, but it doesn't even come close to wrapping around the root. I try again. It hits the root, but won't drop down the other side of it. *Concentrate.* I toss it again and again. I get frustrated. It feels like it isn't going to go in, like my shots are getting wilder and more off course.

Finally, it catches. The end of the leash slips down between the thick root and the earth behind it. But only a couple of inches of it swing down. I reach up but I can't quite grab ahold of it. I need to pull it down so I can hold both ends, test how sturdy the root is. I think, *maybe I can reach it if I jump.* I jump and jump, trying to brush my fingers against that dumb bit of red rope. I'm already exhausted from my earlier jumping, and I get winded faster than I should. Tears prick my eyes. This is stupid. I can't get worked up over this, not now when I'm so close.

I try one more time and finally my fingers catch on the slim cord. As I come back down, the rope comes with me, and I catch hold of the other side to keep it from accidentally slipping all the way through. Now I've got hold of both ends, and the middle part is wrapped around the tree root.

I give it a good tug. Part of me is afraid that the root isn't as strong as it looks, that it'll come straight out of the dirt as soon as I put tension on it, but that sucker is in there good. I tug as hard as I can, pulling my whole weight on the thing, and there's no give at all. None.

I let out a whoop. This is really working. It's going to work.

I couple the two ends of the leash together, pull them out a ways, and start to climb. I brace my feet against the wall and use the rope for leverage, like we used to have to do in gym class when I was a kid. I could climb like a monkey back then.

Give me any jungle gym or pyramid of cheerleaders, and I could scale it in two seconds flat. I've lost a lot of that over the years — both the physical ability and the general gumption — but I pray it's going to come back to me now, in my hour of need.

And, unbelievably, miraculously, it does. Sort of. I'm not nearly as graceful or as limber or as quick, but I'm making it happen. I'm actually scaling this wall. It's slow going and my shoulders ache, but eventually I can reach up and brush my fingertips against the root. That glorious root. When I finally close my fingers around it, I almost weep. I use it to pull myself up a little more, my sneakers scrabbling against the dirt wall, trying to find purchase. But there's nothing for them to grab onto. I know there was a rock shard along here, but I can't see it and I can't find it with my foot.

My arms are starting to tremble and I know I can't hold on much longer. I scuff my feet over and over against the dirt wall, but there's nothing that I can rest my weight on. My hands start to slip, and I'm falling back down. I hit the ground with a thud. I burst into tears.

It isn't the pain of falling — though my tailbone screams at me — it's the shock of the fall and the disappointment of being so close. I let myself cry for a minute or two, long enough to get the worst of my self-loathing and bitterness out, and then I pick myself up. I was close last time. This time I'm going to do it for real.

The second time goes faster. My arms are weaker, but the muscle memory is kicking in and I monkey up there faster than I would have thought possible. Soon, I'm reaching the root again and my fingers close around it triumphantly. This time I know where that stupid rock outcropping is, too — I memorized its location while I was lying on the ground feeling sorry for myself. It was higher than I remembered, closer to where the root is, so this time I bring my leg up even higher and … there it is. My toes connect and I use it to push myself up higher. It holds. Hallelujah, it holds. Slowly, painfully, I push myself up. Pushing from my feet, pulling at the root. And then … the top of my head is out. The taste of fresh air is on my tongue.

The first thing I do is look around for King's slumbering figure. I whisper his name in the darkness — for some reason, I'm still afraid to speak too loudly. Something about the woods at night, about the memory of that bear that wandered through a couple of days ago.

At the sound of his name, King's eyes pop open. He blinks at me a few times in the darkness, then scrabbles to his feet and runs over. He covers me in kisses, and I delight in it, the reek of his breath filling me with dumb joy.

But I'm still barely holding on, so there isn't time for a reunion yet. My foot rests on the rock outcropping, and my hands are still at the root, which is now right around my midsection. My balance is so precarious that I'm afraid to lift my arm up and reach over the side of the hole. What if I fall backward again?

But I'm so close that I have to try. I lean forward and slowly let go with one hand, inch it up the wall until I can throw my hand up onto the grass. There's nothing to cling to — unless you count grass — and my position is even more precarious now. How do I get the other arm over?

I have no choice but to just do it. I take a deep breath, lean into the wall, and reach my arm up.

I wobble a little, but I keep my balance. Now my head,

shoulders, and both arms are completely out of the hole. I can taste the freedom.

It's torture to pull myself over — my arms are weak from effort and there's nothing but slick, dew-covered grass to hang on to, but somehow, inch by soggy inch, I pull myself up and over. When my whole torso is out, I know I'm home free. I scramble the rest of the way out and squirm through the grass for a few feet, until I'm far away from the hole. I have the eerie sensation that somehow it's going to pull me back in.

But no. I'm out. I'm safe. King clambers over me, forcing his big dumb German shepherd body into my lap like he's a tiny puppy and not a beast of a thing. He covers my face in more kisses and I do the same to him. Tears stream down my cheeks and snot runs down from my nose and I don't even care. Because I'm free.

My God, I'm free.

I look around the clearing, the same one I'd run through chasing King so many days ago. It looks different at night. Eerier. Or maybe it's that now I know the evil secrets this place holds. I shiver in the darkness, and it isn't just because of the dew that's soaking my clothes.

All I need to do is find the trail again, the one that'll lead me back to my car. I have no idea exactly where I am, or even what side of the clearing I originally came from. But finding my way out of the woods is a small feat compared to finding my way out of the hole, so I don't feel as worried as I should.

And maybe that's my mistake. I get too cocky.

I stand and brush my pants off, taking long exuberant breaths. The air up here isn't vastly different than the air down there, but it feels fresher somehow. Maybe that's just the freedom talking.

"Okay, buddy," I say to King. "Let's go. Let's go home."

We start to walk, and we're almost out of the clearing when I hear it. A branch snapping. I freeze. King does, too. And it comes to me right away what it is — somehow, I just know. The bear. The bear has come back. Maybe it smelled me, or maybe it would have come back anyway, but it's back and it's going to tear us both to shreds and we're both going to die out here, never to be found again.

I tamp down the panic. "Come on, bud," I say to King. "Let's go. Quiet."

"Not so fast."

Although the voice is deep and gravelly, I know damn well it isn't a bear.

It's *him*.

TWENTY
SIX MONTHS AGO

For nearly a week, Lily doesn't get anything done at work. How can she, when she keeps checking the website for the security camera feeds? The technology allows her to peek into the apartment in real time, and the idea of catching the intruder in the act is too irresistible to pass up. She even downloads the app onto her phone so she can keep it open all day and monitor both cameras at once. She tells herself she'll delete it at the end of the day, before she goes home. No reason James has to see it.

But no matter how long she spends watching, the apartment remains silent and still. Not even a shadow passes in front of either camera. She's both relieved and disappointed.

She's staring at the feeds one morning when her phone chirps with a new email. She's militant about keeping spam out of her personal email account — she's the fastest draw in the west when it comes to the unsubscribe button — so she knows it'll be something she wants to see. Most likely something from James.

Only it isn't James' name that pops up when she taps the phone to open up her inbox. The name on her screen is Connor Franklin.

She stares down at the phone for a minute without opening the email. She should delete it unread. She doesn't want to know what he wants. It can't be anything good. That much she's sure of. But ignoring him could backfire. Forewarned is forearmed and all that.

Finally, she taps the email. The screen shuttles Connor's message open and she reads.

"*Hello Lily,*" it starts.

"*It was a pleasure running into you the other day — what a strange coincidence! I'm sorry you were unavailable when I came to your office. Would love a chance to connect with you again. There's something I really need to talk to you about.*

Please reach out as soon as you can.

Your old friend,

Connor."

She shudders as she reads the message again. On the surface it sounds friendly enough, but she can feel the menace pouring out of it. In fact, she's sure that last bit — *there's something I really need to talk to you about* — is an outright threat. *I know what you did.*

It's clear to her now that Connor Franklin knows about what she did. He's probably figured he can get something out of it. She doesn't know what — money, most likely, but maybe he wants to relive their past exploits. She has no interest in indulging him in either one. As far as she's concerned, Connor Franklin can go fuck himself.

But at the moment, the threat remains. He knows where she is, the name she's living under. If he contacts anyone from back home — any of his old friends, or one of her brothers — everything will implode. She'll have to run.

She should run *now*. Before it comes to that. Buy herself time, a head start. Giana Rossi could settle down in Sante Fe, maybe, or Austin. Start a new career dealing in essential oils or healing crystals. Take up meditation.

But she doesn't want to go. Every fiber of her being fights the idea. She was forced to run before, and she won't do it again. She has a life here. A real life. She has James. She won't be scared away from that.

But she's not sure what it will take to neutralize Connor's threat. Her first instinct is to delete the email and ignore his insinuations, but she has to admit that she hasn't known Connor for more than ten years. She has no idea what kind of person he is now, nor does she know the circumstances of his life. He could be divorced, bankrupt, angry at the world. A man with nothing to lose and no qualms about bringing anyone else down with him. It would be a mistake to dismiss him out of hand.

She's still thinking about Connor when the knock comes on her office door. She jumps, but it's only Aurora.

"Yes?" Lily says, planting her hands on her keyboard and trying to look busy and important.

"We finished the first build," Aurora says. "If you want to come down to the pod and check it out. It needs a bit of work before it can go to the client but …"

"For the Green Acre project?"

Aurora nods. Lily doesn't want to admit it, but she's pleased. She'd expected Aurora to drag her feet all month, just to prove a point. The fact that the first build is already done is a monumental feat, and even though the project will still need lots of going over, she expects they'll be able to make their deadline after all.

"That's great," she says to Aurora, and she means it. "I'll be down in five minutes, okay?"

"Sure." Aurora still looks sullen, but she leaves Lily's office and disappears back down the hallway toward the pod. As soon as she's out of sight again, Lily grabs her phone. It's been a whole ten minutes since she checked on her security cameras, and she's afraid she might have missed something.

She loads up the app and watches the apartment, but it's as still and silent as the last time she looked. She scrubs backward in the footage, making sure that no one came and went while she was distracted by Aurora and by Connor's message, but no, nothing moves within the apartment.

She's surprised to find herself disappointed by that.

———

THAT NIGHT she leaves the market bearing her usual market goodies. Lamb again, fresh basil and mint, thick plain yogurt. She's craving Greek food and hopes James will take the hint. When she arrives home and walks into the apartment, she expects to feel at ease. She knows for a fact that no one's been in here all day — she's got the proof right on her smartphone — but the apartment feels foreign and strange, like it's not the place she lives in but a dream version, with weird funhouse angles and twisted reflections. She wanders from room to room, looking for anything changed. She finds nothing.

Of course not, she tells herself. She would have seen it on the camera. *But what if the intruder bypassed the cameras?* She considers this. They're trained on the front door and the bedroom, but most of the living room is uncovered. So, she realizes, is the balcony. What if the intruder was entering via the sliding door? Sure, their balcony is fourteen floors up, but it wouldn't be impossible. Their neighbor's balcony is only about three feet away from theirs, and in theory, a nimble or clever intruder could manage to travel from one balcony to the next, undetected.

She hurries to the patio door and tugs, but finds it locked. As she suspected. James is good about keeping things locked, and they haven't used the door since the early fall when it was still nice enough to sit outside. She flips the lock anyway and steps outside into the frigid air. The tomato plant she'd tried to grow last summer sits shriveled and shameful in the corner, and the patio furniture is draped in thick plastic covers to protect it from the bitter cold air. Even though they never get snow, James says even the cold will damage it, so in the fall, when the leaves started to turn, he enshrouded it in black plastic coverings.

She steps across the balcony and leans against the railing. From up here she has a view of the market, Elliot Bay. Two ferryboats cross each other, one coming and one going. She looks down at the street below, at the tiny people and cars fourteen floors down. She leans over so far that it gives her a sense of vertigo, and she pulls back, dizzy.

Lily turns and eyes the dark hulking shapes of their covered patio furniture and tries to imagine a person hiding beneath them. That one, the sofa, is more than big enough to envision a person beneath the slick plastic sheeting. A person could stretch out on that sofa, under the tarp, and she'd never even be able to tell.

There could be a person there right now.

No. That's crazy.

But the thought won't leave her alone. She stands in the cold, freezing in her silk blouse and pencil skirt. She wants to go back inside, but she can't make her feet move the way she wants them to. She's frozen — almost literally — to the spot. Then she can't take it anymore and she's ripping at the plastic sheeting, pulling at it and trying to tear it open even though it's far too thick for that. Eventually, she wrestles it off and stands there with it piled at her feet. She stares down at the outdoor sofa — the perfectly normal, perfectly empty outdoor sofa, with its water resistant white cushions.

What is happening to her? Why does she feel so crazy all of a sudden?

"Lily?"

She bolts, stumbling against the railing of the balcony and losing her balance. James' reaches out and grabs her arm, steadying her. His face is equal parts angry and concerned.

"What are you doing?" he asks. Something about his voice rattles her. It sounds anxious. There's a note of desperation to it. James doesn't do desperation.

"I don't know," she whispers.

She surveys the patio, the plastic tarp ripped from the sofa and piled at her feet. And it isn't only the sofa she stripped — all of the furniture stands bare and uncovered. Plastic pools around her. When had she done that? She doesn't even remember. She can't believe she doesn't remember. She looks helplessly at James and the two of them stand there in the March chill for what seems like hours.

TWENTY-ONE
PRESENT DAY

"Not so fast." The voice — *his* voice — stops me dead in my tracks.

King growls and spins around. Not me. I'm afraid to move. Because if I turn and see him, it'll be real. He'll really be standing there. If I don't turn around, maybe I can convince myself that the whole thing is only a dream. A delusion, brought on by dehydration and stress.

"Where do you think you're going?" he says. A shiver runs the entire length of my body. He waits for me to answer, but I don't. "I guess I didn't give you enough credit. I really didn't think you'd be able to get out. I thought I'd dug it deep enough."

"You didn't," I say, unable to help myself. I'm standing here talking to my delusion, I think. Nothing to see here, folks.

I take a few steps forward, then another. If it *is* a delusion, I should be able to walk right out of the clearing. And for a second, I think it's actually going to work, that I'm going to get out of here.

A hand wraps around my arm. A hand I know I'm not imagining. A hand that's strong, large, that squeezes too tight on my tender skin. Such a familiar feeling. There was a time in my life when my arms were constantly covered in bruises, but that time feels like so long ago. Just a dream I had once. Another delusion.

I whip around to face him, steeling myself. If it's a fight he wants, it's a fight he'll get. I've faced worse in my life. He isn't the first entitled man I've come up against, and with my luck, he won't be the last. So bring it on.

When I turn I'm startled to find him still wearing a ski mask. The weather isn't cold, but I guess he thinks this will help hide his identity. His eyes are visible, though, and up close they're a familiar shade of green, almost the same color as the grass at our feet.

"Let go of me," I spit. I refuse to show him any fear.

Under the ski mask, his mouth twists up into a sadistic grin. That scares me more than anything, that grin. There's no sanity in that grin. There's only a sick and twisted sort of rage. My leg muscles turn to jelly, and even though I haven't needed to use the bathroom in almost two days, my bowels suddenly want to void.

"Silly girl," he says. "Silly, silly girl. Did you really think I'd let you get away that easily?"

I don't answer him. I won't. It's what he wants, after all, and I refuse to give him what he wants.

"Come on," he says.

He starts to drag me back toward the hole. No, God, no. I won't go back there. I pull against him, dig my heels into the ground, throw the weight of my body away from him. Anything to get loose. I start to scream, on the off chance there's somebody out here that can hear me, and also just because it's an instinctual reaction. I scream until my lungs burn and my throat feels raw.

And still he pulls me. Closer and closer we get to the hole. I'm not making it easy for him, but at the end of the day, he's stronger than I am and the distance between us and the hole is closing. I twist and turn and wrench my body like a feral cat, but he brings his other hand up, grips me by both shoulders, walks me forward.

King sees me struggle, and whatever bond he's developed with my captor over the last week is eroded by his instinct to protect me. He lunges and leaps at the man, biting into his calf and tearing at it. The man yells, tries to shake King off, but King is ferocious. His loyalty to me makes him wild. For a second, the man lets go of my shoulders, and that's more than enough time for me to wrench myself away from him.

I run. I run like the devil is after me, because, when you think about it, he is. I leave King, even though it kills me to do it. If I'm going to get away, this is going to be my only chance. I run through the tall grass, stumbling and chaotic but with only one goal in mind: to get to the tree line, where hopefully I can disappear.

As the trees get closer and closer, my hope builds. Freedom is almost close enough to taste. The man curses and stumbles after me, and King growls and snarls and lunges after him, trying valiantly to hold him back. I risk a glance behind me. They're both gaining on me, even though I'm running as fast as I can. I must be weak, too weak. But I push on anyway. Almost there now. I can do this.

My foot slides out from under me. The grass is wet and I spin and my ankle turns and then I'm falling to the ground. I try to right myself, ignoring the searing pain that shrieks out from my ankle, but I stumble every time I try to get to my feet. It takes me three tries to finally get off the ground, and by then he's on top of me. He grabs me by the shoulders and lifts. This time he pulls me tight against his chest, wrapping his powerful arms around me. I struggle but his hold is firm, and I'm pinned there like a butterfly on one of those horrible little displays. I kick and bite and scratch, but he's pulling me backward, back to the hole.

King lunges at his ankles, but the man lets loose with one good kick and catches King right in the ribs. I cry out at the same time that he whimpers and slinks low to the ground.

"You bastard," I hiss between sobs. I try to rip at his arm with my teeth but he has on a leather jacket and I can't come anywhere close to penetrating the thick fabric. The worst I'm going to do is bruise him. I can't get out of this.

"Back in you go," he announces cheerfully. My heart is a stampede of horses, thundering in my chest. Fear bubbles inside me.

"No," I say. "Nonononopleaseno." It's a chant. I don't let up. He unwraps his arms from around me and in one swift motion, he pushes me forward. I stumble and fall and he pushes me again and I go right over the side. Back down into the hole.

Back down into my prison.

The fall hurts even more this time than it did last time. Maybe it's because I'm weaker or maybe it's because I went over at the wrong angle. Last time the worst thing I did was bite down too hard on my tongue, but this time a searing, screaming pain rips through my shoulder. I scream, and above me, the man laughs. I turn my back to him, trying to curl into a ball, protect myself as much as I can. But as I do, I realize I'm holding onto something. Despite the pain, I have enough sense to figure out what it is — a ski mask. *His* ski mask. Somehow, in my struggle to get away from him, I'd managed to rip it off.

I crane my neck and look up. It's dark out, so I can't make out much, but I can make out enough. That face. That familiar face.

He doesn't realize he lost the ski mask, because he's still staring down at me and laughing. When I look into that face, I cringe. That horrible face. That horrible, beautiful, familiar face.

He sees me looking at him, and there must be something in my expression because he stops laughing. I hold the ski mask up so he knows. So he knows that I know. Who he is, at last. Who he is.

"James," I say slowly, drawing out the word as if it had more than one syllable.

He doesn't say anything for a minute.

"Well, then," he says finally. "Now you know." He disappears again.

I lie there for a long time, breathing through the pain in my shoulder and thinking through the implications of what just happened.

James. I'd been almost sure, but perhaps a part of me didn't want to believe it. But now I have no choice. It's James, all right. And if he's done this, that means he knows what I did. I don't know how, but he knows.

TWENTY-TWO
SIX MONTHS AGO

James tries to convince Lily to stay home the next day, but she insists on going to work. She doesn't want to be alone in the apartment all day. Besides, she'll be able to watch the apartment on the camera all day, anyway, so it'll be almost as good — better, really — as being home.

But once at work she finds herself wishing she was anywhere else. She distantly sees emails arriving in her inbox, hears the phone ringing on her desk, feels the buzz of text messages landing on her phone, but all she does is stare at the feed from her security cameras. She watches the silent apartment, believing, truly, that at any moment she'll see something meaningful. An opening door. A shadow passing into view. An actual person, maybe, creeping through her space. She imagines catching him in all sorts of perverse acts — sniffing her underwear, jerking off into the soap dispenser, defecating in the fridge. There's no end to the scenarios her mind can concoct. She wonders what that says about her.

But again that day, she sees nothing.

She sees nothing the next day, or the next day either, and then it's the weekend, and she and James are home most of the day and she doesn't worry as much. Still, she finds herself checking the feed, when James is in the shower or when he retreats to his office to work for awhile. It's ridiculous — she's standing right there in the room, she can see with her own eyes that there are no intruders, nothing for the camera to pick up. That doesn't stop her from staring intently at the screen on her phone.

At one point it occurs to her that maybe the cameras are broken. Maybe they aren't projecting a live feed but just a still photo of the apartment. Once she gets the idea in her head, she can't shake it, so the next chance she gets — on Sunday morning, when James goes to the cafe down the street to get them lattes and croissants — she loads up the living room feed on her phone and tests it. She walks back and forth in front of the camera's field of view. Sure enough, she appears on the screen. It's disconcerting, observing herself on the handheld phone at a completely different angle. It makes her dizzy. Like she's living in an upside down world. She wonders if she's going to pass out.

When the apartment door swings open, she's so startled that she drops her phone. James stands in the doorway, frowning at her. "Lily? he asks. "Are you okay?"

"I'm fine."

"You're as white as a ghost."

"I just … I got this wave of dizziness. I don't know." She picks up the phone and there it is again, that wooziness.

"Maybe you should sit down." He comes over to lead her to the couch, but she's afraid he's going to see the screen of her phone, so she snatches her hand away from him. Clutches it, with the phone, to her chest. She realizes right away that it was a mistake, because James frowns at her.

"Lily? What's going on? I want you to tell me right now. Let me see your phone."

"There's nothing going on." Her voice is too high-pitched. Squeaky. Horribly unattractive. She knows James is mad. But she can't tell him. She holds up the phone, deletes the app, and hands the device over to James. "Nothing's going on," she says again. Does she sound convincing?

He takes the phone. He's aware she did something before she gave it to him, only there's no way for him to tell what. He knows it, and she knows it.

She also knows she's going to be punished for it. James doesn't like to be defied. Doesn't accept it. She looks up with her eyebrows raised, practically batting her eyelashes at him. Waiting — wanting — to see what he'll do. She actually craves his punishment, the distraction of it. It feels, sometimes, like a reset button. The same reason people go to confession, she imagines.

But in the end, what disturbs her most is that he doesn't do anything. He only sighs. He looks … disappointed. "I came back because I forgot my wallet," he says. There's defeat in his voice. "Do you still want a latte?"

"Sure," she says. "Whatever."

He looks at her for another minute. "Whatever," he agrees and leaves the apartment. Lily surprises herself by bursting into tears.

LATER, in bed, she wonders if she's having a nervous breakdown. For the first time, she considers the possibility that maybe James has been right all along. With the exception of the dead bird, which they both saw, what proof does she have that anything is really going on? She could have imagined the photograph thing. She doesn't think she did, but if she was mentally ill, she wouldn't, would she? Crazy people always think they're sane.

But what does it mean that she's now considering her own levels of sanity? Does that mean she *is* sane? She goes back and forth like that, her mind circling like a toilet. Down the drain her thoughts go, and with them, any chance of sleep.

———

ON MONDAY, she tells herself that she isn't going to check the camera feed. It's becoming an unhealthy obsession. No one's entering the apartment. She doesn't quite believe that yet, but she figures that if she keeps saying it to herself, it'll eventually be true. Fake it till you make it. It's the only way to change. It's the rule she's always followed, the thing that allowed her to evolve from Stacey Kincaid into Lily Castleman. Fake it till you make it. So she'll fake sanity, confidence, until she gets there.

But by late afternoon, her resolve is weakening. She gets a coffee to distract herself, stops by the pod to talk to Aurora and Bao and check in on how the next stage of development is going. She tries to sound enthusiastic and encouraging, praises them for the work they're doing, the effort they've been putting in. People like to hear that stuff. James would disagree, but she really believes that you get more flies with honey. She's not sure she'll ever be able to win over Aurora completely, but at least she can make an effort.

She manages to kill a half hour down in the pod, but when she gets back to her office, she reaches automatically for her cellphone. The app's not on the device anymore, not since she deleted it yesterday, but it'll take two seconds to download it again, log in, and open up the feed. Under a minute, and she could be looking into the apartment.

It's like an itch, the urge to do it. This must be how alcoholics feel. Or maybe sex addicts — because what she's craving isn't oblivion but release. The release of looking into the apartment, seeing that everything is fine. Her finger hovers over the button to open the App Store, the first step down the path. She thinks, *okay, maybe I'll just click it. Just to see what other apps I could download. That might distract me for a bit. How many people lose themselves in hours of crushing bright little candies?*

So she opens the App Store. But instead of browsing the games or the productivity apps or the meditation apps or the weird karaoke apps, she starts typing the name of the security camera app. It comes up straight away and even the sight of the calming blue and white logo eases something inside her. Only for a second, though, and then the itch returns. She wriggles against her chair, as if it's a spot on her back she can't quite reach.

She can't help it; she clicks the app. It starts to download. She tells herself she won't open it, but she already knows that's a lie. She opens it as soon as it's finished installing. Then she's typing in her username and password. And then there they are. The feeds.

She stares at them in surprise. There's nothing happening on them. Just the still, silent apartment. For some reason, she'd convinced herself that this time — *this* time — there really would be something. Maybe because she'd avoided it for so long. She thought she should be rewarded with something.

But there's nothing.

She closes the app in disgust. She's weak. James is always telling her that, and now she knows it to be true. When it comes down to it, she's weak in the ways that matter.

But wait. There's a whole day worth of feed footage that she hasn't inspected. The apartment has been empty all day. What if someone came in the morning but has left already? All she has to do is open the app and scrub through the timeline.

This time she doesn't even bother trying to stop herself. She's already accepted the fact of her weakness, so what is there to do but indulge it?

She goes through the bedroom feed first, scrubbing through from the time she was in there this morning getting dressed until now. The room is still. Calm, even. The bed made up nice and smooth and perfect, exactly as James likes it.

Undeterred, she switches to the living room camera. She watches herself and James leaving this morning, both of them silent and grim. They haven't spoken much since yesterday. She knows she has to repair things with him, but she doesn't know how. She hopes that maybe it just needs a bit of time.

She's thinking about that — about James — when something moves on the camera.

At first she thinks she's imagining things but when she rewinds it, she sees, yes, there's definitely a shadow that passes in front of the camera. Then, a foot. Right in the corner of the screen — black shoes, the cuff of a pant leg. Definitely a man's. A frisson of nervous excitement zips down her spine.

Part of her can hardly believe that this is really happening, and the other part of her swells with vindication.

"Come on," she says softly to her camera. "Just a little bit further. Come into the room so I can get a look at you."

As if he can hear her, the man steps forward.

Lily gasps. She doesn't know what she'd been expecting but it wasn't this.

James. James is in the apartment.

She checks the timecode on the feed, because maybe she's gotten mixed up. Maybe this shot is from before they left for work. Maybe this is James, standing out there waiting for her to finish spritzing herself with perfume and tweezing a few stray hairs from her brows. But no, the stamp shows that it's just past eleven. Well after the time that James would be at the office.

So what is he doing at the apartment instead?

TWENTY-THREE
PRESENT DAY

The staggering certainty that James is my captor, that James is the one who did this to me, is pushed aside by something far more pressing — the searing pain in my left shoulder. I haven't even been able to move myself into a sitting position yet. The best I've managed is to roll onto my back, where at least the pain isn't quite so excruciating. But even now that the pressure's off it, the agony still rips through me. The shoulder's dislocated. It has to be. Maybe even broken.

I lay there for a long time, trying to get my heart to stop racing. I take long, slow, meditative breaths — in through the nose, out through the mouth — and try to imagine my shoulder is a balloon that I'm inflating with magical white light or some bullshit. It doesn't work at all, big surprise. If anything, the pain gets worse as I draw more of my mind's attention to it.

Finally, after an unknowable amount of time, the pain begins to subside to a dull ache. Or maybe my body just gets tired of feeling it and shoots me up with some of those blessed endorphins. Either way, it's time to try sitting up. I can't lie here on my back forever.

The first few attempts end up with me screaming my lungs out as I accidentally rattle and jostle the inflamed joint. Yeah, it's definitely dislocated, at the very least. I find a way to put my weight onto my right side and kind of torque myself into a sitting position, and use my butt cheeks to walk myself back toward the wall of the hole so I can lean against it. Leaning isn't great either, it turns out, since it moves the shoulder too much, but if I let more of my weight rest against my right side, it's not too bad.

Not too bad being a relative notion at this point, of course.

Once I'm sitting up, my breathing comes slightly easier and I have more time to consider the implications of what just happened. I was so close to getting out of here — so close that the bitter frustration of it makes me weep. James must have come to bring more water, maybe. It was just bad luck that he showed up right as I was making my triumphant escape. If I'd climbed out ten minutes earlier or ten minutes later, I'd be home free right now. I'd be sunk deep into a bath, throwing back a bottle of wine and with all the oatmeal a person could ever want resting on the edge of the tub beside me. I don't care that people don't usually eat oatmeal in the tub, no way am I going to deny myself either of those luxuries. Bath, wine, oatmeal. Then climbing into my softest pajamas and sleeping for a thousand years in my own bed. With King solid and warm beside me, of course.

King. I look up but I don't see him anywhere. It's dark out, but usually I can sense him nearby.

"King," I call out. I no longer care about speaking too loudly. James is long gone, and the bear doesn't scare me the way it did even an hour ago. King, wherever he is, doesn't respond. I try to tell myself that he's just gone off for a piddle, that he'll be back to his usual watchful position any minute now, but the minutes come and go and King doesn't return.

I get worried. James kicked him, but how hard? It didn't look too bad — King had slunk away, but he hadn't appeared mortally wounded or anything. But what do I know? What if he's been up there this whole time, bleeding internally? Jesus. The thought fills me with raw panic. Not King. Anything but that.

"King!" I call again. And then louder, "King!"

I try to listen for the sound of King padding through the long grass, but there's only the sound of crickets, and somewhere in the distance, an owl. No sign of my dog.

The tears, which had started earlier, return with a vengeance. I have to get out of here.

I try to steel myself for it. I got out of here once — I can do it again.

As if on cue, my shoulder throbs. The pain is a schoolyard bully taunting me: *you think you can but I'm going to make sure you don't*. It was hard enough scaling that wall with all my limbs in working order. With my shoulder out of commission, it'll be ten times harder. I don't even know how I'll hold onto the leash.

And then the worst of it hits me — the leash. It's not down here. I scan the hole and touch the ground all around me to be sure, but it's definitely not down here. I must have left it in the grass when I climbed out.

Now the hopelessness really sets in. I got out once, yes, but how could I ever do it again? With a bum shoulder and no rope to aide me in my climb, it would be next to impossible. No, not next to — well beyond.

"I'm going to die down here," I say, to myself and maybe to God, if there is one and if he gives a shit about some girl down in a hole. "I'm actually going to die down here."

No more baths, no more wine, no more oatmeal. No more King. No more Pina coladas or getting caught in the rain. Well, scratch that — I suppose I could still get caught in the rain between now and the exact moment of my expiration. But no more slow dancing and no more licorice and no more reruns of *Friends* and no more Drake and no more beef and broccoli from the take-away down the street and no more pretending to flirt with the delivery driver who was old enough to be my father. This is the end for me. This is the end of everything.

I let myself cry. I don't put a limit on it and I don't try to temper my reaction and I don't try to stay optimistic. I give into the sadness, because it's all there is.

James is going to let me die down here. I have no doubt he has it in him, too. My guess is he's actually enjoying this. Getting off on it, even.

James. Just his name is like a parasite invading my brain. I want to spray Lysol in there and soak him out. *James.* It's battery acid on my tongue.

For a minute I allow myself to remember the day we met. It had been a Tuesday — I still remember this so clearly — and I was coming out of a coffee shop on Union Street. That was when I was still the office grunt and had to pick up everybody's coffee order. I was loaded down with lattes, almost bent double with the weight of cappuccinos and mochaccinos and dense, fruit-filled pastries. James was coming out of the dry cleaners next door. Later I found out that he almost never picked up his own shirts — he, of course, employed someone who did that for him — but on that day, his normal assistant was having a baby and there'd been a mix-up with her stand-in and he was picking up his own shirts. So maybe you could say this was all Deirdre's fault — Deirdre and her dumb baby.

In any case, James was coming out of the dry cleaner. I was coming out of the coffee shop. In true romantic comedy fashion, we crashed straight into each other. Coffee all over everything. His shirt, my shirt, his dry-cleaning bags. I stammered out a flustered and mortified apology, but James was as cool as a cucumber. I liked that about him. Then, anyway. He insisted on paying for my dry-cleaning, even though I was the one with the wayward coffees and should have been covering the cost of his ruined shirts. He took my name and number and insisted he'd transfer me the funds to cover it.

I thought that would be the end of it. Instead, he called me and insisted I have dinner with him. I'd been so young. Young, naive, impressionable. New to the city and realizing my life was nothing like the *Sex And The City* romp I'd envisioned when I first moved here. Where were my designer clothes, my expensive cocktails, my laughably bad but glamorous dates? I had a cruddy apartment, no real friends, and the dates I'd been on were laughably bad but decidedly unglamorous. James felt like everything I'd been dreaming of, everything I thought I wanted in my life. He was sexy, powerful, wealthy, and in control. I fell in love.

And now look at me. Look at where loving him got me.

TWENTY-FOUR
SIX MONTHS AGO

What Lily wants most in the world is to find out that there's a perfectly reasonable explanation for James being home in the middle of the day. What she wants is to go home and confront him and have him explain everything to her. To tell her that it was nothing at all, that he forgot something in his home office and popped by to pick it up. Some files or a contract or a set of schematics that he absolutely needed. It isn't unreasonable, is it, to think there must be a legitimate reason for his presence in his own apartment?

But nothing about this feels perfectly reasonable.

This is what she thinks about the entire way home. If she doesn't want to piss him off, she can't lay into him the second he gets home, demanding to know what he was doing. He already thinks she's losing it. Flying off the handle will get her nowhere. So even though she trembles with anticipation and dread, she goes to the market as she always does, picks up groceries as she always does — couscous, chicken breast, saffron — and tidies the apartment before James gets home.

While she works, she looks for anything that feels off in the apartment. It's become a habit. A meticulous cataloging of James' possessions, their exact placement in the space. For the first time, she's grateful for his minimal style. Nothing stands out. Everything in the apartment is as it should be. Or at least it appears to be.

She tries to tell herself that's good. James wasn't up to anything untoward — he had every right to be in the apartment during the day. It's silly to be suspicious. But that does nothing to quell the pit of dread in her stomach, or slow her racing pulse.

James comes home just before seven, looking slightly disheveled. Which is to say his face is drawn and he has a single lock of hair that's come out of place and flipped down over his forehead in a way Lily finds, despite herself, boyishly charming.

"How was your day?" she asks him, hoping that she sounds cheerful and, most of all, normal.

"Shit," he says. He strides straight into the kitchen, pours himself a generous glass of something amber and strong-smelling. Scotch, she thinks, or maybe Irish whiskey. He doesn't offer her one.

"What happened?" She tries to sound soothing. When he sits down, she goes and stands behind him, puts her hands on his shoulders. Reassuring. Or so she hopes.

"The usual client bullshit," he says. "The city hasn't approved the plans for the development in Delridge, and somehow this is our fault. Because we have *so* much control over that bullshit bureaucracy. I've greased as many wheels as I can, and the damn thing is still at a standstill."

"Hmmm," she murmurs. She reaches down and loosens

his tie, unbuttons the top button of his shirt. He kisses her fingers. "People are idiots."

"You can say that again. Sometimes I don't know why I do this job."

"Because you love it," Lily says.

"Do I?"

It's a conversation they've treaded a few times over the course of their relationship. James is a brilliant architect. But owning his own firm means he's become less hands-on with the work. Now he pays people to do the very things that he once loved to do. He'd never give up running the firm — he likes the wealth and the status too much — but Lily knows he misses the late nights sketching up blueprints and dreaming up concepts. It's actually one of the things that made her love him in the beginning — the knowledge that underneath it all, maybe he was just a normal man with a frustrated passion. That maybe, despite all his power and prestige, he was an artist. Like her.

But is he? She's learned so much about James in the last year that she doesn't know what to believe anymore. She worries that deep down, she may not know him at all. What is he capable of? What really motivates him?

She doesn't have answers to those questions. Wonders, even, if answers exist. Is James a mystery even to himself?

"How was your day other than that?" she prods.

He answers with a shrug and takes a sip of his scotch.

She scoots down onto the couch beside him. "Did you get out of the office at all? Fresh air always helps." Is that subtle enough? Surely he can see right through her.

"Not once," he says, with a tired sigh. "Between meetings

and phone calls and putting out fires, I barely had time for a coffee."

"Oh." Her voice is small and weak, and James looks at her with an eyebrow raised. "That's terrible," she covers. "You work yourself so hard."

"Yeah, well, that's how it is."

The moment passes. James leans his head back and closes his eyes, but Lily's heart and mind are both racing. James would only lie about being in the apartment if he had something to hide, right? Otherwise, he would have mentioned that he came home to pick something up.

She wonders if maybe he just forgot. If his day was that hectic and stressful, perhaps it slipped his mind that he'd been home at one point. She wants to try again, but if she pushes him too hard, he'll be suspicious. After all, she's not supposed to know he was here, and she wouldn't have, were it not for the cameras. She can't admit to having them yet, not until she has the proof she needs that someone has been entering their space.

"I called your office today," she says. "Around eleven. They said you weren't in."

He opens his eyes but narrows them at her. He doesn't like it when she acts jealous, and checking up on him at work certainly constitutes jealous behavior, at least in James' mind. But better he thinks she's jealous than losing it.

"I was probably in a meeting," he says. "Around eleven? Yes, I was in a meeting."

"Deirdre was pretty clear you were out."

"It was a meeting off-site," he says easily. "Duncan and I went down to talk to the Delridge clients. Sometimes they need that face-to-face time. You know what it's like."

That, Lily knows, is true — she puts in her own share of face time with clients — but she also knows for a fact that James is lying. She has the video evidence to prove it.

What she doesn't understand is *why*.

The night passes. She and James eat the chicken and he drinks more scotch and decides to turn in early. They have normal sex, for once, with James almost falling asleep on top of her. By the time Lily slithers out from beneath him, she's shaking. Can she trust James? *Does* she trust him? Why is he lying to her?

She creeps into the bathroom after he's asleep and turns on the shower. For a while she just lets the water run. She needs to be able to think, and she can't do it lying in the dark next to James.

Maybe she really *is* losing her mind. If she can't trust James, why is she marrying him? Why is she even with him? She should break up with him if that's how she feels. But the very notion makes her feel the way she did riding up the elevator of the Space Needle the first time, as if her body had traveled hundreds of feet up into the air but her stomach was still on the ground floor.

She thinks of Connor. If she isn't careful, she may not even have a choice in the matter. Maybe Connor will go to her family, or to the police. Ten years later and there's still an open warrant for her arrest in North Carolina. Well, there's a warrant for the arrest of Stacey Kincaid. Lily Castleman is nothing but an elaborate fiction. But with Connor's information, it won't be long before the cops track down that fiction and she's right back to where she started.

Of course, if Connor really wanted to hurt her, he would

go directly to James. Tell him all the lies that Lily's been spinning, the truth about who she is and what she's done.

Suddenly, she wonders if maybe he already has. The thought seizes her like a hand around her throat. Maybe that's why James has been lying to her. Maybe he knows about her past and is — what? Punishing her? Trying to drive her mad?

She pictures the beady eyes of the dead crow and tries to swallow. She stares into the stream of water pouring forth from the shower head. For the first time in an eternity, she lets herself think back to that day.

It had been a Saturday; August. Her mother was out with Ray and Dale, which meant she was alone with her father. Like she was every Saturday. He cornered her in her room, like he did every Saturday. She kept her eyes closed. It was okay. Now that she was older, he liked her from behind, and that was fine with her. She could keep her face pressed into the pillow and pretend it wasn't happening.

That day, she had plenty of other happier things to think about. She'd been accepted to Columbia, full scholarship, but she hadn't yet dared to broach the subject with her parents. She didn't know how they were going to react, and maybe she enjoyed having a secret to herself.

She waited until he was finished, until he stood and fastened his pants. She rolled over and tugged her shorts up. When she looked at him — at his beady dark eyes, his too-red ears — the thought came to her: *I hate him.* She realized it with crystal clarity, that over the last ten years her love and fear had hardened into something far colder. She also realized she had the power to hurt him.

"I'm going to Columbia," she said as she hugged her knees

to her chest. Her voice was soft but even. Strong. "In the fall. I'm going to study art. You'll never see me again."

"Columbia?" Her father turned, his hands still on his belt buckle. "No fucking way."

"It won't cost you anything. I got a scholarship. I'm going."

He leaned in close. "You think it's about the money, girlie? It ain't about the money. Your ass belongs here in this house until I say otherwise."

"That's not fair."

"Life's not fair."

She had learned that with her father, the best approach was to lie back and take it, but for once she was tired of doing that. She didn't want to take it anymore. He couldn't steal Columbia from her. She wouldn't let him.

In the years since, she's wished a thousand times that she'd kept her big mouth shut. She already had the scholarship, the admittance. She was eighteen. She didn't need their permission to go. She could have bided her time, waited until September, and disappeared into the dead of night. But no. She had to choose that moment to mouth off.

"You can't stop me," she said.

At first she thought he hadn't heard her. He finished buckling his belt, tugging it tight and shoving the tail of his blue short sleeve button-down into his khakis. He walked out of the room.

She laid there on the bed, just breathing. Her cheeks felt hot and her heart hammered in her chest. Even though he was gone, she felt on edge. Unsettled.

He returned. This time bearing a large black garbage bag. He stormed into her room, ripped the black plastic wide open, and started sweeping the art supplies from her desk into the gaping mouth of the bag. Her paints, her brushes, her sketch books, all into the trash. He yanked pictures down off the wall — the only pictures she'd been happy enough with to tack up over her desk. Into the trash. He turned to her bookshelf next, grabbing all her art books. Van Gogh, Vermeer, Kahlo, Klimt. She'd been collecting them second-hand since she was ten. All into the trash.

At first she just sat there, stunned. But as he stripped the room of everything she loved, she started to scream. She staggered from the bed and clawed at shoulders, his bare forearms. She tried to wrench the bag away from him, but he backhanded her so hard she careened into the desk. He turned and grabbed the black portfolio case off the floor. The case contained all her best work — it was what she'd used to secure her spot at Columbia. He shoved it into the garbage bag with everything else.

She did it without thinking. No matter how many times she recalled this moment later, she could never remember a conscious thought to do what she did. She reached toward the nightstand and grabbed the lamp. The base was heavy, a chunk of geometric concrete, but she wasn't thinking about that at the time. All she could think about was her portfolio. How she couldn't let it become trash. He'd turned everything in her life into trash — he'd turned *her* into trash. But this he could not take. This she would not allow him to take.

She swung the lamp.

It connected with the back of his skull. Her father went down faster than a pair of shorts in a pissing contest. That was another one of Daddy's expressions. He blinked up at her.

There was no blood. She hit him again. And again. Then there was blood. A lot of it.

The cruelest irony was that, in the end, she left the portfolio behind anyway. She didn't know where else to go so she went to Mr. Winthrop's. She knew where he lived because she'd once helped him load a truck full of blank canvases that he'd bought at a store-closing sale in Raleigh. He donated them to the school's art class. He was that kind of guy.

The fake ID was his idea. He hid her for two days, helped her concoct the plan that would get her to Seattle. Sometimes she wondered why he'd jumped to that drastic plan. Another adult might have tried to convince her to go to the police, tell them exactly what had happened and what her father had been doing to her. She wondered, sometimes, if she had done that, might she have got off? A sympathetic jury, the right lawyer. She might have got nothing more than a slap on the wrist. She wondered if Mr. Winthrop didn't have his own secrets. His own reasons for not trusting the police, or the legal system.

But the choice had been made, and now so much time has passed that she can never go back.

And she likes being Lily Castleman. She hated giving up her art, but she found a new kind of vibrancy in Seattle, one she'd never known back home. That she could lose that now — that James might know the ugly truth about her — is too unbearable for words.

"Lily?" The bathroom doorknob rattles, and Lily jumps. It's locked, thank God, so James doesn't come in, but she can hear him there on the other side of the door. Breathing. "Lily? Are you okay?"

"I'm fine," she says, on edge again. "I'm having a shower."

"You've been in there over an hour."

"I haven't."

"Yes, you have."

She doesn't answer, but holds her hand under the stream of water coming out of the shower and realizes it's gone cold.

"Open the door," James says.

Lily stares in horror at the door. The last thing she wants to do is open it, but she has no choice. The inflection in James' voice has changed. He's using his commanding voice, his dominant voice. She has to open the door. The tone works on her as effectively as Pavlov's dogs' bells.

She stands and unlocks the door, then sits back down without opening it. A second later, James is in the bathroom. He crouches down in front of her.

"What's wrong?" he asks. "Have you been taking your Xanax?"

He's stopped monitoring her pill consumption every morning. He still checks the bottle to ensure the number of pills is going down, but it was easy enough to dump one down the drain every day. But now she can tell he's suspicious, thinking maybe he shouldn't have been so careless with his monitoring.

"I've been taking it," she sniffles.

"Are you sure?"

His head's bent down close to hers, and she can smell him, warm from sleep, and the remnants of the days the cologne and deodorant. His nearness makes her nervous, and she says, "I don't know."

"You don't know?"

"I ..."

It wasn't what she'd meant to say. She'd meant to tell him

that of course she was taking her medication, no need to worry, haha, this is only a little PMS, let's go back to bed.

"Come on, Lily," he says gently. He takes her hand and pulls her up from the toilet. "Let's go to bed. We'll figure this out in the morning. I'll help you."

She lets him lead her to the bedroom. She wants to believe him, that he'll help her get these crazy feelings under control, but all she can think about is the image of him on the camera feed, creeping around the apartment they share, and then lying to her about it. All she can think about, the word that echoes over and over in her head, is: why? What does he know?

TWENTY-FIVE
PRESENT DAY

I'm dying. No ifs, ands, or buts about it. It's been almost three days since I've had water, and that alone will do it, never mind the lack of food. The pain in my shoulder has subsided to a dull throb. King hasn't returned. I'd hoped that in the morning, when the sun came, he'd be there, lying there at the edge of the hole the way he always was, his muzzle resting on his paws, watching me with his deep chocolate brown eyes. But he's been nowhere to be seen. So I assume he's dead, too.

In a weird way, it's a relief. Worrying about him made me even more afraid to die, because what would happen to him? Where would he end up? But if he's dead, I have nothing to worry about. There's no longer anything tying me to this earth, to this life. I'm finally free to move on to the next chapter, whatever that might be.

I spend the day dying. I don't start out that way, of course. I make a token effort to get myself out of here. I start digging at the dirt again, trying to build my little step-up even higher, but with my bad arm, it's harder to dig, and the process is unbearably slow. I'm weak, dehydrated, in pain. I barely get an inch of dirt added. And without having the leash to help me pull myself up, I'd need at least another foot or two of height on my step, a feat that feels near impossible.

And even if I managed it, what would I do if I got the dirt high enough that I could grab onto the root? With my busted shoulder, there's no way I can pull myself up high enough to scramble out of here. I struggled last time, and that was when I was in the possession of a fully functioning body.

So eventually I give up on the digging, and I lie there using my pile of dirt as a make-shift pillow. I drift in and out of consciousness. Something jams into my ribs, and I realize it's the can of pepper spray. Fat lot of good that's going to do me now. I should have used it when I was above ground, when James came for me.

And why didn't I? Panic, I suppose. Surprise. The plain fact that part of my mind forgot I even had it.

But I wonder, too, if there was something more to it. Like … what if there was a part of me that believed I deserved what was happening to me? After all, it was my fault that —

Well. Let's just say it was my fault. He had to take a lot of the blame, too, but in the end, I was the one who was there that day. So maybe I do deserve this. Maybe I deserve to die in a hole like an animal.

It won't be long now. I can't imagine I have more than a day left. Not without any water. I stare down at the pepper spray and wonder if I could use it to hasten my demise. It must be toxic, after all. I could try to swallow some of it. But in the end I decide it will be too painful — and might not even speed things up, only make my last few hours even more miserable than they need to be. I try to slip the holster off but it makes my shoulder scream in agony. In the end I simply shove the orange can back in the holster and try to get comfortable.

I wait for the end to come. But it doesn't.

James comes, instead.

TWENTY-SIX

SIX MONTHS AGO

In the morning, James stands over her and forces her to take the Xanax. She doesn't fight it. She swallows the pill and allows the wave of uncaring wash over her. Let it come.

James tries to convince her to take the day off work, but she declines. Peter Serrano is coming into the office today — she'd no longer been able to put off his calls, his emails, so she'd let Daphne set up a meeting so they could discuss the status of the project. Aurora was supposed to have a demo set up that they could walk through. The developers hated demoing projects at this stage — the clients always fussed over details that weren't final and ended up making more work for everyone involved — but Lily knew it was the only way to appease him after her poor handling of the account. She almost feels bad about it, but not quite.

When James drops her off at the office, he leans over to give her a kiss, and Lily finds herself turning her head, presenting him with her cheek instead of her lips. He hesitates and then dryly kisses her cheek. She slides out of the car without a word.

Inside, she berates herself. James was the one who suggested she stay home, so surely he wasn't hiding anything at the apartment. Otherwise, he'd want her out. Wouldn't he? She doesn't know anymore. Until she understands why he'd been in the apartment in the first place — and more importantly, why he'd lied about it — she has no idea what to make of his behavior. Everything's gone upside-down. Mixed up and too confusing. Especially now, in her Xanax haze.

She grabs an extra-large coffee at the shop down in the lobby and rides the elevator up to the seventeenth floor. She chugs a third of the coffee before she even gets to her office, and it barely penetrates the haze that emanates from the innermost part of her mind. It'd been stupid to take the pill. She can't meet with a client like this. She chugs back more of the coffee, hoping the caffeine will help cancel out some of the effects of the Xanax. She wonders if it might create a toxic stew, instead.

In her office, she assembles the materials for the meeting, messages Aurora to make sure her team is ready. Aurora doesn't answer, and Lily hopes it's because she's in the boardroom, setting up the projector screen. She tries Bao, but his status is set to 'away', so she assumes — hopes — they're both in there already.

She goes over the materials while she chugs more coffee, but it does almost nothing to beat back the encroaching grayness. What she needs is a walk. She needs to burn off some of that fog.

She finishes the coffee and rides the elevator back down to the ground floor and steps outside. The March air is brisk and sharp. It cuts right through her wool coat. She welcomes the cold, hopes it'll be able to blow back the fog. She walks three blocks west, turns right, another two blocks, turns left. She has no destination in mind, just wants to work her legs. Her muscles. She takes long deep breaths, filling her lungs with shocking cold air. It helps. She keeps walking.

She goes to check the time and realizes she left her phone on her desk. She has no idea how much time has passed. The meeting isn't until eleven, but is it possible that she's already been out for an hour? She stops a woman on the street and asks her the time. Is told that it's a quarter to. Lily turns and starts to hurry back. She doesn't even say thank-you.

She's almost at the office when she hears her name. It's not the most common name, so she stops and turns. Still, she expects to be mistaken. And the very last thing she expects to see is …

"Connor." She swallows.

He closes the distance between them. "Hello, Lily. You're a hard one to get ahold of, aren't you? Did you get my email?"

Shit. Shit, shit, shit. She debates playing dumb, but figures there's no point. "I did. I'm sorry. It's been crazy at work, and, you know…"

"Oh, I know. Work's crazy for me, too. But it's even crazier that we ran into each other, don't you think? After all these years. What are the odds?"

"I don't know." She tries to smile. Her legs are liquid gelatin. She hates that her first instinct is always to be polite. She wants to turn on her heel and get away from this man.

He leans his hand against the brick storefront behind them. Somehow, without her noticing, he's walked them up against the building, and she's pinned between him and the exterior wall of Shawarma Palace. The smell of spicy beef curdles her stomach.

"It's so rare to run into someone from home, all the way out here. And you know, I really had to be persistent after I saw you in the lobby that day. It took me forever to figure out where you worked. Who would have thought you'd change your name? Lily. I like it. What made you pick it?"

She doesn't know what Connor wants, but she can only assume it's nothing good. She stays silent. Connor gazes at her for a minute and then his mouth turns to a grim line. He nods once. "Right. I guess I'm probably not your favorite person. I get that. Actually…" He pauses, seeming to consider her. "That's sort of what I wanted to talk to you about."

She scans the street, searching for a way out. People pass by, but she's terrible at asking for help. No, scratch that: she refuses to. After so many years spent trying to get help from anyone she could — teachers, guidance counsellors, neighbors, the fucking mailman — she's given up on other people. The only way to help yourself is to help yourself.

"I've thought a lot about what happened between us," Connor is saying, as Lily stares over his shoulder. "I guess I wanted to apologize…"

Still looking past him, Lily raises a hand in greeting. She makes sure to plaster a grateful smile on her face. Connor turns his head briefly to see who she's waving at. It's enough. She brings her knee up and connects with his groin, as hard as she can.

He lets out a surprised *ouff* and doubles over. She slips out from under his arm and hurries down the street, tottering on her heels. At least the Xanax haze has evaporated; the adrenalin has made her clearheaded.

"Lily!" he calls out from behind her. "Lily, I was just trying to talk to you. I really wanted to—"

Whatever else he has to say is drowned out by the sound of a cab driver leaning on his horn as Lily darts across the street in front of him. She waves a hand in apology but keeps trotting forward. When the familiar glass office tower comes back into view, she heaves a sigh of relief. And when she at last risks a glance behind her, Connor is nowhere to be seen.

An apology, she thinks to herself, rolling her eyes. He expected her to believe that all of this was about apologizing. Men like Connor Franklin don't apologize, that much she knows for sure. What is he really after?

She forces herself to put her worries temporarily aside and gets to her office with five minutes to spare before the meeting. She grabs her things. Adrenalin makes her clumsy, and she drops her file on the floor, scattering papers everywhere. She collects everything, swearing under her breath, and skitters down the hallway to the boardroom. Just in time to find Damian and Aurora and the rest of the team strolling out, laughing.

"Hi," she says breathlessly. "Am I late?"

Damian looks pointedly at his watch. "I'll say."

The slant of his eyebrows says he's most definitely peeved. Lily glances at the boardroom clock — a Warhol-style pop art thing — but it's only just eleven. Hardly reason for him to get snippy with her. She tells him as much.

His eyebrows slant further. Aurora looks down and drags Bao away, leaving Lily alone with Damian.

"Lily," he says, halfway between irritated patience and utter outrage. "The meeting was at ten. You missed the whole thing."

"No," she insists, still sure this is a mistake. "It was at eleven. I have it right here in my calendar." She holds up her phone to show him. Damian gives it a cursory glance and shrugs.

"Well, I don't know how you mixed it up. It was at ten. It's always been at ten. Peter and his team have come and gone."

"Damn," Lily says. And again, "Damn!" The tang of adrenalin has cleared, sweeping the Xanax fog away with it, and now the only thing she feels is irritated with herself. Missing a client meeting is unforgivable, especially considering her entire job is keeping the clients happy. She's lucky Damian and Aurora were here to cover for her.

"I'm so sorry," she grovels. She looks down at her phone again, clicking the calendar entry open and trying to figure out how she managed to change it. It wasn't like her to mess up things like that.

"Lucky for you, it went okay," Damian says as they walk down the hallway back toward the offices. "Aurora did a killer job demoing the site. They're really happy with how it's going."

"That's great," Lily says. "I'll have to thank her."

"Yeah," Damian says, more pointedly. "You will."

LATER THAT AFTERNOON, Lily picks up a box of donuts and takes it down to the pod. Aurora and Bao are bent over his desk, laughing about something. Lily dumps the peace offering down on the desk beside them.

"I hear I owe you my thanks," Lily says. She isn't too proud to eat crow if she needs to.

Aurora shrugs. "If you're talking about the meeting, it was

nothing. We went in prepared, did our thing, client's happy. No big deal."

What a different song she's singing now, Lily thinks. Compared to a couple of weeks ago when she was convinced they'd never be able to meet the deadline Lily'd saddled them with. She doesn't point that out to Aurora, however. No point in poking the bear.

"It sounds like it went great. I still have no idea how I missed the meeting, though. It showed in my calendar that it was at eleven."

"Bad luck," Aurora says, and something about the way she says it raises Lily's hackles.

"Enjoy the donuts," she says.

She starts to walk back to her office, but she's thinking about Aurora's words, and more specifically, her tone. Aurora enjoyed presenting to the client, Lily knows. The project managers never get that much face time with the client, and when they do, it's usually because there's an issue with the project and they're in there speaking on behalf of their teams. This time, Aurora got to be the star.

Must have liked that, Lily thinks bitterly. *Getting all the glory when I was conveniently away from the office.*

She looks at her phone again, and at the calendar entry, and wonders if Aurora could have possibly changed it somehow. Oh, who is she kidding — with the development team on her side, Lily doubts there's anything she couldn't do. Plus, Aurora's friends with Daphne, who schedules most of their meetings, anyway. One of them surely could have arranged it so the time in Lily's calendar was wrong.

She notices something else as she examines the phone. There isn't one missed phone call, email, or text asking where she is. Usually, if she's even a few minutes late for a meeting, she'll have a slew of messages from Damian, most of which read, "U coming?" It's happened before. Today there's nothing. Neither Damian nor Aurora reached out to see if she was on her way.

She sits there wondering if that's suspicious or not. She's lost all sense of what to worry about. What possible reason could her coworkers have to sabotage her? Unless they just don't like her and this is their way of extracting their revenge. She supposes that's possible, but she can't quite bring herself to believe it. She and Damian have always gotten along fairly well. She can't believe he'd have anything to do with this. Aurora isn't as much of a stretch, but still Lily resists the idea.

Something else occurs to her. Last night, when she'd barricaded herself into the bathroom, she'd left James alone in the apartment. He could have taken her phone and changed the time of the meeting. It would have been easy for him to do. He knew the passcode to her phone — it was one of the things he insisted on — which gave him access to her emails, her calendar, her texts, and everything else. It would have been no problem at all for him to log in and make that one little change.

But to what end? At least if it was Aurora, she could understand the motivation. Aurora wanted the glory, the prestige, of leading a big project. But what possible reason could James have had? None.

If he had been the one to change the photograph, to leave the bird — what was his goal? If he was trying to make her think she was going insane, he was succeeding, but why? To what end?

No, it makes no sense. And yet the idea feels right. James

has the most access to her. There's a reason she hasn't yet been able to figure out how the bird got into the apartment. There's a reason she hasn't yet seen anyone on the cameras except for James. There's a reason she thinks she's losing her mind.

He's orchestrating this. She has no idea how, or why. But she feels sure, in her gut, that he is. It's the only thing that makes sense.

But she needs proof. She has to know for sure, before she does anything drastic.

And what would that drastic thing be, she wonders? She'll have to leave him, she supposes. But James Russel isn't a man you could ever really leave.

She pushes the thought away with a shiver. That thought is for another time. First things first, she needs to figure out how to get the proof she needs. She has to catch James in the act.

TWENTY-SEVEN
PRESENT DAY

James arrives as the sun is coming up. It surprises me to see him so early, and at first, when I look up to the top of the hole and see his shimmering silhouette, I think I'm hallucinating. I'd had strange dreams all night — dreams of black crows flying down into the hole with me, dreams of roots snaking over my ankles and sucking me further down into the earth. I blink up at him and try to make the wavering apparition disappear. Only it doesn't.

Instead, a water bottle thuds on the ground beside my head. I attempt to blink that away, too, but it's as solid and real as my own body. I try to sit up and reach for it. My shoulder wails in agony after the stiff way I'd been sleeping. I think I even scream out loud, because James chuckles.

"Doing well, I see." His voice is cold, and there's no mirth in that laughter. "Drink the water. I'm not ready for you to die. Not yet, anyway."

I want to refuse. If he doesn't want me to die, maybe dying is exactly what I should do. Just to piss him off. To foil whatever twisted plan he's concocted. But my survival instinct is too strong. Stronger, anyway, than my desire to one-up James. I reach for the bottle. My shoulder screams again, and I can barely get the cap off. I have to wedge the bottle in between my forearm and my ribs, and even then I have a hard time twisting that stupid little white top off. Imagine, I think with some delirium, if I died down here all because I couldn't manage to open a bottle of water.

When I finally get it open, I drink greedily. Water spills down over my chin, even though I try not to waste a precious drop. The effects are almost immediate. I come a little more alive, get a little more energetic. A little more angry.

"James, you are one sick fucking bastard," I say, wiping my mouth with the back of my hand. Okay, make that a *lot* more angry.

Above me, he chuckles. "You're one to talk."

I glare at him.

"I'd be willing to let you live, you know," James says. It's as if he's just come up with this idea, even though I know him well enough to hear how practiced it is. James never has a single encounter without planning it down to the micro detail.

I don't bother to answer him.

"Aren't you interested in knowing how?"

"Not really." I know what he wants me to say, but I refuse to do it. A few minutes ago, before the water, I might have done it. That little bit of rejuvenation from the water has made me stubborn and filled me with hatred again. So I try to sound bored. Not an easy feat from down here.

But James only laughs again. It's a horrible sound, slimy and weasel-like. I can't believe I ever found it attractive.

"Here," he says.

He tosses something else down into the hole. More

Zigman's sandwiches. That makes me think of King and the fact that I won't have to share these with him. And thinking that fills me with even more rage. I don't mind. I welcome it. The rage ignites something in me, some latent spark of life. Even when I'm dying, I can still hate him.

"All you have to do," James continues, as if I've said nothing at all, "is tell me the truth. About what happened that day. About what you did."

"I didn't do anything," I say indignantly. It's what I've been telling myself for six months now, and I've gotten pretty good at believing it.

"You didn't do anything," he mocks. "Right. Do you really expect me to believe that?"

"What happened was an accident." Also true. "And if it hadn't been for you, it never would have happened."

"Oh, so you're saying it's my fault." That sarcastic, asshole-ish smile again.

"Yes." I hold my chin out.

I can smell the ham from the sandwiches, and it makes my mouth water and my stomach clench, but I refuse to let myself reach for them. Somehow, it feels like that would be admitting weaknesses. Never mind that food is a basic human need. James has never cared for basic human needs. I can recall many nights of 'play' where he made that abundantly clear. In his mind, having me down here is the ultimate assertion of his control over me. He's in charge of when I eat, when I drink. How much and how often. He's in charge of whether I live or die. The ultimate control.

Knowing that he brought me to the edge of starvation would play right into his sick fantasy. So instead I let the sandwich sit there, untouched, while my stomach cramps in need.

"Right," he says. "Well, if that's the way you want to be..."

He turns. I want to call out, to stop him. It's an instinct, one I barely have the strength to fight. He pauses in the grass above. At least, I think he pauses. Maybe I'm imagining it. But I picture him waiting up there, ready for me to give in. To say I'll confess if only he'll stay, let me out, help me somehow.

When I don't speak, he moves on. The clearing is silent again, except for the cacophony of birds and, from somewhere in the distance, the crackle of gunfire. People shoot target practice out here all the time, but the sound fills me with an icy dread.

When I'm sure James is gone, I rip open the sandwiches and shovel half of one into my face. My stomach starts cramping as soon as I swallow it, and for a second I'm sure I'm not going to be able to keep it down, but I take a few deep breaths and it stays put. I eat the rest of the sandwich more slowly. It gives me strength. Desperately needed strength.

And with that strength comes understanding. James may have the ultimate control down here, but I still hold one card. One single, solitary card, but damn if it isn't an ace. I know what James wants now. What he wants most of all is to hear me tell him that I did it, that what happened was my fault.

And now that I know that, I can use it.

TWENTY-EIGHT
SIX MONTHS AGO

Lily buys two more cameras. It's the only solution she can think of. The only way she can catch James in the act. Last time, she only captured enough to know he entered the apartment, but not enough to know what he did when he was in there. That was a mistake. But she can still correct it. As far as she knows, he hasn't discovered the cameras yet. It's a risk to add two more, but it's a risk she can't afford not to take.

She has to divide her time wisely, so she buys them one night but doesn't install them so she can still make it to the market, still pick up groceries and even an extra bottle of chianti to go with the fresh farfalle pasta. She forces herself to act normal, or as normal as possible under the circumstances. James is still feeding her Xanax, but she's gone back to spitting them out into the sink when he isn't looking. But in the evening, she acts as if she's swathed in a pleasant pink fog. She drapes herself over James' shoulder as he watches the news, acts supple and pliable and good. Just how he likes her.

She feels bitter about that now, about all the time she's wasted playing the good girl for him.

She remembers the day they met, the chilly early spring air that bit through her sweater, the way his creamy white business card felt so officious between her fingers. Could a man seduce you with a business card? She never would have thought so, until she met James. He was so smooth, so calculating, even then. She'd been mortified at running into him like that, spilling coffee all over his shirt. Hers, too, though it took him pointing it out for her to even notice. That's how smitten she was, right from the word go.

A few months ago, in a hazy, post-sex glow, he'd admitted to her that he orchestrated that meeting. He'd glimpsed her at the coffee shop once before, and felt desperate to meet her. He'd gone to the coffee shop every day for a week, learning her schedule and finally staging the dry-cleaning run-in. It had made her feel unbalanced, somehow, to think of him following her like that without her knowledge. She loved the story of their meeting, the serendipity of it. But she had to admit it didn't surprise her — not entirely, anyway — to find out that James had manipulated the situation. It was, after all, his specialty.

She supposes that was what she liked about him. She saw a version of herself in James — careful, deliberate. Two steps ahead of everyone else in the room. And she liked the way he he'd allowed her to forget her past, to reinvent herself into the woman he saw. That was all she'd ever really wanted. To be brand new.

Now she wonders if maybe she's only ever been replaying past patterns. First her father, now James. A girl in the shadow of a man.

She feels like she's tearing at the seams. A rag doll that's been through the wash one too many times. Her stuffing lost, her limbs pulling away. All that remains of her is her glass bead eyes. All she has is her eyes. And for once she can see clearly.

The next day she installs the new cameras.

AT WORK, she no longer makes any pretense of doing her job. She watches the camera feeds all day long. There are four now, so she loads one up on her desk computer and one on her phone. Every five minutes or so, she alternates them both so she can check on what's happening in the rest of the apartment. But nothing moves in the open space. Not in the bedroom, not in the hall. Not a flicker, not a shadow.

"Come on," she whispers to herself, as if coaxing a dog or a small child. "Come on."

Damian schedules a meeting with her and Aurora and some of the development team, to go over the final steps for the Green Acres project. Lily doesn't go. She doesn't see the point. They hadn't needed her at the last meeting, so they could do this one without her, too. She ignores the texts that ding through on her phone, the ones from Damian saying, "Where r u?" and "Started 5 min ago." She has better things to do now. More important things. She swipes the messages off her screen without a glance and concentrates on the bright, quiet interior of her apartment. Her home.

For days, she goes on like this. No need for Xanax; the feeds lull her far more efficiently than any pharmaceutical. Yet the cameras continue to show nothing. Each day, she watches and each day, the apartment remains empty and still. But instead of forcing her to step back and question her assumptions about James, this fact only thrusts her further into the surety that he knew exactly what he was doing, that he was pushing her buttons in an elaborately orchestrated quest to drive her mad. She still has no idea of his motive, but she doesn't let that get in the way of her plan. She will not let him get to her. She's already one step ahead of him, and there she intends to stay.

On Tuesday of the following week, Aurora arrives at her office with a box of donuts. "We missed you at the meeting," she says.

Lily blinks. She isn't aware she's missed another one, but she can't bring herself to care. Aurora sets the donuts down on her desk, though Lily already knows she won't touch them.

"Peter Serrano was very happy with the result," Aurora says carefully. She slips into the chair across from Lily's desk and studies her. "So, I guess you were right — we were able to get it done in time, after all."

Lily almost smiles. She loves hearing Aurora say that she was right, and two weeks ago, she would have gloated all day. Today all of that seems far behind her.

"Peter will probably call you," Aurora says. She bites at the corner of her thumb. "He wanted to thank you *personally*." She gives Lily a self-consciously bitter smile.

Lily doesn't blame her for being annoyed — she can't take any of the credit for this one, but she's still the face of it as far as the client is concerned. Life's not fair, she wants to tell Aurora, but she says nothing. She blinks.

Lily wants Aurora to leave so she can go back to watching her feeds, but Aurora's settled in. She sits across from Lily and scans the office, her gaze taking in the African mask James had brought her back from one of his trips overseas, the stupid stuffed bear he won her at the carnival last summer, and the framed photo she keeps on her desk — her and James in front of the Space Needle, his arms wrapped around her, her hair whipping around to cover half her face. She hates heights, but James couldn't believe she'd never been up before and he'd insisted on taking her one weekend. The entire time they'd been up there, she'd had to fight a wave of nausea so strong it kept triggering her gag reflex. It didn't matter how many times James explained to her the technical details on how the glass was structurally reinforced. She cried when he dragged her onto the new glass floor. She kept imagining the glass dissolving somehow, saw herself plummeting to her death, smashing into the ground 500 feet below. She'd smiled for that photo, but it was only with the relief of finally being back on solid ground.

"Are you alright?" Aurora says. She twists a coil of copper-colored hair around her finger.

"I'm fine." Lily blinks in surprise again. She can't stop blinking. She feels like some kind of dull amphibian.

"Are you sure? Because … I might understand, you know." Her eyes flick to the photograph again. "I might understand more than you even realize."

Lily hesitates. She almost tells her. She's never felt close to Aurora — just the opposite, in fact — but maybe that's why it's less scary to talk to her. Aurora already thinks she's a flake, so what harm could it do to say, *"I think my soon-to-be-husband is trying to drive me insane"*? But in the end, she keeps her mouth clapped shut. Instead, she picks up a frosted donut and starts picking off the sprinkles with her fingernail, popping the tiny candies into her mouth one by one.

Aurora waits for a long time. At least, it feels to Lily like a long time. But eventually she gets up and leaves, taking a cinnamon-dusted donut for herself on the way out.

AN HOUR LATER, Damian arrives at her office. *What is this,* she thinks, *Grand Central Station?* She reluctantly tears her gaze away from the camera feeds, and he comes in without knocking, slinking down into the same chair Aurora had occupied.

"We need to talk," he says.

She knows what he's going to say before he says it. She doesn't blame him, either. If anything, she wonders why it's taken him this long to come to it. She lets him speak.

"Your performance lately has been substandard. If there's something going on, I can try to help you. HR can try to help you. But you need to talk to me."

She finds herself smiling. It's sweet that he wants to help her. That he thinks he can. That he thinks he or HR can have any impact at all on her particular issue. *James would squash you like a bug,* she thinks. It makes her giggle. This doesn't go over well with Damian.

"Lily, come on. See this from my perspective. We got lucky on this project — Aurora was able to hit it out of the park. The client's happy. But I had to keep covering for you. It ended up being more work for me, and the last thing I need is more work. You get that, right?"

Lily nods. She does get that, absolutely. She knows she could make this easy on him by quitting right now, but she decides she wants to hear the words "you're fired." She's never been fired from anything before.

Damian sighs. He's got one leg crossed over the other knee, and he stares down at his expensive sneakers. Sneakers that probably cost almost as much as a pair of James' fancy leather brogues. And men say women are obsessed with shoes. "I think maybe you should take some time off. We can put it through as medical leave. You'll just need to get a note from your doctor. Something that says you're under too much stress here."

Lily's so surprised that at first she doesn't say anything. Then she blurts, "You're not firing me?"

"God, no. Lily. No. I just think you need some help."

"You should fire me." She knows she shouldn't say it, but it's the truth. After her behavior these last few weeks, she deserves to be fired.

"Well, I'm not. That's my decision. Get a doctor to vouch for you and we'll put you on stress leave. Come back in a month or two. When you're ready."

"Thank you," she says, because it's what he expects her to say. He isn't moving from the chair, and she realizes he's waiting for her to get up. "You want me to leave right now. Right?"

"I think it would be best."

"Alright." She stands and starts robotically packing up her things. There isn't much she needs to take. Her phone. The spare blazer she keeps on the back of her office door, in case of spilled coffee. She looks at, considers, and ultimately leaves behind the photograph, the stuffed bear, the African mask.

"Goodbye," she says to Damian. "And thank you. It's been

a pleasure," she adds, almost as an afterthought. She hopes he can tell that she means it.

She's surprised to find a tear forming in the corner of her eye. She's suddenly quite sure she won't ever see Damian again. She doesn't think she'll ever set foot inside the doors of DigitaLuster again. She isn't sure how she knows, but she does. She nods goodbye to Betsy the lucite ostrich, and heads out.

TWENTY-NINE
PRESENT DAY

I bide my time. I conserve the water and the sandwiches as much as I can. If I burn through them too fast, I'll be weak by the time he returns. So I make them last. It's easy now because my stomach is the size of a thimble. And because I have a fire inside me.

In the end, I get lucky, if you can call anything about my current situation *lucky*. James comes back the next night. I hear him crossing the clearing; I've become attuned to the sound of his footfalls, and I know it's him from the very first snap of a branch.

I want to stand strong, ready to face him. But I don't. I need him to think he has the upper hand. There is nothing he likes more than a small woman, so that's what I'm going to be for him. I stay supine on the earth floor, cradling my shoulder. Shuddering and trying to look like I'm near the end. It's not so far off, really.

"Wake up," he says.

I squint up at him, his silhouette grey in the twilight. He never wears the mask anymore. I suppose there's no need. I know it's him, and he knows I know. We're free to be ourselves. At last.

I hold my hands up against my eyes, like the light hurts me, like I've become a mole-person after being down here so long. Also not so far off.

"I brought you some water," he says. He holds out the bottle.

I want to tell him that he can shove that bottle up his fiery asshole, but instead I reach my hand out. Pleading. Weak. I can already tell he isn't going to make this easy. Normally, he just tosses the bottle down to me, but he's getting frustrated. He doesn't know why I haven't broken yet. He wants to make sure I do.

"Do you want it?" He holds the bottle out, dangling it above the hole.

"Yes," I say. "Please." I'll beg for it, James. If that's what you want.

He slowly untwists the top of the bottle and takes a small sip. He makes a face. "I hate when they taste like plastic. You know what I mean?" He slowly starts to pour the water out. Not the whole thing, but enough to make my blood course with need and desire. Even though I'm entirely fueled by anger now, I still ache to see the water seep into the ground.

"Well," he says, shoving one hand into his pocket, while his other hand grips the water bottle. Real casual, like we're chatting at a networking event. "I suppose you've had lots of time to think."

"I have," I answer.

"And what have you thought about?"

I don't answer. His mouth forms a straight line.

"I've spent the last hundred and fifty days thinking about

this moment," he says. "As if you might be able to give me some sort of explanation, a way that all of this would make sense."

I remain quiet while he stares down at me, considering me. Or contemplating his options. I have no doubt that what he says is true, that he's been obsessing over this — you don't dig a hole in the woods to trap someone if you've adjusted in a healthy manner.

Finally, I play my card.

"If you want me to talk," I say. "I want something from you in exchange."

James snorts. "I think you're forgetting who has the upper hand here."

"Maybe I have," I say. "But you've miscalculated something."

"Oh?" He raises one eyebrow in an amused fashion, but I can tell he's curious.

"You gave me too much time to think," I say. I make myself sound completely defeated. "You gave me time to adjust to my circumstances. I've already accepted the fact that I'm probably going to die down here. So why would I give you anything you want? If I'm just going to die, anyway."

James sneers. "You aren't serious," he says. "No one gives up that easily. You want to live — I know you do."

"Maybe once I would have," I say softly, more to myself than to him. "But that was before I met you. Before you beat me down. It's been ages since I truly wanted to live, I'm just too chicken shit to kill myself. You'd be doing me a favor, really."

"Come on," he says, his face incredulous. "You can't really expect me to believe that."

"You can believe whatever you want." I shrug. "If I die, I die. But if you want me to talk, you're going to have to let me out of here."

He grins. "There it is," he says. "The ploy. You're trying to get me to let you out."

Of course I am, I want to scream. *You sadistic douchebag.* Instead, I shrug again. "Maybe we both want something."

"You know even if I let you out of there, you won't be able to get away," he says. He lifts the hem of his jacket, revealing a gun holstered around his waist. I shiver. If I had any doubts about James, they're erased now.

"I know. Believe me, I know. I'm not asking for much. I just want to breathe fresh air. And …" Here I don't have to fake my emotion. "I want to bury my dog. I want to tell him goodbye."

Above me, James is still grinning his sardonic grin. I hate him. I want to claw that grin right off his face, slice his lips off with a hunting knife. The force of my rage shocks me, but it also galvanizes me. Ignites me. I take power from my hatred.

Somehow, being down here has changed me. It's like the dirt and the darkness have been my crucible. I can face him now, the way I should have faced him then.

"I know what you want," I tell him. "You want to know why I did it."

"I know exactly why," he spits. He's angry now. Good. If he's angry he's more likely to make a mistake. "But I want to know how it happened. Exactly. At the end. The video only captured the door of the balcony, and not the whole thing."

Just like that, everything clicks into place. There was video. Of course there was.

"I can tell you," I say. "Everything that happened. Every detail of those last few minutes."

James is almost salivating now, and I know my gamble is paying off.

"I'm going to die down here, anyway," I tell him, not giving him a chance to disagree. "And I have no problem going toward the light without ever saying a word. Or … you can let me out of here. Let me see one last sunset. Let me bury my dog. And I'll tell you everything you want to know."

THIRTY
SIX MONTHS AGO

When Lily leaves the office, she's in a daze. So much so that she doesn't notice the rain pouring down, even though it soaks her wool coat and plasters her dark hair to her face. She hails a cab. She goes home because she has nowhere else to go.

She hasn't decided how she's going to tell James about losing her job. Sorry, 'medical leave'. She isn't even sure *if* she'll tell him. Because at this point, she can admit that she doesn't trust him. The notion capsizes her.

She's let James do many things to her over the years. Things that have repulsed her, things that have frightened her, things that other women would have walked away from. But she's done them with her eyes open. Consensually. What he's doing to her now scares her more than any of those things, mostly because she doesn't understand why he's doing it.

When the cab pulls up in front of the apartment building on Beckham Avenue, she hesitates. She thinks about directing the driver to take her to the airport. She's got money, a credit card, a whole other identity waiting to be assumed. She could be halfway around the world before James even realizes she's missing.

He'd find her, though. She knows he would. James Russel is not the sort of man who can let things go.

While she's sitting there, the driver cranes his head back to glare at her. "You gettin' out, lady?" he barks. "'Cause if not, I'm going to keep the meter running."

"I'm getting out," she says, and she realizes as she says it that it's true, her hand's already on the door handle and she's already stepping back out into the rain. She's wet and freezing. The calendar has just ticked over to April, bringing with it a never-ending assault of cold and rain. Instead of running away, maybe she'll have a long, hot bath.

She rides the elevator up to the fourteenth floor and unlocks the door to the apartment. All she wants to do is peel off her wet clothes, which is probably why she doesn't pay too much attention to the empty apartment, or to the cameras.

As she walks to the bedroom, leaving a trail of drips behind her, she thinks how peaceful it is to have the place to herself for a few hours before James gets home. Maybe she won't even bother telling him that she's on leave. She'll let him drive her to the office every day and then she'll take the bus home and change back into her pajamas and spend the entire afternoon watching daytime television until he gets home for dinner. God, that idea sounds delectable. So many hours where she wouldn't have to be *on*. Not for James, not for Damian, not for her clients. She can wear her rattiest pajamas and eat Cheez-Its and maybe even drink wine straight from the bottle. Things she used to do in the early days of her emancipation. After she'd left her family behind, but before James. It will be like a mini-vacation. A trip back in time.

It doesn't solve her larger issue — namely, why James insists on torturing her — but it will buy her some time and the mental space to figure it out. And if she's home all day, he won't be able to sneak back to do anything funny. If he does, he'll find her already there, possibly slightly drunk and covered in a fine coating of cheese powder.

The thought makes her cackle as she peels off her damp turtleneck. The shirt momentarily gets stuck on her wet hair and she dances around the room trying to wrench it off. She's so distracted by the shirt shenanigans that she almost doesn't hear the thud from the living room.

Lily freezes, arms up in the air and the black turtleneck covering her face. If she could see herself, she'd find the image downright comical. But instead she's straining her ears, trying to listen to the apartment, working through the possibilities of what that noise could have been.

She paws at the sweater, finally gets it off, and throws it down on the ground. She doesn't bother to put on a new one right away. She wants to see what that noise was. Is it possible James has come home? Maybe she can catch him in the act.

The thought fills her with a smug satisfaction, and she strides back out to the living room.

There's no James. There's nothing at all. She scans the apartment, confounded. She knows she heard something. She'd stake her life on it. But nothing looks amiss. She stands in the middle of the room and turns in slow circles, considering all the angles. She still can't see anything. She remembers the cameras.

She grabs her phone from her bag — the battery's almost drained, since she's been using it all morning — and opens up the security app. The sight of the camera feeds fills her with a sort of relief. Even though she's standing right here, in the actual apartment, the cameras have become a security blanket for her. A thing she can cling to. She scrolls through the main living area feed, shivering in her bra, when something catches her attention on the screen. Just a flicker. A shadow.

At first, she thinks she might have imagined it, but when she scrolls back, there's definitely something. Not right in the sight lines of the camera, but off to the side.

She's freezing suddenly. Aware that she's standing there in her bra, still dripping onto the bamboo floors. Exposed. She forces herself to take her eyes off the phone and scan the room. It's still. Quiet. But that flicker on the screen, it meant something. She knows it.

She tries to breathe through the fear. She tells herself that maybe it was just *her* on the camera. Stalking through the hallway, peeling off her coat. Yes. She sighs, sagging with relief. It must be her. Her own shadow, the hem of her Burberry coat.

But what if it wasn't?

She gazes down at the phone again. With trembling hands, she drags her fingertip along the timeline. Since she's going backward, everything happens in reverse. Her, stomping backward from the bedroom to the front door, shrugging into her coat. Her, entering the foyer, looking sodden and crazed. Video Lily pulls the door of the apartment closed and disappears out into the hallway. The images are eerie, but nothing more than she expected. Just her, Lily, alone in the apartment. She watches as it drops back to the stillness of the room in the time before she arrived home and tells herself she might actually be losing her mind.

Then she sees it. Not just a flicker, but a figure. A real person. Crossing right in front of the camera's path.

She nearly drops the phone. Her heart kicks up six notches and she wonders if it's possible for it to thud right out of her chest completely. For a split second, she imagines James arriving home to find her dead on the floor, her still-beating heart hammering away six feet from her corpse. A wild giggle sputters from her lips. She chokes it back.

She focuses on the phone and scrolls back and forth through the timeline. Yes, there it is. A figure entering the apartment, creeping slowly past the camera's field of view. A chill runs through her. She scrolls forward again and watches herself enter the apartment, storm off toward the bedroom. A minute or two later, there she is, walking past the camera in her bra, her hair dripping onto her shoulders.

All at once, the realization hits her. Someone came into her apartment. It's real. Someone really has invaded their space.

The second realization hits her even harder, like a tidal wave of cold fear. Someone came into the apartment … and they never left. Whoever came in is still here.

THIRTY-ONE
PRESENT DAY

I barely dare to breathe while I wait for James to answer, but he says nothing. He simply gazes down at me from above, and there's something so starkly familiar about it that I shudder. This is the James I remember. Ruthless. Cold. Sick.

Then he's gone.

Without a word, he disappears from the edge of the hole. I hear him moving through the clearing. I want to call out, but I'm too stunned. I was sure that I had him. That he'd agree to my bargain. I know he wants to know what happened that day. He wouldn't walk away when he's so close to getting the answers he craves.

And yet, he has. He did.

I slump down onto the ground. My shoulder throbs. The adrenalin of my confrontation with James had allowed me to forget about it for a few minutes, but now the pain returns in double time. If I had tears left in me, I'd cry. Instead, I just stare at the wall of my prison.

I lose track of time. An hour goes by, maybe. And then

there's a noise in the clearing. A whisper through the grasses. And something else. A metallic clanging. It gets closer and closer. Footsteps, I think. But the metal sound — I can't quite place it.

And then I don't have to, because the source of the sound plunges down into the hole with me.

I jolt, rolling out of the way of the extendable ladder. My shoulder screams. I might scream, too, I don't know. James is back. He must have walked to his car, wherever that is, and retrieved the ladder.

I stare at it in disbelief. Can it really be this easy?

But *easy* isn't the right word. Not really. He's still going to kill me when this is all said and done. He just wants to hear the truth about what really happened that day. As soon as he's satisfied, I'll be dead. No one will ever hear a gunshot out here; if they do, they'll just think we're rednecks out doing target practice.

But beyond that, there's a more practical matter right in front of me. Namely, my broken-or-possibly-dislocated shoulder is going to make it damn difficult to climb that ladder. I look it up and down. It's only about ten feet high, but it might as well be a hundred. I can hardly stand up, never mind climb.

"Well," James snarls from above me. "You wanted to get out. Now's your chance."

I approach the ladder. My upper body tenses, preparing for the searing bolt of pain that's ready to lance through my left side.

You can do this, I tell myself. And then, more acidly, *you've got no fucking choice.*

I lean into the ladder. Using my good arm, I hold onto a

bar slightly higher than my head, and I manage to step up onto the first rung. So far, so good. But my left arm hangs lamely at my side. I try to lift it enough to grab onto a rung but it screams in agony. Nope. Not happening. I twist a little on the ladder, trying to find a way to balance so I can brace myself for another step.

Above me, James laughs. "Always so stubborn," he says.

"You taught me that."

"I didn't think I taught you anything."

"More things than you'll ever know."

"I'm flattered."

"Don't be."

"I miss our repartee."

In a sick and twisted way, I do, too. But I'll never tell him that. Instead, I turn my attention back to the task at hand: somehow getting myself up this ladder and onto solid ground. I never thought I'd be so close to freedom and yet have such difficulty taking those last few steps.

I grit my teeth and renew my focus. I *am* getting out of this hole and I *am* getting away from James. I'm going to survive this, no matter what he might think.

After some shifting and wriggling, I finally find a way to scale the ladder, by bracing my chest against the rung in front of me and using my right hand to pull myself up. My left shoulder still throbs and I'm attacked at each step by a wave of pain so dizzying that I almost pass out, but I hold on. While I inch my way up the ladder, I use the time to think about what I'm going to do when I'm there.

Half of me fears this is all a trick — that as soon as I get to the top of the ladder, James is going to plant a boot in my face and push me back down. One final *fuck you* from him to me.

But there's nothing I can do about it if that's the case. For once — and it kills me a little to think this — I have to trust him. I have to take him at his word.

But even if I get out of here, even if he lets me stand up there on the grass and face him, I have no idea what I'm going to do then.

Panic starts to bubble up inside me, but I tamp it down. James feeds on fear, and I refuse to nourish him with my own.

Slowly, slowly, I inch my way up the ladder. I'm aware of James standing above me, of the air that gets cooler the higher I climb, of the birds that are singing their night songs.

Finally, my head is above the ground. It's even more miraculous than the first time, when I'd dragged myself up here using nothing but my hands, a dog leash, and a tree root. This time the miracle is that James has allowed it to happen. I brace myself, waiting for the trick, for the boot to the face. It doesn't come. Instead, James leans down and grabs me roughly by the arm. My good arm, thank God, but even that sends a sharp spasm of pain and terror through me. But James only lifts me from the ladder. I fall onto the grass at his feet.

"Up," he commands, and for a second I'm back in his bedroom, kneeling in front of him while he twists my hair around his fist. The same familiar terror and revulsion courses through me. How did I not see him for who he was? How did I ignore so many warning signs?

But there's no time to think about that. James wrenches me to my feet and I stagger against him. With so much open space around me, I have to fight off a wave of vertigo, and I barely notice when he reaches down and pulls the ladder back out of the hole. He leaves it sprawled on the grass beside us, ready to take back to wherever his car is parked. He's starting his clean-up already, I realize. Making sure there's nothing left here that will tie him to me. Just in case someone finds my body some day.

I shudder again. I know I only have this one chance. I stand tall, as tall as I can, and I face James. I try to look unafraid.

But he isn't buying it. He knows me too well, is intimately familiar with all my tells and the tiniest tremor of my lip. He smiles in his sadistic, twisted way. Moves the hem of his jacket aside. Makes sure I haven't forgotten he's armed. He never stops smiling. He gestures around the clearing.

"There's your sunset," he says. The sky is pink and it makes the trees grow with a golden light. It's really quite pretty, everything else aside. "Now, I believe we had a deal," he says. "I gave you your last taste of freedom. Now I want to know the truth about how Lily died."

THIRTY-TWO
SIX MONTHS AGO

Lily stands in the middle of the living room, chilled to the bone. She wants to go back to the bedroom and get a shirt, but she's scared to move from the spot she's in. Her eyes scan the apartment, taking in every slant of light, every dust mote, every possible hiding space. With James' minimal style, there aren't exactly a lot of them. Whoever is in the apartment is not in this room.

She has a thought: if it *was* James in the apartment, he wouldn't have bothered hiding. He could have made up some excuse for being home — a headache, a forgotten contract, a need for a change of clothes. He wouldn't have hidden like a child when he heard her at the door. He would have greeted her face-to-face.

So. Not James. She understands this now, a crystal clear certainty that hardens her fear into anger. Someone — she has no idea who, if it isn't James — is torturing her. Trying to ruin everything she's worked so hard for. And she has no interest in taking it. Not anymore.

James owns a gun, but he's never given her the combination to the safe, so she goes for the next best thing. His prized chef's knife. She's pretty sure he paid something ridiculous like four hundred dollars for it, and he keeps it meticulously sharpened. On the way to the kitchen, she passes her coat, still on the floor, and considers shrugging it onto her bare shoulders, but decides against it. The bra might be revealing, but it offers her a freedom of movement that she might need.

She creeps toward the kitchen, trying not to make a sound. Maybe there's no point — without knowing exactly where the intruder is, she has no idea if he's watching her right now — but she isn't taking any chances. As she rounds the corner to the kitchen she slows and braces herself, but when she finally faces the entrance, there's no one there. She slides the drawer open slowly — it's silent anyway, thanks to James' fancy Italian cabinets — and slips the knife out. It feels good in her hand — weighty, sharp, powerful. She stands with her back against the island, gripping the knife in her fist and surveying the portion of the apartment she can see. There's still no sign of anyone. If she hadn't seen it on the camera, she'd think she was imagining the whole thing. Unlike the last time, she doesn't even have the sense of someone in the apartment. Not even the hint of a presence.

But he has to be here somewhere. And she's going to find him. No one threatens her. Not if they want to live.

"Come out, come out, wherever you are." She moves through the house on a cat's silent feet. She goes to James' office first because it seems the most likely place, but when she swings the door wide open, she finds it empty. She creeps around the desk, checks there, peers behind the wingbacks, under the sideboard. The room is empty, nothing disturbed.

Next is the bathroom, but she finds that empty, too. As she clears the apartment, she should feel safer and more at ease, but she only feels more agitated. Where is he hiding?

She clears the guest room, the powder room, the walk-in closets in the master bedroom, the ensuite. Lily gets increasingly agitated with each one. She's running out of places to look. By the time she returns to the living room, she realizes the only place she hasn't looked is the hall closet. Right in front of her. Suddenly, she's sure that's the answer. Maybe whoever's in the apartment hid in there when he heard her key in the lock, expecting her to open it first thing in order to hang up her coat. He could have been planning to ambush her. She'd foiled his plan by letting her coat fall onto the floor. She sets her mouth in a grimly triumphant line. Without even realizing it, she's turned the tables on him. Now she'll be the one to ambush him. He won't be expecting her to confront him, and he especially won't be expecting the chef's knife.

For about five seconds, she considers calling the police instead of opening the closet door. It would be the smart thing to do, after all. The reasonable thing. But she doesn't want to involve the police. She's spent her ten years in Seattle trying to avoid the police. She doesn't dare bring them in now, not when she has no idea what this intruder's motives are and what he might or might not know about her. If it's Connor —

She pictures him crouched in the closet, waiting. Not just the scruff-covered face of the Connor she ran into the other day, but the clean-cut, baby-faced Connor of ten years ago, too. Both of them waiting and wanting to destroy her. She won't take it. She won't.

Lily approaches the closet, quietly and carefully, and all at once she swings the door open, thrashing the knife around wildly.

The closet is empty. Her knife slices open an innocent winter coat of James'. Down spurts out the tear in the sleeve's outer shell. Lily stands there, breathing heavily, heart racing wildly. She can't believe the closet is empty. She claws at the coats as if they might still be hiding someone behind them, but of course she finds nothing. No one.

She spins around and glares at the apartment, as if it's to blame for this. As if it's somehow complicit in hiding this intruder from her. She flexes her fingers around the handle of the knife, runs the blade lightly over her palm, relishing the feel of the cold, smooth steel.

She needs some air. She glances at the balcony and it hits her. How obvious. The balcony. That's why she couldn't sense the presence of anyone else in the apartment. Because no one was *in* the apartment.

She flips through the app on her phone, calling up the feed that's trained on the balcony doors. She scrolls through and, even though she's expecting it, she gasps when she sees the hooded figure scurry into the frame, yank the door open and dart outside.

Lily tosses her phone down onto James' obscene coffee table and creeps over toward the sliding doors, still clutching the knife. She can't see anything. Is he still there? The camera feed captures the entrance to the balcony only; the glare from the glass doors makes it impossible to make out what happens beyond that. Lily tries to peer out. Maybe he's crawled across to the neighbor's balcony. He could travel the entire length of the building that way, if he was agile and industrious enough.

Maybe eventually find a balcony door that's unlocked. He could be out of the building entirely by now, escaped down onto the street.

When she slides the door open, she's already convinced this is the case. She'll step out there and find it as empty as the rest of the apartment. He'll have gotten away with it once again.

Something tickles her nose. A scent. Citrusy. But bitter, like orange rinds.

It takes her a second to parse the huddled form on the far side of the outdoor sectional. In fact, she almost misses it completely. But as her eyes focus, it's unmistakable. It's the rounded back of someone crouching down, trying to be smaller than they actually are. Not under the tarp but beside it, trying to blend in.

Her grim smile returns. "Come on out, motherfucker," she barks. She feels wild and unleashed.

At first the figure doesn't move. Lily takes a step closer, then another one, closing the distance between them. Still, the huddled figure doesn't move.

She's close enough to reach out and touch him. She could plunge the knife right down through his back or the nape of his neck. She tries to decide which area is softer, which might be more fatal. She doesn't think about the consequences, only about defending herself. The same way she did so many years ago, in a Pepto-pink bedroom in Bryson City.

But instead of reaching out with the knife, she uses her foot and plants a solid kick in the intruder's side. He topples over, and Lily hears a groan that sounds surprisingly familiar. The scent of oranges pricks her nose.

She doesn't make the connection until the figure moves and she glimpses the red hair beneath the hoodie.

"Aurora?" Lily drops the knife down to her side, her mouth gaping like a fish. "What the fuck?"

THIRTY-THREE
SIX YEARS AGO

Aurora Watts is wrangling coffees. That's what she does at Linchpin, the advertising firm where she works. She wrangles coffees. Oh, and books meeting rooms and sets up webcasts and prints out slide decks for clients who still need to hold something physical in their hands when they're in a meeting. Clients who think 'something physical' also includes her ass. The best part of it is, she isn't even getting paid. She's an intern, the lowest plebe of them all, given the shit jobs and the thankless tasks all in the name of experience. And she's loving every single minute of it.

She balances the tray of lattes and tries not to turn over on her ankle as she shuffles her way from the coffee shop to the office. She's not used to wearing heels — more of a jeans and sneakers kind of girl, really — but she wants to make a good impression. For years now, ever since she first watched *Mad Men*, she's never wanted anything other than to work in advertising. And even though Linchpin is nothing like Sterling

Cooper, she still loves every single minute of it. She feels like she's at home.

She rounds the corner of 5th Avenue and Union Street. She doesn't see the man in the expensive suit, not until she's already run smack into him. Hot coffee spills over her wrists, over her blouse, her skirt — and all over him.

"Fuck!" They both say it at exactly the same time, and it surprises Aurora so much that she starts to laugh. She often does that, laughs at inopportune times. It's something she's always done, something she can't help.

The man in the expensive suit glares at her, but eventually he starts to laugh, too. Soon they're both laughing, doubled over, reeking of espresso. Aurora notices for the first time how handsome he is.

As she stares at him, he stares back. His eyes crease — even more handsome — and he frowns. "Do I know you from somewhere?"

"I don't know," she stammers. "I don't think so."

"Do you know the Hendersons?" he asks. "That party in Laurelhurst?"

She snorts. She most certainly doesn't, and she's never been to any parties in Laurelhurst — that's the most expensive part of the city. She doubts she even knows anyone who knows anyone who lives there. "No, definitely not." She notices that he's carrying dry-cleaning. "Do you come here often?"

He grins — still even more handsome, it's stupid really, how handsome he is — and says, "Is that a line?"

She flushes crimson. "No! I just meant … I work near here and sometimes I come in here."

He laughs. It's a rippling sound, like a peaceful river.

"Relax. I'm teasing. And no, I don't come here often. I normally use the dry-cleaners near my office, but my assistant dropped them off here because ... honestly, I don't know why." His grin is so disarming that Aurora has forgotten she's almost completely covered in coffee.

"I'm Aurora," she blurts, and her face flames. But the man just smiles his disarming smile again.

"James."

AURORA FLOATS BACK to her office. It cost thirty dollars to replace all the spilled coffees, but James insisted on paying. He'd also insisted on getting her number, though she's sure he's not going to call. Positive. But she puts her cell on the corner of her desk, anyway, so she can glance at it every five seconds all afternoon while she's cataloguing images from the Carson Brewery photoshoot. But she's sure he's not going to call. He's a hotshot architect who wears Armani suits; she's an intern who can barely afford knock-off Rayban sunglasses. Even if he did call her — even if — there's no way anything would ever happen.

Four hours later, she's having dinner with him.

THE FIRST TIME she goes home with James, Aurora thinks she's died and gone to heaven. His apartment on Beckham Avenue is modern and stylish and expensive-looking, the complete opposite of the hipster musician types she normally dates. He's a grown-up. A real one. He pours her wine that probably costs more than her entire outfit, and they drink it out of glasses that look like crystal. He turns on a gas fireplace using a remote — a remote! For some reason, it's that tiny detail that blows her away the most. The only fires she's ever had have been camping bonfires that involved her father cursing a lot over wet kindling. And here James has fire at the click of a button. It seems to her like the ultimate form of sophistication. A harnessing of the elements that speaks to James' charisma, his sheer magnetism.

She lets him take her to bed and she doesn't even blink when he ties her wrists to his bedposts.

THE FIRST TIME he really hurts her is after they've been dating for two months. Aurora has spent nearly a hundred percent of their time together on cloud nine. She tells herself that his sexual proclivities are a sign of his sophistication. Something she herself can't quite grasp because of her station in life. The same way she can't taste the difference between a two hundred dollar bottle of wine and a jug of plonk from Trader Joe's. She can let James cultivate her sexual palate the same way he's honing her taste for fine foods and wines. She's twenty-two years old and ready to have her eyes opened to the world.

But on that particular night, things take a turn. As he strips off her clothes, she throws her head back, delighting in his ministrations. When his teeth drag against her nipple, she leans into it. A searing pain erupts. She screams. She throws her head forward so fast her teeth snap. She looks down. Blood pools around her nipple.

"Jesus Christ." She tries to pull away, to go to the bathroom, to get a cold wet facecloth, but James grabs her wrist.

"Where do you think you're going?"

Her mouth opens and closes a couple of times like a fish. "You hurt me." There's surprise in her voice.

"Did I?"

She gingerly touches the nipple, inspecting it. "I think I might need stitches." She stares at him in disbelief, waiting for him to freak out, to apologize, to fall all over himself taking care of her. Instead, he arches his eyebrows.

"If it bothers you so much, you can leave," he says plainly. "But I wasn't under the impression that you were such a child."

Aurora gapes at him. He sits down on the edge of the bed, waiting. A challenge. Aurora swallows. She looks back toward the living room, to the door of the apartment. She could leave right now, she thinks, and chalk this up to another relationship that wasn't meant to be. Or she can grow the fuck up. Meet James where he is, and let him take her to places she's never been.

She crosses the room and stands between his thighs.

THE DAY she moves in with him, Aurora feels like she's won the lottery. James pours them champagne, orders Thai takeout, and makes gentle love to her in his king-sized bed. He presents her with a key, attached to a little daisy keychain, and tells her that it's not just the key to his apartment but the key to his heart. But that night, she lies awake for hours, staring at the ceiling. His body looms strange and foreign beside her.

JAMES HAS A NEW THING, a new game. Something he calls *Closet Time*. He binds her wrists with one of his expensive leather belts, and he locks her in the closet. It's a big closet, the walk-in style, but he encloses her in the area where he keeps his suits, which is closed off from the rest of the space. She stays on her knees in there until he comes to let her out.

He used to do it to punish her, like when she bought the wrong cut of beef from the market or when she wore the red underwear instead of the black ones he preferred. Now he does it whenever he feels like it. He does it on her birthday, after promising her an extravagant night out. He does it when she has the flu.

The sessions get longer, too. She misses work one day because he won't let her out in the morning. Most of the time he comes in to visit her, to tenderly feed her pieces of fruit or to escort her to the bathroom. That day he goes to the office and leaves her there. She tries to hold her bladder for as long as she can, but eventually the pain in her abdomen is too intense. She pisses herself. It seeps into the carpet, into the air, into James suits. He's furious when he gets home.

She tells herself it's not abuse, because it's a sex thing. She's always considered herself openminded, and she would never 'yuck anyone else's yum', as her friends at the liberal arts college she went to used to say. This is James' yum, and she won't yuck it, even if she doesn't understand it, even if it makes her feel scared and ashamed. Real abuse is when a guy uses you as a punching bag because he's mad at the world. What James does is a kind of play. He's just sexually adventurous.

And the rest of their relationship is good. He's attentive, gentle, a wonderful cook. He takes care of her. He's already talking about the things they'll do 'when they're married.'

She loves him. She knows she'll never leave him. But she can't walk past the bedroom door without flinching, without getting a faint whiff of phantom urine.

AURORA HASN'T BEEN to work in a week. Every time she tries to leave James' apartment, she's hit with a wave of panic so crushing it knocks her to her knees. James doesn't know what to do with her. He puts her in closet time for hours at a time, forces her into scalding hot baths, makes her stand naked on his balcony. Nothing can snap her out of it. He brings her Xanax and she gobbles it down like candy.

THEY CALL IT MEDICAL LEAVE. A polite term for 'girl, you lost it'. She would feel like a failure, if she had the energy to care.

JAMES HASN'T TOUCHED her in weeks. She's secretly relieved. She sleeps in the guest room, which also secretly relieves her. But she misses their closeness. The comforting weight of his arm slung around her shoulders while they watch TV, of his hand slipped through hers when they walked down the street.

One night he comes home smelling of sex. Aurora pretends not to notice. When he jumps in the shower, she locks herself in the guest room and cries.

———

JAMES NEVER COMES home on time anymore. Every night he 'works late' or 'has a dinner meeting'. Every night, he comes home reeking of sex and expensive perfume. Aurora keeps pretending not to notice, keeps closing herself in the guest room and away from the truth. Then one night the truth comes home with him, and she spends the night listening to them fucking through the walls.

———

THE MEN ARE ROUGH. Russians, she thinks. They have calloused hands and dusty steel-toed boots. They pack up all her belongings and toss them haphazardly into cardboard boxes, which they seal up with tape guns that make a terrible ripping noise. She cries. James looks bored. The Russians don't say a word.

She moves into her new apartment that afternoon. First and last month's rent paid for by James, under the condition that she not contact him ever again. She agrees, because she has no choice. He's done with her. He's been done for months.

SHE SPENDS another eight months off work. She calls it her mourning period. It would be longer, too, except her mother and sister come up from Portland, and they buy her new curtains for her bedroom, groceries for her kitchen, fluffy white towels for her bathroom. Most importantly, they get her a therapist. Dr. Monica explains to her about healthy, consensual BDSM relationships — how both parties have to be willing and enthusiastic participants, how most would argue that the submissive holds the balance of power. She shows Aurora the ways in which what she experienced was different, that it really was abuse. She even asks Aurora if she wants to press charges. Aurora is stricken; it's the last thing she wants, her weakness on full display to the world. The only thing she truly wants is to put this entire thing behind her. But she thinks a lot about what Dr. Monica said, about the balance of power. She wants to take her own power back.

SHE GOES BACK to work on a Monday in March. It should be the happiest day of this past year, but instead she shrinks from it. Everyone treats her with kid gloves, like she might freak out at any minute. She starts looking for a new job. She still wants to stay in the industry, but she knows she has to leave Linchpin. She gets an interview with DigitaLuster and nails it. They offer her the job a week later.

YEARS PASS. Aurora thrives at DigitaLuster. She gets promoted to project manager. A dream job. She kicks ass at it, too. She knows how to rally her troops, how to push back when needed. They're loyal to her, and she's loyal to them, and it just works. She likes the clients, the projects, the other people she works with. Even though some of the account managers drive her crazy, she still respects them. She never thought a job could feel this good.

AURORA IS SITTING in Lily Castleman's office. Lily is one of the account managers who drives her insane, but Aurora's gotten better at handling herself around them. She doesn't let them intimidate her. Right now, she's staring Lily down, telling her no way can they make that deadline. Lily won't hear it. She just keeps shrugging and saying 'do your best."

Aurora is about to give up. She throws her hands up in the air and stands, ready to go back to her office. That's when she sees it. The picture frame. Lily, and a man that Aurora hasn't thought about in months. A chill runs down her spine and cold sweat pools in the small of her back. She realizes she's panting, mouth open, like a deer in the hot sun.

"Are you okay?" Lily looks concerned. It's the most human Aurora has ever seen her.

"I'm fine. Nice picture," she manages to croak.

"Oh, thanks. That's my boyfriend, James. We took that on the weekend, at the Space Needle."

"Right. Cute."

Aurora isn't sure how she manages to make it back to her desk.

THIRTY-FOUR
PRESENT DAY

I take a deep breath. Standing face to face with him, being this close to him again, is twisting up my insides. I'm flooded with memories. Not just of that life-altering day on Beckham Avenue, but of everything that came before it. All the hurt, the denial, the naivety. All my mistakes. It's amazing how clearly you can see things in hindsight.

"Stop wasting my time." James folds his arms across his chest. "Unless you want to go back in the hole.

No. Going back in the hole is the absolute last thing I want. I cast a glance over my shoulder, wondering if I can make a run for it, but James reads my intentions.

"Don't even think about it," he says, taking a step toward me. "You think you can outrun me? Not even on a good day, Aurora, and certainly not in your current condition."

I have to admit he's right. "Why did you do it?" I say, because I think that if I can keep him talking, I can buy myself some time. "Why'd you trap me here like this?"

For the first time, he looks pleased. "Inspired, wasn't it? I remembered how much you disliked small, enclosed spaces.

At first, I thought maybe a storage locker, but that seemed risky. I started following you, hoping for inspiration. When I saw you routinely came out here — out here to the middle of fucking nowhere, Aurora, really — the idea just came to me. No one can hear you scream out here. It's a beautiful thing."

"It must have taken some coordinating, though. Digging it. Getting me into it." That's been a question I've wondered about before — what are the odds, in a hundred-thousand-acre forest, of stumbling across a single eight-foot by eight-foot hole? Not very high, I'd wager.

"Getting it dug was easy. Never even had to get my hands dirty. My line of work puts me in contact with all kinds of construction companies. You have no idea how easy it is to get someone to do something like this. Find someone without a Green Card and pay them a couple grand, and I guarantee they won't ask a single question."

I shake my head. It shouldn't surprise me, James exploiting undocumented workers like that, but it's another low in a never-ending series of lows.

James shakes his head. "As for getting you in here, that was also surprisingly easy. Do you know how much your dog likes bacon?" *King.* I groan. James grins. "It's why I've never liked pets, myself. No *real* loyalty. Anyway, all I needed to do was get him to lure you to the clearing. I'd planned to push you in myself but then you ..." James stops to catch a breath, and I realize he's laughing. He's *laughing*. "You just fell right in."

He doubles over — exaggerated, I'm sure — and I see a window. While he laughs, I turn and run. I'm three feet away from him, then four feet, then six, and I almost think I'm going to get away with it when his fingers seize around my arm. My bad arm. He yanks me back and I scream in agony.

"Not so fast, darling," he says. "We're not done talking. But tell me what I want to hear, and who knows? Maybe I'll be struck by a sudden burst of compassion and let you go."

I know the odds of that are about the same as the odds of James getting struck by lightning in the next two minutes. I look up at the cloudless sky and take another deep breath. Pain still courses through my arm, and I try to focus on that while I speak.

"It was an accident," I say. If he takes nothing else away from this, that's the one thing I want him to hear. "I didn't mean for it to happen."

James doesn't say anything, so I go on. "I only wanted to warn her. To tell her about the things you did to me. I didn't want her to stay with you. I actually liked her."

"Which is why you broke into our apartment and came after her?" He looks skeptical, and for once, I can't say I blame him.

"I know it sounds crazy. I wasn't thinking straight. Lily had just been let go at work —"

I pause, waiting to see if he shows any surprise, but his face remains neutral. I guess that information had come out during the investigation into her death. I hadn't been privy to any of the inner workings of that investigation, but I knew it had eventually been ruled a suicide, and I guessed that her medical leave was assumed to be a contributing factor. I'd had one cursory interview with a bored-looking detective, during which I'd told him, honestly, about the stress Lily had been under recently at work and how scattered and unfocused she'd become. He'd taken about two lines of notes, thanked me for my time, and asked me to show the next employee into the boardroom, where he'd set up for the morning. I was pretty sure they'd already decided on the cause of death; the interviews were merely a formality.

"Anyway, as soon as I heard she'd been let go, I rushed over there. I was worried that if she didn't have a job to go to anymore ... I don't know. I guess I thought she might become so isolated that she'd never be able to get away from you." I can't look at him. I think about how isolated I was when I lived there, stashed away in the guest room like the mad wife in a Bronte novel.

"I got to your apartment and went in—"

"How did you get in?" It's the first time he's interrupted me.

"One of your neighbors let me in."

"I mean into the apartment, not into the building."

"The door was unlocked."

He raises his eyebrows. "I doubt that's true."

"Cross my heart." I make the gesture to show how serious I am. "I knocked first but there was no answer. I assumed Lily was already in the apartment, and I was concerned about her, so I let myself in. When I didn't find her anywhere, I thought of the balcony. I had this horrible thought that maybe she'd ..."

"Jumped?"

I nod. My lip quivers. "I was just about to go out there when I heard your apartment door open. I panicked. I hid."

"On the balcony."

"Yes. I didn't know what else to do. I had come to talk to her, to support her, but I knew if she found me there in your apartment, there was probably zero chance she'd talk to me. And even less chance that she'd actually listen to me."

From somewhere in the distance, an owl hoots. I shiver. James is still waiting for me to continue, so I force myself to go on.

"From there it all happened so fast. She must have known I was in the apartment — or at least that someone was. She came out brandishing this huge kitchen knife. I stood up and tried to calm her down, to tell her that it was just me and that I wasn't there to hurt her. But I don't know. She snapped, I guess. She rushed at me with the knife. All I did was move out of the way. I swear, James. I was trying not to get stabbed. That's all. I dodged when she came at me and she hit the railing of the balcony and she — I guess she had too much momentum because she just …"

I trail off. I don't want to finish the sentence. But James still waits. I realize he needs this. This closure. I force myself to say it.

"She went over the side. Just like that." I shiver again, this time unrelated to the local wildlife. Watching Lily plummet over the side of that balcony had been the single most surreal moment of my life. Reliving it here with James Russel is a close second. "There was nothing I could do. I watched her fall. She was so quiet. All the way down, she was so quiet."

THIRTY-FIVE
SIX MONTHS AGO

A strange thing happens when Lily falls, twisting and turning through the chilly Seattle air. She isn't Lily Castleman anymore. She isn't Stacey Kincaid. She isn't James' fiancee. She isn't her father's daughter. She isn't anyone.

She's only, finally, free.

The sidewalk rises up to meet her, and she closes her eyes and lets it come.

THIRTY-SIX
PRESENT DAY

"And that's the whole story," I say. I hold my hands open. A strange — and I'm sure temporary — aura of peace has descended on me. Maybe speaking those words, even to James, has eased my conscience somehow.

A myriad of expressions play out over James' face. He'd been impassive while I spoke, coolly evaluating my story, probably weighing it against what he already knew. Trying to figure out whether I was lying to him. But he had to know there was no point in lying. It's just us here, alone in the woods. Just us, alone at last.

But now, standing in front of me, James' jaw ticks. The muscles in his cheek tighten. His Adam's apple bobs. I realize he's ... fighting back tears. That surprises me perhaps more than anything else on this long, strange nightmare. As I watch, stunned, his eyes pool with liquid, rendering the green of his irises watery and surreal. He blinks the tears furiously away.

"I can't believe it," he says. His voice sounds choked.

"Trust me, neither can I." Part of me has been waiting for this moment since the day it happened. Dreading it, but maybe ... maybe craving it, too. The moment of reckoning.

"I loved her," James says. His voice is soft in the twilight.

"Right. The same way you loved me."

"No. I never loved you." He says it plainly, not as an arrow designed to hurt me but as a simple statement of fact. "But I loved her. And she loved me. I know that my needs are strange to some, and I know — now — that perhaps I forced them on you too aggressively. But Lily didn't just understand those needs, she embraced them. She came to love them, too."

"I don't believe you," I say. I hold my shoulders strong and firm. I *can't* believe him. James is making it sound fine, like he just happens to like it a little rough in the bedroom. What he did to me was more than that. It was the torture of it. The fear he instilled in me. That's what he got off on. If Lily had truly liked it, she wouldn't have been afraid, and that wouldn't have been enough for him. He needed us to feel terror, so that he could lord his power over us. I've had years to think about what he did to me, to analyze his behavior, to sort it out in therapy with Dr. Monica. To think about that balance of power.

"I don't care if you believe it," James said. "Lily had her own darkness. She didn't share that with people. She didn't even share it with me, though I hoped that in time, she would. I already knew her secrets, and I loved her anyway. Maybe I even loved her because of them. Her strength, her will, her determination. It was a beautiful thing. You killed a woman who was happy, and all because ... what? You were jealous?"

I snort in laughter. Two hours ago, I would have thought I'd never laugh again, and the sensation feels foreign and painful. There's no humor in it, either. James is too deluded for there to be any humor in this situation. "No. Jealous was the last thing I felt. Try fear, terror, hatred. Those might get you a little closer to the mark."

"Hatred," he sneers. "I've become intimately familiar with the feeling, Aurora." He pauses, looking up at the sky and around the clearing as if we were on a daytime stroll in a pretty little park. He regards me again. "You know, I was going to shoot you, but now I think I'd prefer to strangle you with my bare hands. I thought about doing that so many times, when you'd be huddled in my bed sniveling. That time you pissed in my closet."

James looks absolutely disgusted, and my face flames red. *Shame.* There's another emotion I never expected to feel again. But mixed with the shame is cold blue terror. Because I know he's going to kill me. When we were together, when he would punish me for whatever imaginary transgression I'd committed, I'd been scared. Of course, I had. Scared of the pain, of upsetting him. Of losing him. But I'd never truly feared for my life. Not like I do now.

Without even realizing I'm doing it, I start to walk backward. All I want is to get as far away from him as possible. But as soon as he notices, he stops laughing. He takes a couple of steps toward me, closing the distance between us again. I take another step back. We do that dance for a few feet. My heart is racing in my chest. I want to turn and run but I know if I do, he'll be on me like a wild jungle cat. There'll be no outrunning him. He was right about that, at least — I'd have a hard time of it under the best of circumstances, and right now I'm too dehydrated and weak to get far. I don't even dare count on my adrenalin to carry me through.

No, the only choice I have is to stand and face him. If I could get his gun, I'd have the upper hand. That's probably my only chance. When he reaches for my neck, I have to go for the gun.

But that means I have to let him reach for my neck. I take two steps backward to buy myself another couple of seconds. I suck in a deep breath and still. It takes every ounce of willpower I have not to wrench myself away from him as he closes the last foot of space between us.

But instead of reaching for my neck, closing his strong hands around my tender skin, he knocks me to the ground. He mounts me, using his thighs to lock my arms to my sides. I wriggle and flail beneath him but he's too heavy, too powerful for me to throw off. I realize I've greatly miscalculated. There's no way I'll be able to grab the gun now, not with my arms pinned down like this. He's going to strangle me right here on the ground, and I won't be able to fight him off.

James is preternaturally calm as he sits astride me. I keep thrashing, but he's smart enough to wait, knowing that eventually I'll tire myself out. I can't stop, though. Dying here, at James' hand, would be worse than dying in that hole. I can't — I *won't* — give him the satisfaction.

But the flailing gets me nowhere. I pause to take a breath — maybe one of the last I'll ever get. That realization sends a wave of awareness through my body, and in that second, I feel everything. The rending agony of my shoulder, the dry dirt and grass under my back, the weight of James' body above me, the dull ache of his kneecap digging into my side.

Wait. That's not his kneecap. His knees are on the ground beside me. But something sharp is gouging at my side. I wriggle my fingers enough to touch the edge of it.

The bear spray.

It's still in the holster, the one I couldn't slip off because of my shoulder. And right now, it's pinned to my side, but if I can just wiggle the safety off, maybe I can —

James' hands wrap around my neck. I stopped moving for too long and he made his move. His thumbs press into the hollow of my throat, and the pressure plants stars in my field of vision. His hands close tighter, and when I look up to his face, I find him smiling peacefully, like this is what he was born to do. And maybe it is.

But I was born to do this, too. I was born to take this motherfucker out. I jab at the can, trying to find the safety. James' hands tighten around my throat. The safety comes free. My vision darkens. I can't wrench the bottle out but if I can hit the nozzle, maybe enough of the gas will come out that …

My legs thrash. I can't control them. I'm dying. It's happening. I'm going to die here, with James' hands around my neck. I jam the nozzle and a squirt of gas emerges from between my side and James' knee. It's not enough to do any damage, but it's enough to make him pause. His grip on my neck loosens and he shifts his thighs so he can look down and see what that was.

I take my opportunity. I yank the bottle from the holster. I'm already squeezing before I can bring it front and center, which means I get as much of it as James does. But I can prepare myself — I close my eyes and my mouth, bring my other hand up to cover my nose, even though I'm desperate for air.

James screams when the pepper spray hits him. It's a vile thing at any time, and when it catches you unaware, it can feel like you're dying. James leaps off me and begins scrubbing at his face with his hands and, when that doesn't work, with the hem of his shirt. I get up after him. I turn my head and try to take a couple of desperate breaths. I'm so dizzy that I'm in danger of passing out, but I force myself to take a couple of steps toward James, blast him again with the bear spray.

"You fucking bitch!" he roars. He must realize there's no point in running, because instead he changes direction and lunges right at me. I hit him full in the face with another shot of pepper spray and he screams so loud I think he's going to rouse every animal in the forest.

But James doesn't stop coming for me. He's relentless. He charges at me and I hit the spray again. This time nothing comes out. I hit it again and again, shake it, try again, but nothing. The can's empty. James laughs.

There's no sanity in that sound. None of James' usual cold calculating style. It's pure madness now. He means to kill me, no matter how. He'll never stop coming for me.

I lunge at him. I have no idea what I'm going to do, I only know I can't let him pin me to the ground again, because this time I won't survive. I tackle him football-style and he staggers backward a few steps, surprised. I try to remember everything I ever learned about self-defense, which isn't much. I bring my knee up toward his balls — I barely connect, but it's hard enough to get a frustrated *ouff* out of him. I bring my foot back down on his. Again, it barely does anything. The eyes, I think. Go for the eyes. I raise my hands up to his face and aim my thumbs at his eyeballs. One thumb hits his cheekbone, but the other connects with the soft bulging part of his eye. James screams and staggers backward.

Then he disappears.

I stare in disbelief at the place he was just standing. I take a cautious step forward.

The hole.

I stand at the edge and peer down. James is sprawled at the bottom, in the very place I'd been eating and sleeping and pissing for ten days. He looks dazed. Blood flows from his eye, and his left arm is bent at an odd angle. He's knocked out, I think.

But his eyes flutter open. "You fucking bitch," he croaks. "I'm going to fucking kill you."

"Good luck with that." I shouldn't taunt him, but standing up here, looking down over him like this, sends a wave of power coursing through me. "You're never going to hurt me again. You're never going to hurt anyone again."

He fumbles for something, and a flash of metal rocks my heart. The gun. I forgot about the gun. James fires wildly, and the bullet sails by so close that I can hear it whistle past my ear.

I dive into the grass, out of range. I lie there panting for a minute. The true reality of this situation hits me. James is in the hole. I'm free. And I have two choices — get help, or leave him here.

Except it's not really a choice at all. I already know what I'm going to do. I don't even have to think about it.

THIRTY-SEVEN
PRESENT DAY

James fires the gun twice more. It's an idle threat — there's no way the trajectory can reach me — but each shot sends a lance of fear ricocheting through me. Despite the fact that it's a relatively modern technology, there's a primal fear that's triggered at the sound of a gunshot. Even when I know I'm safe, I cower.

Slowly, I crawl over toward the hole. I know he can't climb out — I spent enough time down there to know it's virtually impossible — but I still hold the baseless fear that I'm going to get to the edge and find him hanging just below, ready to pull me down with him. Or straight up shoot me in the face. So I don't go close enough to give him that chance. I only go as far as the ladder, and I pull that even farther away from the hole. Just on the off chance that he somehow found a way to reach it, if he has rope or something in his pockets. I want him to feel as helpless, as hopeless, as I did.

It's cruel, I know. It makes me no better than he is. This won't be truly over until James Russel is dead. So I've decided to let him die.

From down in the hole, James is screaming at me. A string of barely coherent obscenities erupts from his mouth. His voice is already going hoarse; I guess that's the pepper spray. I don't know how long he'll live down there. It'll depend on how recently he drank water, whether he happens to have a water bottle stashed in his pocket. But it should only take a few days at most. A few days, and I'll never have to worry about him again.

I take a minute to catch my breath. My lungs still hurt from the bear spray, and my eyes feel as if I've rubbed hot peppers all over them. I hunt around and find the half-empty water bottle James had been holding earlier, the one he'd started to pour out onto the ground. Even though I can think of nothing but guzzling it down, I use it instead to douse my eyes. I don't know what kind of permanent damage pepper spray might be able to do. It's not enough to really flush them out, but it brings me a pinch of relief.

But I'm not out of the woods yet. Literally or figuratively. I need to find the trail again, somehow find a way out of this forest. Otherwise I'll die out here as surely as I would have died in that hole.

If King were here, he'd probably be able to help. King. My chest tightens at the thought of him, and I scan the clearing for his body. I can't remember where we were standing when James and I had our first confrontation, when James kicked him like that. I don't see his body anywhere. Maybe he slunk off into the woods to die, I think. Or maybe an animal got to him. The thought nearly gags me with grief.

The twilight sky has turned to almost full night. The forest will be a maze of blackness, and if I try to find my way to the trail now, I risk getting completely turned around. Maybe ending up even deeper into the woods, maybe walking in circles for hours. Expending what precious little energy I have left and getting nowhere. But I also know, in a way I can't explain, that I won't survive another night here in the clearing. I don't know when I last had water, but it had to have been at least twenty-four hours ago. If I'm going to survive, I need to go now.

James is still screaming. It's not even intelligible anymore, just wordless howls. Even if it weren't for my life-threatening dehydration, I don't think I could live through a night of those screams. They make my blood feel like battery acid.

I look around the clearing again. I have no idea what direction that trail is in, so I simply pick one.

A COUPLE OF HOURS LATER, the reality has become clear: I've picked wrong. I only chased King for five or ten minutes on my way out here, so if the trail was in this direction, surely I would have found it by now. Even accounting for my slower pace and the poor visibility. But turning back would be futile. There has to be a way out. It only took James an hour to get that ladder from wherever he was parked, so there must be an access route around here somewhere. My best chance is to hope I run across another trail. This forest is littered with them — hiking trails, motorcross trails, logging trails. It's a working forest. I should eventually stumble across some sign of life.

Not that I haven't already sensed plenty of life out here. All night it's felt as if something was lurking close behind me. Something big and with far superior night vision. The bear again, maybe, or a coyote. Are there wolves in these woods? I shiver every time a branch cracks behind me. And every time, I'm haunted by the idea of a far deadlier predator tracking me — that James has somehow escaped the hole and followed me through the forest, that he's going to kill me like he'd planned all along. I almost pray that it *is* a wolf. At least a wolf will be quick.

As the night wears on, I wear out. Every step takes a pound of energy, a pint of will. I drag myself forward. Branches scrape at my face in the thickest sections, tree roots threaten to trip me with every footfall. I don't know where I find the strength to keep moving. It must come from a different part of me. Maybe we all have that survival instinct — to keep moving forward until we can't anymore, and then to go a little bit further. Only most people will never be in a position to discover it.

Lucky for them.

I push on. My legs ache, my shoulder throbs, and my eyes weep tears I can ill afford. I think about my mother and my sister. What they'll do if my body is never found. Do they even know I'm missing?

Maybe it's because of them that I push on. Or maybe it's the desire to put as much distance as possible between me and James. Or maybe it's sheer stubbornness.

Just as the sky is starting to turn pink with the sunrise, I take a quick break. I don't sit down, because if I do, there's a good chance I'll never get back up. But I lean against the trunk of a tree, taking a few long, deep breaths and letting my eyes drift closed. When I open them again, the sky is a shocking orange and yellow, and the sun sits far above the horizon line. How many minutes have passed? Twenty? Thirty?

Groggily, I force myself away from the tree and back onto my feet. The sun is directly in front of me now. Is that a good thing or not? I'm not great with directions at the best of times, and right now my brain can hardly compute up from down. I try to think. The sun rises in the east. The trailhead I'd started out from so many days ago, the place my car is parked, is on the eastern edge of the park. I trudge on in that direction.

After another couple of miles, there's still no sign of the trail. I'm no longer sure I'm going the right way. This time I'm truly ready to give up. My legs simply won't move any further. I'm done.

And then I hear it. The unmistakable purr of a car engine. Close, too. So close. I thrash through the trees in what I hope is the right direction. The sound is gone now, but I press forward anyway.

And then ... there it is. Like an oasis in the desert. The solid grey asphalt. The gleam of a car. *My* car. I stagger toward it and yank on the door, but find it locked. Of course. I pat down my pockets for the keys and realize I don't have them.

It hits me. They're back in the hole. Along with my dead cell phone. I have no way to get into or start the car, no way to contact anyone. There are only two other cars around, with no sign of their drivers. The road beyond is silent. I've come all this way — made it out of the hole, made it out of the woods — and I have no way to get any further. I'm going to die here. After all that, I'm going to die here, on the side of the road, like nothing more than a piece of roadkill.

My legs finally give out. I sink down against the car, leaning my back against the tire and putting my head in my hands. That's the last thing I remember before I lose consciousness.

WHEN I WAKE UP, I'm surrounded by light. Not the warm light of heavenly hospitality, but the cold sterile light of a laboratory. No, not a laboratory. A hospital.

I try to turn my head, but everything in my body aches.

"There she is," a voice says. I blink a couple of times, and a nurse leans over me. She's got caramel-colored skin, and when she smiles at me, there's a gap between her two front teeth. "We were wondering when you were going to join us."

"What happened?" I say. At least, I try to. It comes out as more of a strangled cough.

"Don't try to talk," she says. "You were severely dehydrated. We've had you on fluids for two days now." She pauses. "Would you like some water? Your throat will be dry, so take it slow."

I'm able to nod, and she holds a plastic cup with a bent straw up to my lips. My instinct is to gulp it down; my brain has never wanted anything more. But my lips and my tongue and my throat are all so raw that I can hardly get more than a small mouthful down.

"You keep taking sips," the nurse says kindly. "That'll go away soon enough. There's no permanent damage. You dislocated your shoulder and fractured your collar bone, but we got you all patched up."

She makes some notes on a chart at the foot of my bed and straightens my blanket. "The doctor's going to be by to see you shortly. You've also got some people who've been waiting for you to wake up. Do you want to see them?"

I nod again, and she whisks herself out of the room. I try to run my tongue over my lips, but it's like rubbing two pieces of sandpaper together. The door opens again and my mother and sister swoop in.

"Oh, Aurora, my baby." My mom descends on me, not quite hugging me but patting me gently all over. "We were so worried about you. What happened?"

"I —" I stop. If I tell her about the hole, what will happen? There will be more questions. How I got out, how the hole got there. The police will be involved, maybe the park officials. They'll want to find the hole, fill it in. People will be looking. They'll find James.

"I got lost in the woods," I say instead. "King got loose, and I chased after him and, I don't know, I just lost my bearings. I wandered around forever. I thought I was going to die." I choke up at that last part, because after all, it's the one bit that's true. I really did think I was going to die. I still kind of can't believe I didn't.

"How scary," my mother says. She's still patting me down like I'm a ceramic doll that fell from a high shelf and she's inspecting me for cracks. "I knew you shouldn't be out in those woods all alone. With that damn dog."

"It wasn't his fault." Thinking about King closes my throat up. I can't do it right now. "How long was I gone for?"

"Ten days," Mom says softly. "Ten long days. It was your office that called us. That nice young man."

"Damian?"

"No, he had a foreign name." She taps her lip.

"Bao," my sister supplies.

"That's right."

Bao. Of course. Of all the people at DigitaLuster, Bao would know that I'd never miss work without a reason. I feel a small sense of satisfaction that at least there was some effort made to find me. That I matter to people.

"He's here if you want to see him," my mother says.

"Who?"

"Bao," she says slowly, as if my brain might have been bumped somewhere along the way. "From your office."

"Oh. Um. Sure." My mother leaves and I straighten the blankets, comb my fingers through the ends of my hair. I realize how ridiculous that is. I haven't washed my hair in almost two weeks, so finger-combing it is about as useful or attractive as plaits on a pig. And anyway, it's just Bao.

"Heya Watts," he says, as he slips into my room. He's wearing an Atari t-shirt and those black-rimmed glasses he always wears, and he's so familiar and friendly-looking that I cry. Well, I try to. My tear ducts are still about as dry as my throat.

"Hi," I eke out and give a dry little laugh.

"You know city girls don't belong in the woods, right? This is the kind of shit that happens."

"I know that now," I say, offering him a grim smile. "I just thought the walks would be good for the dog."

"Trust me, he's a city dog, too. He's been plenty happy watching Netflix and eating my leftover moo shu pork."

"Yeah. Wait, what?"

"He's an awesome dog. Super chill. His favorite is *Breaking Bad*. I think he might have been a drug-sniffing dog in a past life."

"You ... he's alive?"

Bao's eyes widen in surprise. "He turned up a few days ago, on the highway near Capital State Forest. That's why the cops figured you were there."

"And he's okay?"

"Great. He was a bit dehydrated, and the vet said he's got some bruised ribs, possibly from scrambling over logs or rocks. But he's doing great now."

Somehow my body makes enough liquid to generate tears, because they start to stream down my cheeks. "Oh, thank you, Bao, thank you."

Bao looks embarrassed. "Hey, don't cry. He's fine. You're both fine."

"Yeah." I wipe away the tears and let out my first real laugh. "I think maybe we are."

THIRTY-EIGHT
THREE MONTHS LATER

The hunter has the deer in his sights. A nice buck, an eight-pointer. It's going to look awesome on his garage wall. He imagines drinking a beer with Buddy and Gill and shooting the shit while this bad boy gazes down over them. Yeah, it's going to be sweet, that's for sure.

The buck hasn't noticed him yet. It's still meandering between the trees, its steps careful and deliberate. The hunter tracks silently behind. He's a large man but he's as elegant as the deer when he's out here, almost on tiptoe in his big muck boots.

But so far he hasn't been able to get a clean shot. The trees are dense and the buck seems to know it, always keeping a few trunks between his flank and the hunter. But the hunter is persistent. It's almost the end of the season and he isn't going to get too many more chances. Especially not any as sweet as this one, that's for sure.

So he's patient. He's steady. He tracks the deer until finally it emerges into a small clearing. The buck stops to graze, and the hunter knows he's got his shot.

He raises his rifle to his shoulder but the deer — blast their damn good hearing — perks up at the sound. The animal hesitates for only a moment, then bounds off through the clearing, toward the tree line on the other side.

"Dammit," the hunter mutters, moving on silent feet across the same grass the deer was just munching. He doesn't let that beast out of his sight; that animal is going to be his.

But as he watches, the buck disappears.

The hunter blinks. Swivels his head. One minute the thing was right there, and now it's …gone. He's sure it didn't make it to the trees, he would have seen it go in. It's more like it … fell out of sight.

He slows his pace and walks toward where he last saw the deer. He hears an unmistakable grunting, the noise a buck'll make when it's trying to show its dominance. He hears the soft thudding of hooves against earth. It seems to be coming from below him.

He slows down even more, and thank God he does, because he doesn't see the hole until he's almost on top of it.

"Well, shit." He peers down into the hole. The buck's charging back and forth, panicked. He's barely got room to maneuver; the hole is maybe only eight feet by eight feet, and the buck's more than half that. It stomps its feet and turns in tight circles and butts its horns against the side of the hole. Panicked. The hunter's seen them like that a few times, usually when they've been shot but not killed. But now it's just stuck. Stuck and scared.

The hunter sees something that scares him, too. The deer ain't alone down there.

"Hey," he calls. "Hey, you okay?" But he already knows it's pointless, because no way is that guy okay. That's for sure.

POLICE. Firefighters. Ambulance. State rangers. Animal control. They all show up, each trying to figure out how to get the buck and the body out of the hole, each thinking their own agenda should take precedence.

The hunter gives his statement half a dozen times, embellishing it a little each time. "Yeah, dropped out of sight right in front of my eyes. Like the earth opened up and swallowed it right in, you know? Like Jonah and the whale. Right weird, that's for sure." He hints that he should get first crack at the buck once they get it out, but that doesn't go over too well. One of the officers tells him that he should go home, that they have his contact info in case they need him for anything else.

The hunter leaves.

The officer, a ginger-haired rookie named Lorne Cooke, gets the honor of being the first down the hole once they've extracted the buck. The buck did a lot of damage, and probably a lot of evidence has already been destroyed, but he still tries to be careful as he does an initial inspection of the body, as he reaches into the pockets to try to find a wallet.

No wallet, but he does find a cell phone. It's dead, but they should still be able to get an ID off the number, unless it's a burner, and no real reason to think that at this point, though the situation is certainly strange. He bags it and climbs back out of the hole. He doesn't say anything — would never admit to this, even on the witness stand — but the hole gives him the creeps. It feels like death down there, like a kind of hopelessness and desperation that takes him several hours to shake off, even once he's back above ground.

THE GUY *in the hole* is the talk of the station for the rest of the day. They've all seen some weird deaths, but the idea of starving to death in a hole in the middle of the woods is one that haunts everyone a little bit more than usual.

Officer Cooke charges the guy's phone at his desk. He should have entered it into evidence, but no one is thinking this is anything more than a tragic — albeit bizarre — accident. They'd found a ladder not too far away from the hole, so they figured this guy had been digging out there and somehow fallen in. The only slightly unusual thing was that they'd recovered a second phone from the hole as well — different brand, this one with a pink case. Officer Cooke had that one charging at his desk, too.

When the first phone finally comes back to life, the one he'd found in buddy's pocket, Officer Cooke starts it up right away. He's really hoping to be able to make an ID. The body had been down there quite a while, and the deer had done a real number on it, making it relatively unrecognizable. If he couldn't get a name off the phone, they were going to have to try DNA or dental records and that was always a pain.

But when the phone comes to life, he's surprised to find a message on the lock screen.

"When you find my body, listen to the audio," it says. Officer Cooke looks around to see if anyone else has noticed this, but no one is paying him or the phone any attention. He taps into the audio screen. There's no passcode — the guy must have removed it at the same time he was creating that custom image for the lock screen. Officer Cooke feels a tremendous amount of respect for him. That took foresight. Smarts.

In the audio section, he finds two files. One is short, less than a minute long. The second one is just over twenty minutes.

He listens to the shorter one first.

"My name is James Russel. I live at 498 Beckham Avenue, apartment 1412. I was left here to die by a woman named Aurora Watts. She was also responsible for the death of my fiancee, Lily Castleman. In the attached audio recording, you will hear her admission. My fiancee did not commit suicide. I want the world to know. She did not kill herself. Neither did I. Aurora Watts is responsible. For all of it."

The man's voice is breathless and weak, but there's a certain strength to it, too. A conviction. Officer Cooke also recognizes the name — James Russel. That missing architect. He realizes that what looked like a simple accident just got a whole lot more complicated.

He goes to find his boss.

AURORA AND BAO are sitting on her couch with King between them. She can't keep the smile off her face. James' death should have made her feel guilty, but it's had the opposite effect. She's only, finally, free.

Bao flips through television stations, looking for something that isn't inane drivel, when Aurora hears something that makes her ears perk up.

"Breaking news in the case of missing businessman James Russel…"

"Stop," Aurora says, putting her hand on Bao's. "What's that?"

He flips back to the 24-hour news station. "Isn't that Lily's fiance? God, that story is so messed up."

Aurora doesn't answer. She stares transfixed at the television as the dark-skinned, perfectly coiffed news anchor speaks earnestly into the camera.

"The body of Seattle architect James Russel was recovered yesterday in Capitol State Forest, about an hour and a half outside the city. Russel has been missing for approximately three months. He was thought to have possibly taken his own life, following the suicide of his fiancee in the spring. Police are treating the death as suspicious but have yet to release any further details. We'll continue to follow this story as it develops."

"So messed up," Bao repeats, slinging his arm around Aurora and turning the television to the Seahawks game.

When the apartment buzzer goes off, Aurora already knows who it will be. She hits the button to unlock the building door without even speaking to them. This is her moment of reckoning. She'll face it head on.

But when she pulls open the apartment door and discovers two uniformed officers standing there, the reality sinks in and a hint of dread starts to creep into her veins.

"Yes?" she says. Her throat burns. It always feels dry now, maybe a lingering effect of the dehydration, or the bear spray.

"Aurora Watts?"

"Yes?"

"Do you know a James Russel?"

"Yes." She swallows. Blood is pounding in her head. Like she's upside-down.

"And did you also know a Lily Castleman?"

"Yes."

"We'd like to ask you a few questions. Down at the station, if you don't mind."

"I..." Aurora swivels to look at Bao and King.

Bao is frowning, and King emits a low deep growl. She turns back to the officers. One is older, maybe in his fifties, with greying hair and the start of a paunch, but the other is young. Very young. Probably as young as she was when she met James. He's got a babyface, complete with freckles and a mop of red hair that looks incongruous with the police uniform. Both of them are watching her with blank expressions.

"Yes," she says. "I'll come with you." She's surprised to find there's no hesitation in her voice. She turns back to Bao. "Take care of King, okay? I might be awhile."

She lets the officers lead her out of the apartment, and when they sit her in the back of the squad car, she leans against the window. She has a pretty good idea of what they have on her. If they found James' body, that means they also found her phone and her car keys. Easy enough to track her down from that, but she suspects something more.

She's known all along that there was a good chance James recorded their conversation out in the clearing. James was always two steps ahead, and that meant he would want to preserve her confession, such as it was. Just in case. In case the police ever came after him, in case he ever had to justify what he did. Not that it would be enough for them to let him off the hook, but it might have bought him some sympathy with a jury. A bereaved man, the jealous ex who'd driven his fiancee to her death.

That's why she'd been so careful about what she said to him. She admitted to being there when Lily fell from the balcony but she can't imagine she'll get more than a slap on the wrist for that. She left the scene, yes, and she retrieved the knife from the gutter near where Lily fell — it was easy enough, with everyone so distracted by the body that they didn't notice Aurora emerging from the lobby and discretely hunting around for that glint of steel. She supposes that might count as obstruction of justice, but in Washington State, that's only a gross misdemeanor. Less than a year in prison, and that's if they even decide to pursue it.

James' death is another question mark, but she isn't worried about that one. She has plenty of evidence of what James did to her when they were together, and her mother and sister would both testify on her behalf. Yes, she let him die alone in that hole, but she can say that when she left him, he was standing in the clearing, unharmed. If he fell into a hole that *he* dug, well, surely she can't be held responsible for that.

She leans back, confident. This is most likely a formality. Just the police doing their due diligence, making sure they aren't missing anything in the death of a prominent architect.

The drive to the station brings her, ironically, past James' apartment building. Or maybe it's intentional, she thinks, as she catches the younger officer watching her in the rear view mirror. She tries to look scared, traumatized, but something else slips through. A bit of smugness. Because after all, she got what she wanted. James doesn't have Lily anymore. He doesn't have anyone anymore. The balance of power has been restored.

James set all of this in motion, the day he kicked her out of his apartment with not even a kiss goodbye. After she'd given up everything — literally everything — for him. Did he really think she was going to let that go?

The funny thing is, she might have. She'd made good progress with Dr. Monica. She had a life of her own now. And then she'd seen James' picture that day, in Lily's office. She could scarcely believe it. What were the odds that he'd end up dating someone she worked with? Was the universe trying to mess with her?

A week later, she'd plucked up the courage to ask Lily how they'd met. The story stunned her — Lily had met James in the exact same way Aurora had. It was *all* the same — the spilled coffee, the soiled dry-cleaning. She realized it wasn't the universe trying to send her a message but James himself. He'd orchestrated this whole thing in the hopes that it would get back to her. She didn't know why, but she didn't understand why James did half the things he did. She knew how his mind worked, though. And now, there was poor Lily, going on about their meeting as if it was oh-so-romantic. As if it was so original. The poor dumb cow.

Dr. Monica told her to let it go. She thought Aurora was reading too much into it. Hyperfocusing. Obsessing. But Aurora couldn't let it go. Not when the facts were staring her in the face like that. The game had begun again.

She waited for James to make his next move. She thought it might happen at the DigitaLuster Christmas party, where everyone was bringing a date, but he'd pointedly ignored her, not even catching her eye over the canapés. She saw it for what it was, though: a challenge. And she knew she was up for it. She was older now. Wiser. She could play his games.

Then it happened. An off-hand comment from Damian that changed everything. The week before Valentine's Day, he'd stopped by her desk and mentioned that Lily wouldn't be in on Friday. Her boyfriend was whisking her away to San Francisco for a romantic weekend. He was planning to propose. It was a surprise; Lily didn't know.

Aurora has thought of that moment so many times in the days and weeks and months since it happened. Why would James communicate his plans to Damian like that, unless he wanted the information to get back to Aurora? It was another one of his psychological games. He wanted to see how she'd react. What she'd do.

She stole Lily's keys. It was stupidly easy. DigitaLuster didn't believe in office doors, and Lily was too dumb to lock her purse in her desk. Aurora snatched the keys out while Lily was in the bathroom Thursday afternoon, easy as you please. When she saw the daisy keychain, she felt a smug elation. It was identical to the one James had given her. She was doing the right thing. She knew it for sure now.

After that, it was simple. All she had to do was make Lily think she was going crazy. A feat that, again, turned out to be stupidly easy. Who knew Lily was already so close to the edge? She'd barely had to flick her — a bird in the apartment, a changed meeting time. Child's stuff, really — and the poor girl was halfway to checking herself into the nearest head hospital. Aurora had laid in bed every night, too wired to sleep, imagining Lily uncovering her little surprises, picturing James' face as he realized it was her. She knew he would, too, especially after the photo. Puget Sound, their first vacation together. It was inspired.

Aurora hadn't meant to kill Lily, of course. Not really. She only wanted to undermine her, to make her so crazy that James would abandon her the same way he'd done to Aurora.

But when they both stood on the balcony that day, she finally understood. This was the game. In order to win, in order to truly restore the balance of power, she needed to take James' queen. Lily had been so fragile by then that it had been easy. One firm shove, and she was gone. Checkmate.

After, she waited for James to come to her. For months, she'd been waiting. She should have known he wouldn't make it simple. That was James, oblique as always. The hole, though — that she truly hadn't seen coming. She would give him points for that, at least. But even then, the game was already over. It was over the moment she took his queen. Everything after that was just an inexorable march toward an ending that was already written. She had won; James had lost.

Aurora leans back against the seat of the cruiser, satisfied. She sees that baby-faced cop staring at her again, his eyes bright blue in the rear view mirror, so she gives him a sad smile and bats her eyelashes once, twice. He looks away.

She isn't bothered. She isn't bothered by any of this. She'll get through it with a little patience.

After all, she's always been patient. She has many, many flaws — she's emotional, disagreeable, and she holds a grudge like no one else, to name a few — but a lack of patience isn't one of them.

ABOUT THE AUTHOR

Marissa Finch spent most of her life asking herself 'what's the worst thing that could happen right now?' so she decided to make a career out of writing those thoughts down.

When she's not writing, she enjoys reading thrillers, watching crime dramas, and browsing Pinterest for pictures of haircuts.

She lives in the country with her husband and two very bad cats.

Printed in Great Britain
by Amazon